Prodigal

A Novel

Phyllis Gobbell

Prodigal

A Novel

Histria Fiction

Las Vegas ◊ Chicago ◊ Palm Beach

Published in the United States of America by
Histria Books
7181 N. Hualapai Way, Ste. 130-86
Las Vegas, NV 89166 USA
HistriaBooks.com

Histria Fiction is an imprint of Histria Books. Titles published under the imprints of Histria Books are distributed worldwide.

Library of Congress Control Number: 2024931093

ISBN 978-1-59211-478-8 (softbound)
ISBN 978-1-59211-489-4 (eBook)

Chapter 1

2000

The sky was filled with light.

The fireworks were spectacular, for a little town, that first Fourth of July of the new century. Bursts of color rained sparkles and left faces down below brilliant, full of wonder. All of it unforgettable, for a moment.

But not far down the street, a smaller flash of light was unforgettable in the way that can last a lifetime.

A single gunshot at the Back Home Market changed everything for the clerk who was shot, the juvenile delinquent who pulled the trigger, and the Baptist preacher's son who ran away, leaving everything he knew and loved, sure it was forever.

The fireworks whistled and boomed as the unlikely pair arrived at the market to buy beer — Joe Ray, in trouble since he was twelve, and Connor, the youngest of the preacher's kids, all "Yes sir" and "Thank you ma'am" since he could talk.

The parking lot was empty when they pulled up in Joe Ray's battered truck. There were no customers inside, just the clerk behind the counter, looking at a girlie magazine. Joe Ray had bragged, "Raleigh, he's the black guy at the Back Home, he'd sell me his sister if I asked."

Connor could see through his big talk, a boy not yet eighteen trying to stretch himself into a man. Joe Ray Loomis, bad teeth and broken knuckles. But in Mercer County, the only beer a nineteen-year-old could buy was root beer, so Connor went along with the younger kid. He was a little buzzed already from the beer somebody had sneaked into the picnic at the City Park. And he had a thirst in him, burning from knowing he couldn't have the girl he wanted.

Joe Ray said, "Get the beer, preacher boy," and he marched up to the counter, slapped it hard, and said, "Hey, bud. Put your girlfriend down."

Raleigh, propped on a high stool behind the counter, darted Connor a wary glance. Back at Joe Ray, he mumbled, "You didn't say nothing about him."

"Don't worry. This is between you and me," Joe Ray said.

Connor slouched past the chips and candy and burnt coffee to the back of the store. At the cooler, he felt that first cold whisper, something wrong about this. But he was nineteen and bruised up down deep, and he hadn't learned yet to listen to what some would call conscience. His daddy would say an angel was watching over him, but that angel hadn't done him much good lately.

So he kept walking, straight toward trouble.

Connor grabbed two sixes. He turned into the aisle past a Little Debbies rack and had a clear view of the check-out counter. Of Raleigh's face. Of Joe Ray's back. Of the gun.

Joe Ray had a gun turned cockeyed the way he must've seen gang bangers do it in the movies. A gun pointed at Raleigh.

Connor yelled, "*No-o-o-o-o*!" and Joe Ray's arm jerked and the gun popped.

Just one shot. A *pop,* like a firework exploding too close. Raleigh howled and fell off the stool, crumpling to the floor.

Joe Ray raised the gun and stared at it, like a snake handler surprised by the snake bite.

Connor dropped the beer and ran down the aisle. "You stupid sonofabitch! You shot him!" He heard Raleigh wailing behind the counter and got a glimpse of him holding his leg, blood oozing between his fingers. Blood splattered on the wall. Connor remembered just enough about praying to murmur, "God... please... *please* don't let him die."

Joe Ray made a sound. A cry, like he was the wounded one. He suddenly seemed much younger, just a scared kid, in the moment before he stumbled away.

Connor stood looking at the clerk, all that blood, like his life was spilling from him right there. Then Connor looked at Joe Ray, heading toward the truck.

And he had to decide.

Next thing he was in the truck, screaming, "What the hell, man? You crazy?"

Joe Ray cursed under his breath. His hands trembled as he tried to light a Marlboro. "Wasn't s'posed to go down like that." He made a fist and punched the dash. "Nothing ever happens like it's s'posed to!"

Connor stared at the explosions of light above the City Park.

Fireworks fade away into darkness, but a gunshot can change light to dark in a heartbeat. And in that forever kind of dark, it's always so hard to find your way home.

Joe Ray turned the key and the engine caught. And the old truck carried the juvie and the preacher's son out into the darkness.

Montpier, set like a jewel in the rolling Tennessee hills, was a patriotic little town, a God-fearing town, a love-your-neighbor town. The Fourth of July was serious business and it took the whole day to observe it properly.

The parade at noon had kicked off the celebration of freedom. There were flags waving along the parade route and fresh-faced majorettes high-stepping. There were earnest high school band members hitting mostly right notes on their Sousa renditions. And there were the men from the VFW, marching proudly in the uniforms they wore when they were eighteen that strained across their eighty-year-old bellies, others stooped, their eyes cloudy with memory, and all of them sweating. It was hot. It was always blistering hot on the Fourth of July.

An afternoon in the City Park always followed the parade. Horseshoes for the old men and softball for the young men, mamas fussing over babies that yowled from heat rash, and little boys chasing each other with sticks. And then the picnic, the best chicken in Mercer County and deviled eggs that might have been out in the sun too long.

As the languid afternoon slid into a gentle twilight and then dusk, the fireflies came out. Children ran about trying to capture the little flashes of light, if only to let them go again to dance against the darkening sky. The chatter grew expectant as volunteers from the fire department left for the far side of the park to man the fireworks.

Some observant residents of Montpier would remember seeing Connor Burdette and Joe Ray Loomis high-tailing it out of the park about that time and wondering why anybody would want to leave when the big fireworks show was about to start. Thinking back on it, remembering that old truck spinning gravel, some said they knew it was trouble, sure enough.

That day had all the makings of a small-town, old-fashioned Fourth of July, time-honored traditions that carried on without much change in the years to come. As time passed, no one could quite remember which year it was that the mayor, Grand Marshal of the parade, fainted from heat, and paramedics arrived, but on his orders took him to his house for shade and sweet tea. Or which year a rainstorm blew up out of nowhere and upended the 4-H Club's float, and a goat ran free through the streets. But always, as the town walked itself home in the dark after a day of celebration, someone would bring up the shooting at the Back Home Market. And though memories faded, like one of the old Polaroid photos that has lost its sharp colors, Montpier remembered which year it happened. For the first Fourth of July of the brand new century to be stained, like blood on the wall of the Back Home Market, it seemed like a bad sign.

And the memory was still a raw, open wound for the Burdettes, Connor's family, who hung on to the notion that somewhere he was alive and might eventually come home, though years passed without a word from him. Daniel, the Baptist preacher, feared he'd been too hard on his son when Connor began to stray from the straight and narrow. And Kitty, Connor's mama, wouldn't think of letting their new cell phones replace the landline, because that was the number her boy knew like he knew his own birthday.

Russ, his brother, didn't like to imagine the terrible things that could've happened to Connor, but anger was a stronger force than worry. Anger that a brother would vanish like that, like he'd never felt a thing for the blood and love between them.

Russ's wife Nikki tried not to think of him at all, but sometimes she couldn't help it. She thought of how broken he was, and she thought she was the only one who knew why, but she could never say.

Connor's sister Ivy, who knew he understood that she would keep any secret, kept thinking that of all the family, *she* would be the one her little brother would reach out to, somehow he'd contact *her*, just to let her know he was alive, he was all right. But he didn't.

And then there was Lady Burdette, the mighty matriarch of the Burdette family. No one who knew her could have imagined how often disturbing visions of her grandson visited her in the blackest hours of night, how she longed to find him, and how, toward the end of her life, she resolved, *I'll do it, by God. I will.*

Chapter 2

Ten Years After the Shooting

Lady Burdette had spent her long life confident in her bones that she knew what everybody else ought to do. Quick to voice her strident opinions on finance and medicine and politics — and other people's personal matters, how ridiculous it was to nurse a baby that already had a mouthful of teeth. "Is she gonna bring him home for lunch when he starts to school?" Most everybody she knew was making wrong turns. She was the only one with the map.

But anyone who meddled in Lady's business had better have a goddamned good reason. She didn't care much for lawyers or doctors or preachers — her son notwithstanding — but they were all sometimes a necessary evil.

Don Petrie, her lawyer, had drawn up a new will for her. On Monday, the week before July Fourth, it was ready for her signature. Over the disorderly paperwork on his desk, he fixed her with his keen gray eyes. "Against my better judgment," he said, his deep, rich voice so out of kilter with the rest of his bony self. Pale with sparse white hair, so fragile looking, he looked like a stiff north wind could blow him over. But that voice, the sound of authority: "Are you absolutely sure you want to do this, Lady?"

She snatched the pen from the girl with downcast eyes who was going to witness the document, and scrawled her signature. "There! I know *exactly* what I'm doing," she said.

Three days later, coming home from the country club, Lady was not so rock-solid sure of herself. She had no doubts about her heir. It wasn't that. Lady Burdette understood money. She'd been using money her entire life to push people around, but this... this was a pull. Something pulling at the bottom of her heart. And when she closed her eyes, she'd heard it whispering in her blood, singing in her bones. This was not a thinking thing. It was a feeling thing that could not be argued with or talked down.

But something had gone wrong that she couldn't quite put out of her mind.

Don Petrie had clasped his hand over his heart and put on a wounded face when she'd mentioned the need for absolute confidentiality. "Lady. *Lady*, have you ever heard a *murmur* from *anybody* to make you doubt my discretion?" He went on, swelling up like a July tick. "And what about the work I've done for you? All these years? Have you had any complaint?"

No. For more than fifty years, Don had handled her business and Jack's, before he died. She trusted him, as far as she trusted anybody. But the girl, the witness, was another story.

Now Lady took the stairs as quickly as she could manage, clutching the handrail with one hand, her purse with the other. At the top of the staircase she paused to catch her breath. It felt as if every one of her eighty-four years was laying heavy on her lungs. Just last summer she was on the tennis courts twice a week, paying no attention to her heart. Till she had to. These days, when she went to the Country Club, it was to have a martini with her old doubles partner and nod to the pretentious thirty-somethings she used to trounce with her wicked lobs.

Still breathing hard, she went to her bedside table and took out her copy of the will that she'd read again last night. She flipped to the signature page and saw what had been troubling her. It took the air out of her. She sank to the side of the bed and whispered, "*Damnation*," seeing the name of the witness, remembering that girl when she was one of a pack of runny nose kids, children of a no-good daddy and a mama that had no spine. The pretty girl, her mama made over, had pulled herself up to the kind of life her people would never have dreamed of. A paralegal for Don Petrie was no small thing. But that didn't mean she was trustworthy.

Lady pushed back a strand of white hair and tucked it into her French twist. She yanked off her earrings, dropped them on the bedside table, and dug out her phone from her purse. She pressed a number and finally heard, "This is Ivy. Leave a message."

Lady huffed. She didn't do that voicemail thing unless she had to. She sure didn't want to sound desperate, just urgent. Everyone counted on Lady's independence. Maybe she ought not involve family at all... but wasn't this *all* about family? And if she had to trust anybody, Ivy was the one. Smartest of the whole lot, Ivy could appreciate the storm on the horizon.

So Lady left a message.

As she laid her phone on the bed beside her, a voice from downstairs startled her. She wasn't certain what she'd heard. Silence took over for a moment, and Lady thought she might have imagined the sound. Surely she hadn't left the door unlocked, but she'd rushed inside, anxious to look at the will, and lately, she was forgetful sometimes.

Again, "Lady? *Lady*! Are you here?" It was not her imagination.

And no mistaking the contempt behind the words. Same as when they'd talked on the phone at the club. But Lady had thought there would be more time.

People had the notion that she was tough, but truth be told, Lady Burdette had grown to despise confrontations. She could still whittle someone down to size, most times, but she could tell her tongue, once sharp as a scalpel, had grown blunt. It was discouraging. She used to never doubt herself.

"Yes, yes, I'm up here." The voice that came out of her was an old woman's she barely recognized. She rolled up the copy of the will, held it in her fist and raised it like a club, but she suddenly felt older than she'd ever imagined she would feel. Too old now, too weary, for the fireworks she knew were about to ignite her family, and explode.

Oh, she knew it would happen. She'd just imagined it wouldn't happen till she was dead.

Chapter 3

The ache was always there when Ivy thought of Connor. A kind of phantom pain. Like a missing arm or leg that still hurt. Only this was a missing brother. Lost? Or was he dead? The Fourth of July only made it worse, and the holiday was coming up Tuesday.

But that afternoon, Ivy Burdette wasn't dwelling on the Fourth of July. She wasn't dwelling on her Twenty-first Century Lit class or the student who had whispered to her that she was pregnant, and her parents were pressing her to go away to some place for girls in trouble, like some character from a Victorian novel. The summer term was nearly half over at the community college, the dread of Ivy's future looming over her, but she wasn't dwelling on that, either. Her mind was stuck on Lady.

Ivy had checked her voicemail at the end of class, as students checked theirs. One message, a message from her grandmother. "I need to see you... Now this is just between you and me..." Knowing Lady dispensed advice freely but rarely asked for it, Ivy tried to imagine what had prompted the message. What could she need from Ivy? And though Ivy had kept many secrets, she would never have expected her grandmother to confide in her.

She could remember only one other time that Lady had called her. Ever. Last year, trying out her new cell phone, apparently calling everyone she knew. "They say it's a Me-phone or something like that," she'd said. A smile curled the corners of Ivy's lips as she thought about it. In that conversation, her grandmother happened to mention that she'd won her division of tennis singles in the State Senior Olympics, her opponent a young upstart, seventy-three years old.

Ivy and Lady didn't call each other simply to chat. They weren't close, never had been close. And yet — this message.

The last student waved and called out, "See you Tuesday. Have a happy Fourth!" Happy was not a word Ivy associated with the Fourth, but she waved back and said, "You, too."

Now the classroom was empty. Ivy touched *speaker* and listened again as she crammed test papers into her canvas bag.

"I need to see you." The strong voice was insistent, just short of demanding, but Ivy imagined Lady didn't often leave messages; the cadence had that kind of awkwardness. The old voice started to waver, even as it rose to a higher pitch. "Now this is just between you and me, Ivy, you hear?" Lady sounded every day of her eighty-four years when she said, "It's important. I don't know what to do."

Ivy headed to the stairs at the end of the hall. The Humanities Building was a two-floor rectangular brick box, like the other buildings on the Cumberland Regional Community College campus. No arches or bell towers here. No modern glass and steel. This was not a university with chests of money. *Community college!* the unimpressive buildings seemed to shout.

Ivy wouldn't have taken the sluggish elevator, but there was Gwenna Wallis, holding the door open for her. The Humanities secretary was a chunky fifty-something, five feet tall in high heels. She could benefit from a little exercise. Nine inches taller, Ivy smiled down at Gwenna as she stepped into the elevator, thinking she could've been to the parking lot by the time they'd reach the ground floor, trying to hide her impatience. She needed to get to Lady's house.

"Serendipity," Gwenna said in a voice hinting of secrecy. Ivy gave her a dubious glance. The elevator doors closed with a bump. "Good thing I needed a cigarette, same time your class was over," Gwenna said.

As cryptic as Lady's message, Ivy thought. She didn't say it, but Gwenna would've known who Lady was. Everyone in Montpier, in fact everyone in Mercer County, knew Lady Burdette or knew *of* her, if, for no other reason, because of her vehement Letters to the Editor printed periodically in the *Mercer Gazette*. The Burdettes were Democrats in a county of Republicans, seventy percent Republican, but Lady criticized Democrats, too. She didn't spare anyone she felt was being a "dolt," a favorite word of hers. The *Gazette* loved her letters.

As the elevator began its laborious descent, Gwenna said, "Would you be interested in a full-time position here, Ivy?"

The secretary had no authority to pose such a question, but according to campus gossip, reported as gospel-truth, Gwenna was much more than a secretary to

Dr. Keller, Dean of the Humanities. Someone had told Ivy, "Gwenna knows where the bodies are buried. Dr. Keller had better keep her satisfied."

"I'm just here for the summer," Ivy said.

"So you say." Gwenna gave a knowing look. Ivy felt a surge of discomfort, not exactly embarrassment or irritation, just a keen awareness that everybody in Montpier knew everybody else's business, and no doubt the talk was *Ivy Burdette came back home to lick her wounds.* And she guessed it was the truth.

Gwenna, to her credit, didn't press the point. She added a breezy "Keep it under your hat till it's official, but looks like we'll have an opening for a full-time English position in the fall. Patty Rayburn's retiring. Moving to Phoenix. Can you imagine — that gosh-awful heat?"

The elevator lurched to a stop and groaned. The doors opened. Gwenna led the way down the hall. She walked fast for someone with her short legs, but it was an easy pace for Ivy, tall and long-legged and a runner. "Thanks for the heads up," she said.

"I'll keep you posted." Gwenna dug in her purse, coming up with a pack of Virginia Slims, and they left the air-conditioning for a blast of heat that felt like a punch in the face.

As she walked to her car, Ivy tried to call Lady to let her know she was on her way. The call went to voicemail. Lady was hard of hearing and too vain to get a hearing aid. If the phone was in a distant room or another floor of the large Burdette family home, Lady might not hear it ring. Ivy wasn't alarmed. The whole thing just felt peculiar. But then so was her grandmother.

Cumberland Regional Community College was eleven miles outside the Montpier city limits, connected by a four-lane highway that the State of Tennessee had built in the seventies to accommodate all the traffic to the new college. Now, nearly forty years later, Ivy drove home at what would be rush hour in places like Nashville without a glimpse of another car for five whole minutes. Her mind flew to these thoughts on the quiet drive. The only radio stations she could get were talk radio of the Rush Limbaugh variety or local preachers, none as reasonable as her father, or decent country music from Nashville stations that cut out, like cell phone service, at certain dips in the valley.

It was a pretty, peaceful drive, through farm land and woods. June rains had made the vegetation a brilliant green, more like the first growth of spring than summer. Ivy contemplated the beauty of the hills and valleys and pastures, which she hadn't appreciated before she left. When she was a senior at Montpier High School and Wexler-Fitzhugh Bible College had offered her a full scholarship, partly because of her grades and partly because she was a Baptist preacher's daughter, she couldn't wait to live on the Gulf Coast. She'd gone from undergrad to grad student to teaching assistant, to full-time faculty, to tenure track. Then the bottom fell out of what might have been a promising, even rewarding, career. Because she fell in love. It was bad enough that her fiancé was a liar and a cheater. Worse that he was the Academic Vice-President.

Ivy loved the Gulf, the white, sugary sand, the mild winters, and she had loved Preston Gorman for five years. She had loved him in spite of rumors and doubts, loved him until she could no longer lie to herself, after she caught him in bed with the red-haired grad student. And even though that one was just the latest in a long line of co-eds, Ivy couldn't say absolutely that she didn't love him still, in some twisted way.

It was a Southern thing, Ivy guessed, to come home with tail tucked in when life got too hard. Lick her wounds, yes, then go back. She'd been offered the summer class because of someone her daddy knew. She'd never dreamed it might lead to a full-time position. Now, well, it was something to think about. At Wexler-Fitzhugh, she'd never again have the Academic VP's support. She could forget tenure. Preston would love to get rid of her. He'd said as much. No remorse, just a promise: "I'll see you get a good reference if you apply somewhere else."

Ivy came to the square, the town center, dominated by a red brick 19th century courthouse. She had noticed, coming back this time, that the building seemed worn and weary, that it had shrunk from the courthouse in her memory. The empty parking spaces told the sad story of the businesses on the square. Some had moved to the commercial strip on the north side of town, near the bypass that was still a painful subject to those whose businesses on the square had gone under. Lady Burdette had written a Letter to the Editor stating an opinion shared by many, that the bypass was as unnecessary as the highway between Montpier and the college. Furthermore, Lady said, the road builders had the State Building Commission in their pockets.

From the square, Ivy headed west toward Lady's house, just outside the city limits. She pulled into the shaded driveway that climbed upward and made a turn before it revealed the house that was hidden from the road. A grand old house befitting the grand old lady who lived there. The landscaping was impeccable, as always, clipped shrubs and colorful annuals lining the stone walkway that led to the porch — the portico, Lady called it. Everyone used the front door.

Ivy rang the bell. No answer. She tried again. Even hard of hearing as Lady was, even if she was napping, she would surely hear the doorbell. Ivy pressed it a few more times, with more urgency. She tried the big brass door handle, then called again. Again, she was sent to voicemail. This time she left a message: "Where *are* you, Lady? I'm at your front door." Her tone was what her grandmother would call *petulant.* She couldn't imagine anything was wrong, but she couldn't just turn and go away, not knowing. Anybody else might, but not Ivy.

She walked around the house. If the back door was locked and she couldn't find a key under a flower pot or some other obvious place, she'd call her father. Lady had never given anyone a key except Daniel Burdette, her only son.

Ivy got as far as the garage and thought it was worth a peek to check on Lady's car. The free-standing structure was some distance from the house. The garage was big enough for two cars, but Lady owned just one, a Chrysler the size of a tank. She'd driven a Chrysler for as long as Ivy could remember, trading it in for a newer model from time to time but never a brand-new car. The essence of frugality, Lady Burdette, for all her money. After Ivy's grandfather died, Lady sold his nearly-new Suburban to Ivy's brother, Russ. That had been a bit of a sore spot with Russ. He'd thought she was going to *give* him his grandfather's car. He should have known better. No one could accuse Lady of being generous with her grandchildren.

Ivy peered through the small window of one of the garage doors and let out a heavy sigh. Irritation — mixed with relief. She hadn't realized how anxious she'd been, unable to rouse Lady.

The Chrysler was not there. Lady, who had seemed so eager to see her a couple of hours ago, had gone somewhere. Probably forgot all about calling Ivy, sounding such an alarm. Ivy left another message for her grandmother's voicemail as she walked to her car: "I'm leaving your house now, Lady. Call me when you get home. Let me know everything's OK."

She wondered if her grandmother was getting dementia.

Chapter 4

Every time the phone rang, Kitty Burdette felt her heart speed up. Just for a moment, she felt hope tug at her, felt a prayer rise in her: *Dear God, let it be him.* Always listening for her youngest son's voice: *Mama — it's me.* That old phone, hanging on the wall in the kitchen, didn't just connect her to the people in her life. It connected her to hope. She and Daniel had both bought new smart phones but they didn't give out those numbers freely. Calls came in on the landline every day, and every day, with every heart-aching ring, Kitty let herself hope it was Connor.

She knew he was alive. But she couldn't tell anyone else in the family, not even Daniel. Sometimes she thought she couldn't bear that secret anymore, that kind of betrayal, but she had to. She couldn't risk driving Connor away forever.

"Daniel's not at the church. Thursday's his day to visit shut-ins," she said to the plumber who was supposed to fix the ladies' toilet at First Baptist. "Just as long as it's working Sunday."

Sacks of produce from the farmer's market sat in a line, kitchen counter full of home-grown vegetables and fruits. Corn needed to be shucked, beans needed to be strung, and mothers needed to worry. The worry climbed down into the bottom of her heart where it lay turning over and over. Kitty had let herself get carried away at the farmer's market. Stressful times, times something heavy was weighing on her, she found working in the kitchen and digging in her flower bed gave her the greatest relief.

Most of the corn and green beans would wind up in the new freezer at the church. First Baptist had the best-stocked food pantry in Montpier, and a $5,000 commercial freezer that would make any restaurant proud. Daniel had fought for it. Some of the deacons believed Daniel's social programs took away from what ought to be the church's mission. And what might be the church's mission, if not to do good? Daniel had asked them. Frank Steele, chairman of the deacons, argued that in these times the church ought to be standing against the enemies of Christianity, those "free money liberals trying to destroy the morals of our country."

Frank, known as the Colonel, had persuaded a vocal handful of deacons that carried more weight than they should. They chimed in, "Amen!" Take a political stand from the pulpit is what they meant, and Daniel refused. So the deacons voted not to put the freezer in the budget.

Every time Kitty thought about how her husband had handled that dispute, it sent a warm rush through her. He went to the Bible. He preached a stirring sermon one Sunday, taking his text from a scripture every good Baptist knew. Matthew 25, where Jesus was teaching about feeding the poor, clothing the needy, taking in the stranger, visiting the prisoner. If you've done it to one of the least of these, you've done it to me. Kitty told Daniel she could almost hear a grumble from the pew where the Colonel sat with his cronies and his young new wife. Daniel said it was the sound of a conscience wrestling down its own weakness.

Daniel didn't have to ask the congregation for money. After the Sunday service and in the next few weeks, people started giving him checks designated for the freezer. All in all, $4,300 came in. Kitty and Daniel took $700 out of their savings to make up the rest.

Sometimes Kitty had to marvel that she'd wound up a preacher's wife. And that the life suited her so well. Her daddy, a general practitioner in Durbin Falls, used to joke about the boys that hung around his tall, willowy daughter. Couldn't beat them off with a stick, he said. Kitty had expected to marry a doctor, like him, or a lawyer or banker. She almost did marry a banker's son, Johnnie Polk, whose father was president of the Mercer County Farmers and Merchants Bank. Johnnie claimed to be a descendent of President James K. Polk, for all that was worth.

Kitty's senior year of high school, her daddy's big heart suddenly stopped. Still trying to manage the persistent ache of grief, she watched her mama, always a little unstable, slowly give in to the crazy at her core and finally head to Alabama with Milburn Vick, the county school superintendent. He left his wife and three children, the oldest daughter, Kitty's best friend Helen.

Kitty's world shattered. A world once defined by her father, beloved in Durbin Falls, in all of Mercer County, really, now defined by her mother's scandal. It was a wonder she graduated at all. Or that she got a clerical job at the courthouse. Hired out of respect for her daddy.

And then, Kitty went a little wild.

She and her brother Boone remained in their parents' house. Boone was four years older, but he was no parent. His drinking buddy Johnnie Polk was home from college that summer, working at his daddy's bank, and Boone had a job pumping gas. Weekends, though, Kitty might have been living in a fraternity house. Beer and whiskey flowing freely. A rowdy crowd Johnnie knew from college. Older girls who were pretty, stylish, had the perfumed smell of money, but Kitty knew what her daddy would say about the likes of them. "Fast and loose. Not a cupful of common sense in the whole lot." Even so, Kitty found herself admiring their careless ways. She watched how they lit up a cigarette, threw back a shot of whiskey, draped themselves around the boys. And she learned a thing or two about life on the low side.

It wasn't long before she was Johnnie's girl. Though he was seldom sober, always a flask on him, Kitty was drawn to his Paul Newman good looks and his worldliness. And his prospects. She had crossed so many lines that his assurance she wouldn't get pregnant, he'd take care of it, was good enough. Even better, he said he loved her, and then, that he wanted to marry her.

The September night before he returned to college, in the back seat of his GTO, as *The Thomas Crown Affair* played on the drive-in's screen, Johnnie vowed he would have a ring for her at Christmas. "At the end of every semester," he said, "Daddy gives me money for not flunking out." He'd already blown his reward money for spring semester.

Though he didn't actually *ask* or even put a dime-store ring on her finger, Kitty said yes. Engaged! It felt she'd latched onto something solid after she'd been left adrift in the world.

She didn't know yet that she was about to meet Daniel Burdette.

One day, Helen Vick came with her mother to the courthouse, and the girls who had once been best friends met in the hall in front of the ladies' room as Helen was going in. They looked hard at each other.

"We're losing our house," Helen said, finally.

For a moment longer, the girls stood there, silent. And then they threw their arms around each other and began to weep. Helen had weathered the scandal better than Kitty. It was Helen who got Kitty back into church. It was Helen who invited her to go along to a Young Christians Assembly at a Baptist camp one weekend that fall.

And there she met Daniel.

It took just one long weekend of Daniel Burdette, late-night walks around the lake, talks about God, life and death — and love — and the very idea of sharing a marriage bed with Johnnie Polk seemed like infidelity. She had already given some essential part of herself to Daniel.

Kitty didn't tell Daniel about the banker's son. She went home and immediately broke it off with Johnnie in a letter. His letters had never been heartfelt, like hers, and each was shorter than the last. Kitty had been feeling the temperature drop. Now the only thing that mattered was what Daniel would think of her. Almost every day letters flew between her and Daniel, and each confirmed what she'd known from the beginning. They belonged together.

That winter, Kitty's mother came home, took to her bed, and died before spring.

The day of the funeral, Daniel was there, comforting Kitty, saying all the right things. And that night, he asked her to be his wife.

Kitty had to tell him about Johnnie Polk. She had to tell him everything before she could say yes because Daniel would be expecting a "nice girl," one who remained a virgin until marriage. "We were engaged," she said, but not with conviction.

Even now, in the parsonage's kitchen, Kitty could see Daniel's brows pull together. Hear the hurt in his voice. The awful silence. And then, "Why didn't you tell me at the Assembly?"

"I was afraid, Daniel," she said. "I couldn't imagine marrying Johnnie. Not after I met you. And I couldn't bear it that you might not want me because I'd been... not completely honest." The word was *deceitful* but she couldn't say it. Even at that juncture, with all they meant to each other, Kitty had trembled, fearing Daniel would never trust her again.

After the longest time, he had reached for her hand. "Kitty," he said, in a voice she knew now he used only for those he loved most, "we can't keep secrets from each other anymore."

Truth untold is the shadow of a lie, Kitty knew. And now she'd done again what she promised she would never do.

Kitty set the sack of peaches aside. Some of them would find their way into a cobbler tonight. Peach cobbler, Ivy's favorite dessert. Kitty's children each had their favorites. Russ's was pecan pie. And Connor — his was chocolate cream pie with meringue two inches high. Kitty hadn't made a chocolate cream pie since that Fourth of July, ten years ago.

Now the Fourth was a test Kitty had to pass every year. Daniel and Ivy, too, she imagined. Russ, she didn't know. Before Connor went away, something was going on with him and Russ. But all these years, Russ never said a word about it. Once, when he was a little boy, Russ had an inch-long splinter in his foot. Would've gone gangrene if Kitty hadn't noticed his limp. It was impossible to know what her oldest son was thinking. Always had been.

Kitty was peeling peaches when Ivy came in.

"Mama, do you think Lady's getting dementia?" was the first thing Ivy said.

Kitty said, "Seems to me she's like she's always been — you know."

Neither had to say *eccentric.* They both laughed a little.

Ivy told her about Lady's message and how her car was gone when Ivy went to her house, but Kitty was not convinced there was anything wrong with her mother-in-law's mind. "Something probably came up, and she didn't have the good grace to call you back and save you a trip." Kitty exchanged a look with Ivy, and neither said any more about Lady.

The First Baptist parsonage that was the Burdettes' home had a small kitchen typical of 1920s bungalows. The kitchen was Kitty's domain. She didn't allow anyone to get in her way. She let Ivy set the table, then said, "I'm making BLTs for supper. Nothing else for you to do."

The bacon was sizzling when Daniel came in. He gave her a peck on the cheek and poured himself a cup of coffee. Daniel drank gallons of coffee throughout the day and evening. Kitty couldn't tell it ever bothered him.

He took his place at the table and wrapped both hands wrapped around his cup. Squinting, he stared into the coffee as if it held an answer to some profound question. Kitty, who always knew when something was on her husband's mind, asked, "What is it?"

"I'd like to do something for Lonnie Briscoe and his little children," Daniel said.

Kitty didn't look up from the skillet as Daniel told that Lonnie Briscoe's wife had run off with a vinyl siding salesman, and Lonnie was trying to hang on to his job, driving a truck. "Four children, not even school age. Cute little rascals," Daniel said. "Lonnie's stepmother tries to help out when he's on the road. She came by the church today for clothes. Had to nearly pry it out of her that they needed food, too. A proud woman, Amanda. She had all four with her."

Daniel's voice began to sound like it was pulling up the world, but Kitty wouldn't let herself be drawn in. Her mind had flown to the past. The Briscoes, Lonnie's parents. One of those families living on a shoestring, on government aid, maybe a daddy in the picture who might have been disabled. Hard to remember. It was their connection with Joe Ray Loomis that made Kitty's spine stiffen. "You've got too much forgiveness in you, Daniel," she said.

"Lonnie and his kids have done nothing to forgive," Daniel said. "You know that, Kitty."

That was his way, the way he had of soothing all of them.

Bits and pieces came back to her as she lifted bacon onto a platter. All that had bubbled up when Joe Ray Loomis and Connor got into trouble. The sympathy around town for Joe Ray, arrested after Connor left. Sympathy because his daddy had beat his mama to death and burned the body. A gruesome murder, unspeakably terrible. Joe Ray's mama and Lonnie's mama were sisters, so the Briscoes raised him with their kids. Wild as a bobcat, people said, but the Briscoes took him in because he was family. Kitty thought how different *her* family's lives would have been if Joe Ray had gone off to foster care somewhere when his daddy got life in prison.

"I can't forgive Joe Ray," Kitty said. "How he lied about Connor, and people believed him! I know Connor didn't bring a gun to the market. He didn't shoot that clerk. Not my son!"

"Kitty," Daniel said. Just that word, his voice so gentle that she had to turn her face toward him and meet his gaze.

After a moment, a private moment, filled with all that their years together had forged between them, she said, "I know Lonnie's children shouldn't suffer." And then, "I can make up a basket of produce, but *you'll* have to deliver it, Daniel."

Chapter 5

Ivy kept hearing Lady's message, like a song you couldn't get out of your head. What had Lady meant? Ivy supposed her mama could be right. Something came up and Lady didn't have the good grace to call back. Ivy knew as well as anyone how inconsiderate her grandmother could be. But this had a different feel to it. Her call went to voicemail yet again.

"Where *are* you, Lady? Are you all right? We're getting a little worried."

Ivy had left three messages now. That ought to be good enough. She imagined Lady at the club for cocktails and dinner with her tennis friends. "Would you listen to this?" she'd laugh, and play Ivy's message. "My granddaughter needs a man, that's what."

The man she'd had, or thought she'd had, used to say, "Lighten up, Ivy, for God's sake. Lighten up." Turned out they'd had vastly different ideas about what it meant to be responsible.

She propped a pillow against the headboard and stretched out her legs. To her mama's credit, Ivy's room no longer looked like it belonged to an eighteen-year-old about to leave home. The unframed art posters, the mottos she'd lived by that seemed so trite, now at thirty-two, so stunted and lifeless — all gone. "Try to be a rainbow in someone's cloud" popped into her mind. It embarrassed her. She didn't know who she felt worse for, the naïve girl or the weary woman.

No more pink-flowered wallpaper. The walls were painted a cool barely-blue. Kitty had replaced the frilly curtains with shades and the Laura Ashley bedding with an upmarket duvet. When Ivy had returned in May, there was no room in the small closet. It was full of trinkets from the chest of drawers and dresser, all boxed up. Ivy got to choose what to keep and what to toss. Just like life, she guessed. Always leaving part of you behind for the new invention of yourself.

She'd tossed everything except a couple of sweet artifacts. A music box from her tenth birthday that played "Edelweiss" only slightly out of tune. A half-filled bottle of some cheap perfume that reminded her of summer dances, of boys that smelled like Juicy Fruit and beer, of dreaming about how love might someday feel.

It looked like her mama hadn't touched the shelves of books in her bookcase. Books from high-school literature classes. Romance novels. All she'd needed to know about history and calculus and love. And there were the books on fireflies that she used to read, thinking someday she might want to study fireflies. They seemed so frail and full of light, so broken, but still always quietly beating against each evening's deepening darkness.

Wexler-Fitzhugh had no department for studying anything like fireflies. And the longer she stayed at the college, the darker those halls became.

Only two framed photos remained in the bookcase, the rest stored in drawers. One was of Ivy and her parents, the day she received her master's degree. It was August, Connor gone one month, all of their smiles trying too hard. The other, a picture of her and her brothers on moving-in day, the summer before she started junior high. Like Russ, who was going into high school, she was sulking in the photo, both of them figuring their lives were over since they'd been ripped out of their comfort zone, just so their parents could come "home" to Mercer County. But Connor, peering over the top of a box he carried, wore the expression that Ivy remembered so well. That beaming openness to whatever might come next and a willingness to believe it would be fine. Confidence that life was a straight line and happiness was just a matter of time.

Sure, moving to a new town wasn't such a big deal when you were eight years old, but most kids wouldn't have made it look so easy. Connor was riding bikes with boys in his new neighborhood that very afternoon. His disposition was just naturally sunny. Until it wasn't.

The Fourth of July always brought back a flood of memories, sweet and painful. Even the sweet memories were painful.

Ivy had not opened the door of Connor's room since she'd been back. She suspected her mama had not so much as picked up a stray sock since the day Connor left. Sometimes she put her ear to the wall that separated their rooms, hoping she might hear the echo of her brother.

She smelled bacon and heard her daddy's voice, and then she heard a little trill of a laugh from her mama. Ivy crossed the room, but at the door she stopped and for a moment just listened to the consoling back and forth of her parents' voices and hoped this Fourth of July would be easier for all of them. It had been ten years, after all.

Ivy's parents had always lingered at the supper table, even in the days when they'd had to excuse their three fidgety children. Ivy had come to understand that there was so much more to the ritual than just letting their food digest. Her daddy, his earnest face, and her mama with her smiling eyes, leaning toward each other. Ivy joined them after she had cleared the table, brought back a cup of coffee for herself and refilled her father's cup.

Her phone's ping jolted her. She grabbed it, thinking, Lady, finally! It was just a colleague from Wexler-Fitzhugh texting about a tenure meeting, but now Lady was back in her mind. The notion that her grandmother was just out at the club was losing steam. Lady didn't like to drive at night — and it would soon be dark. Ivy couldn't keep this a secret.

"Listen." She held out her phone for her parents, and Lady's voice came on.

Her daddy asked, "When did you get that message?" She told him what she'd told her mama. He got a familiar furrow in his brow that Ivy took as a mild rebuke. He scooted his chair back. It made a loud scraping sound.

"I think we ought to go see about Lady," he said.

As the car climbed the winding drive, Ivy could see a light coming from behind the house, but before she could feel too optimistic, her daddy said, "Those back yard lights are on an automatic timer. I made her do it. It's so secluded back there, too easy for burglars."

Neither had said much on the short drive. Ivy was second-guessing herself. She should've told him earlier that Lady was not responding. He was protective of his mother, as much as Lady would allow. Ivy sensed there was an edge of worry to his silence, the set of his jaw.

He pulled up next to the garage, switched on the pocket-size flashlight he'd brought from the car and shined it through one of the garage door's small windows. "Her car's gone," he said, put away the light, and took long strides toward the kitchen. Ivy followed, something comforting in having him take charge, even for someone as self-sufficient as Ivy liked to believe she was.

The back porch was well lit. Her daddy turned off the flashlight, stuck it in his pocket, and found the key to open the kitchen door. "I've tried to get her to put in an alarm. It was like pulling teeth to get the yard lights," he said. "I swear, she's the most stubborn woman I know."

He flipped the switch next to the door, and the kitchen flooded with light.

Later, when Ivy would remember the next couple of minutes, she'd wonder why she'd stopped just inside the kitchen, why she'd remained motionless except for the sweep of her gaze as she studied everything, when it all seemed perfectly normal, except that Lady was absent. Had she suspected what was coming, how the ground was about to shift? She would wonder if her daddy had suspected, too. She would remember how resolutely he'd headed to the dining room, straight through and on to the foyer. Ivy heard the cadence of his footsteps change. Slow at first, then faster. And his voice — a groan, and then, "Ivy, don't come in here!"

She didn't obey her father.

Where the curved staircase spilled into the foyer, Lady's body lay sprawled on the floor.

Chapter 6

Daniel knew he'd have to have it out with God about the lie he was telling the Sheriff, but his voice was steady as he said, "No, I didn't move her. Felt for a pulse is all."

A sin of omission was a sin all the same, and he had failed to mention that he'd pulled his mama's dress down, but Lady was so proper, so modest. How it would've mortified her if Sonny Bellingham had seen her skirt hiked up, showing her unmentionables.

On her stomach, one hand reaching out, the other hand hidden under her body, his mother looked almost peaceful. Her skirt covering her, lady-like.

The sheriff, who'd brought his deputy, didn't question Daniel's word. Why would he? Daniel, pastor of First Baptist Church, had a sterling reputation in Montpier.

The deputy, chomping on a mouthful of gum, stood back, arms folded, legs spread. He stared at the chandelier hanging from the high ceiling, the sweeping staircase with its shiny bannisters, the marble floor, surveying the foyer like it was the first time he was ever in a fine house.

Daniel had on his pastor face. That's what his family called it. Hundreds of times he'd witnessed Death's unwelcome visit, but this one had set up an ache in him that he hadn't known before, even when his father died. The deep sorrow he felt for his missing son at times consumed him, but he could still pray that Connor was alive somewhere. The finality of death had a bite all its own. He stared at his mama there on the cold floor and swallowed hard. There would be time for tears. Time for grief to wash past him like a tidal wave. But all of that later.

The sheriff let the silence hang for a moment.

"Seems like — I don't know," Daniel said, gazing upward, to the top of the stairs. "She must have lost her footing." He thought of all the ups and downs she'd worn into those stairs.

The sheriff's nod was non-committal. "No one else in the house?"

"Nobody but my daughter and me."

"Did you go upstairs?"

"No. We just went to the kitchen. I made a couple of calls. You got here lickety-split."

The sheriff nodded again, this time smiling, barely. Sonny Bellingham was forty-something, Daniel figured. He was tall and slender, with an intelligent face. Put him in a tweed jacket instead of khakis and he could pass for a college professor. But there was something besides intelligence. His gray-blue eyes suggested iron-clad honesty. Daniel could not have explained why he thought this, but he did. Honesty didn't necessarily go with intelligence, but honesty always had a look all its own.

"Wait in the kitchen if you don't mind, Daniel. I'll be in there shortly," the sheriff said.

Most people addressed Daniel as Brother Burdette, but he liked being on familiar footing with the sheriff.

"My parents and your grandparents were big card-playing buddies." Daniel wasn't sure why he said it, but it brought a comforting feeling, thinking of those days, his parents so vital.

"Yep." Sonny smiled. "Salt of the earth, Lady and Jack Burdette. My granddaddy said it many times. And I won't forget that Letter to the Editor Lady wrote when I was running for office. Hell of a letter. A real boost to my campaign."

"She ran the Republicans down the road for all the drugs in Mercer County."

Sonny made a little grunt. Daniel had heard the meth problem kept getting worse, even with a lawman like Sonny Bellingham doing his best.

"Coroner's on his way," Sonny said. "I need a word with him, and then I'll have some questions for you and your daughter. What's her name?"

"Ivy." Daniel was thinking, if it wasn't for Ivy, it might've been days before Lady — her body — was discovered. The notion that it could've happened like that made him queasy.

Daniel sat across from Ivy at the round Formica table in Lady's perfect kitchen, straight out of a 1960's women's magazine — just like the rest of Lady's house.

"How you doing, Ivy?" he asked. Looked like she'd cried a little. Daniel knew she wasn't close to her grandmother. But this had come as such a shock.

She sniffed and touched a tissue to her nose. "Can't believe this is happening."

Car lights swept across the driveway. The vehicle wasn't visible, but Daniel said, "Must be the coroner. Sonny said he called him."

Death was not an everyday thing in a small town like Montpier, so the coroner couldn't make a living on death. Daniel knew he was an EMT with the ambulance service. He didn't look old enough to shave, but apparently he was a competent medical examiner, a good man who, with wife and baby, slipped into the last pew at First Baptist from time to time.

Daniel had rung up Russ and Kitty after he'd made the 911 call. Russ wanted to come over, but Daniel told him there was nothing he could do here. Kitty was content to wait at home. Not that she didn't love Lady — in her own way. Kitty was a respectful daughter-in-law, but Daniel knew that in his wife's mind, Lady had belonged to him. Maybe to their children a little, but mostly to him. Not to his wife.

Fifteen minutes later — though it seemed longer — Sonny took a chair across from Daniel, leaving an empty chair between himself and Ivy. He glanced at her and smiled what seemed to be a condolence, then pulled out a notepad.

"Was Lady expecting you tonight?" he asked, looking back and forth between them.

Daniel saw Ivy reaching for her phone. He answered. "Lady left a message for Ivy. Asked her to come by, and she did. But when she got here, her car was gone. No sign of Lady."

"What time was that?" Sonny said.

"Two-forty," Ivy said. "The message came in at two-forty. You want to hear it?"

Lady's voice filled the kitchen. It was all Daniel could do to keep his pastor face. This was the first voice in his world sixty-three years ago, and now he knew he'd never hear it again.

Sonny scribbled in his notepad and asked Ivy what time she came to the house. Around four, she thought. Her class was over at three-twenty. Again, Sonny jotted something down.

"You say the car was gone?" he said.

"Still is," Daniel said. "I checked before we came inside."

He noted the almost imperceptible arch of Sonny's brows as he asked Ivy, "Do you know why she wanted to see you? Any idea what she wanted to keep between you and her?"

Daniel thought his words could've been kinder, but he was just a father being protective.

Ivy shook her head. "I wish I knew. I called her a couple of times but she didn't answer."

"I'd like to get a copy of that message, if I can take your phone," Sonny said. As he reached for it, another set of car lights swept across the dark. "I called my investigator," he said. "Something like this, we want to take a good look, make sure we're not missing anything. J.D.'s a fine investigator."

"What do you mean, something like this?" Ivy looked at the sheriff and then at Daniel, her eyes wide. "She fell, didn't she?"

Daniel said, "Sometimes if it's a death in the home, something sudden, an accident, they just have to rule out foul play." He spoke with authority. He had some experience with these things. His church members were likely to call him even before they called 911.

"Foul play? Are you saying... murder? You can't be serious!" Ivy said.

"Your daddy's right." Sonny took over. "We want to know what happened here. You want to know. We have to cover all the bases." His voice had turned gentle, speaking to Ivy. "Let's go upstairs now and see if anything's been disturbed. See if all her jewelry's there." He tucked his notepad in his shirt pocket.

Daniel could see in her eyes that Ivy hadn't been satisfied by Sonny's words. But she said, "I don't know much about her jewelry. I don't even know if she has a jewelry box."

There was a note of regret in her voice. Daniel regretted, too, that his daughter wasn't close with his mother, like grandmothers and grandchildren ought to be.

Russ wasn't either. Just Connor. If Connor hadn't started doing God-knows-what with God-knows-who, Lady would've given that boy anything. It was puzzling why she favored him, but clear to all, she did.

As they all got up from the table, their chairs scraping the quarry tile floor, Daniel said,

"I wouldn't know much about her jewelry, either, but I'll do what I can."

The coroner had covered the body. The stark white sheet made walking past what lay beneath it almost bearable. Daniel nodded to the investigator, who had a camera.

Upstairs, Sonny led them from room to room, opened the doors, and they looked in. "Let me know if you see anything that looks out of place," he said. "Please don't touch anything." All the lights were on, Daniel noticed. Seemed Sonny had already been in these rooms while he and Ivy were waiting in the kitchen.

Daniel couldn't remember the last time he'd been upstairs. It was the kind of house that had more rooms than any one soul could ever hope to use. Five bedrooms on the second floor. Lady's poster bed was nicely made up, everything in its place, clean surfaces, nothing that said anything about who had lived here except for the closet, with its racks of clothes, shoes lined up, and a hint of Lady's powdery smell that set off a new wave of sadness through Daniel.

With a pen, Sonny flipped open the lid of a wooden jewelry box on the dresser and moved aside. "Take a look. See if you think anything's missing."

Daniel hung back and Ivy edged forward. She peered over the few pieces of heavy necklaces and clip-on earrings, all costume jewelry, and said, "I don't remember ever seeing her wear any of this. It must all be old."

"Lady wasn't much for jewelry," Daniel said.

"I'm no expert, but none of it looks expensive," Sonny said.

Daniel gave a little laugh that rang with a note of nostalgia. "I know what you're thinking. She could've had the good stuff, but it wasn't something she cared for. And she was pretty tight with her money. Always afraid of another Depression, I think."

"She was wearing a gold wedding band," Sonny said. "No diamond rings?"

Daniel explained that his father had bought Lady a wedding ring set for their fiftieth anniversary. "A nice-sized diamond and a bunch of little ones — baguettes, I think they're called," he said. But after Jack Burdette died, Lady had put the rings in a safe deposit box in the bank and had gone back to wearing the simple gold band that her husband had slipped on her finger when she was barely twenty.

"The tennis bracelet," Ivy said, suddenly. "I don't see the tennis bracelet."

"I forgot about that," Daniel said. "Daddy bought it for her not long before he passed. She did wear that tennis bracelet sometimes."

Ivy described the elegant bracelet, tiny diamonds linked together. "It was expensive. Not Tiffany's but the real deal, not cubic zirconia."

Sonny tapped the lid of the jewelry box and it closed. "That sounds like the bracelet she had in her hand," he said.

The image flashed in Daniel's mind of his mama's body on that cold floor. One hand reaching out, the other hand hidden.

"The bracelet was broken," Sonny said, something in his voice that Daniel hadn't heard before. "Hard to see how it broke in a fall and wound up with her clutching it like that."

Sonny had to be thinking she was pushed. Was it a robbery? Was that what Sonny had in mind? Daniel suddenly felt weak, thinking of a stranger putting his hands on Lady at the top of the staircase, trying to rip away that bracelet. She would fight. Lord, how she would fight!

Could've been some kids high on meth, no intention to kill. But seeing the body like that, they might be too panicked to think about anything but flight.

Daniel's heart beat out a prayer that it didn't happen that way. *Please God.* Not her life ending like that. *Please.*

Chapter 7

Something swept over Russ like a sudden breeze that makes the leaves tremble and then passes on. Death brings on a quiver as the word speeds into you and whispers, making you think about *your* time, when and how, and who would ache at the sound of your beckoning. Russ felt all of that, but he was a young man, and like all young men, he was sure he would live to be an old man and Death was an enemy he would not face until he had lived out all of his dreams.

The sadness that lingered was for his daddy, who had called with the news. Russ stood still in his tracks, his phone in hand, as if he expected more, as if he'd missed something that ought to make him sorry for Lady. But all he could think of was how sad it was to lose your mama. Even one as cold-hearted as his grandmother.

Nikki's footsteps sounded light and quick as she came from tending to the boys after their baths. Nikki was particular about their boys. Even though they were eight and nine, she had to check behind ears and make sure they'd brushed teeth and fuss a little about the soggy towels.

Before he could tell her, her eyes widened and she whispered that feathery womanly consoling tone. "Russ — what's wrong?" Sometimes his wife could read him, like that.

"Daddy called. Lady fell down her stairs," he said. "She's — gone."

"Gone?" Nikki gasped. "Dead?" Her hands flew to her face, and tears welled up in her eyes. Russ reached out to her, and she moved into his arms. Russ, exactly twelve inches taller than his wife, laid his cheek against the top of her head, her strawberry-scented hair, and held her like that for a minute, feeling her breath catch again and again.

She pulled back finally. "I'm so sorry," she said, wiping at her eyes.

"Yeah. Hard to believe." It was all Russ could think to say. He heard the rough edge in his voice, but he didn't say what he was thinking, that Lady never meant a thing to him, and he never meant anything to her. Somehow, he imagined the old woman would find a way to shout out from beyond the grave. Death wouldn't have the last word, not with his grandmother.

He let Nikki go and went to the refrigerator, where he was heading when he got the call. He grabbed a beer. "You want one?"

She shook her head. "How'd you say it happened? She fell?"

"That's what Daddy said."

"Awful," Nikki said, still blinking back tears.

Russ took a long pull on the beer. "Awful for anybody to fall down the stairs and die," he said, knowing how it sounded. He tried a kinder tone. "I hate it for Daddy."

After a few minutes, Nikki pulled herself together and began loading the dishwasher. Lady didn't deserve his wife's tears, Russ thought. And then Nikki said, "Once, a couple of summers ago, Lady asked me to play with her in a round robin at the club." A little smile in her voice now, but it was still shaky. "She bragged on me. Said I was a force to be reckoned with."

Maybe that was it, Russ thought. Lady treated Nikki better on the tennis courts than she ever did because she was family. She got no special treatment for being his wife.

He finished his beer. "I need to go see about Mama. When Daddy and Ivy get back home, I'll find out more about what happened. Sounds like it was just a fall. She must've hit her head."

"Happens to old people," Nikki said. "They fall all the time."

Night had the heavy feeling that a late hour brings, though it wasn't even nine o'clock. Several cars were parked around the parsonage, the house lit up like a party. Or like exactly what it was, people waiting at Brother Burdette's house to tell him how sorry they were that Lady was dead, and maybe pick up a few more details to spread, as the news hurtled through the town.

Not long after Russ arrived, his daddy and Ivy entered at the kitchen door. His mama met them, hugged Ivy quietly, and reached out to his daddy. As he held her in a long embrace, he squeezed his eyes shut, then patted her back, and the moment was over. Russ understood that kind of Morse Code between husbands and wives. And then he could see his daddy resuming his role of pastor to everyone else crowded in the small kitchen. Even squeezing *his* shoulder, like a pastor, though he did whisper, "Son." And Russ felt chastened, somehow. Maybe he should've stood, should've stepped over to his daddy instead of the other way around.

The sorrow that hung here in his parents' kitchen seemed to be weighing on everyone's shoulders. Except his. Russ felt like he was on the outside of something, looking in.

Boone Mangrum, his mama's brother, took more than his share of air out of any room. Boone was six-three, bear-like, with a scruffy, gray-streaked beard. Russ figured his uncle had to weigh two-fifty, maybe more. He always smelled like cigars; he smelled like he'd just finished one this evening. Sometimes he gave off a scent of stale whiskey, but not tonight. He didn't own a shirt without a stain on it, and he couldn't find a belt to fit so he wore suspenders, but his belly still spilled out over his pants.

"Kitty called me. I cain't believe it. God! What in holy hell happened?" Boone roared.

Russ expected his daddy to say, "No cause to take the Lord's name in vain." He'd said it before, but this time all he said was, "Hey, Boone. Thanks for coming."

"Lady — well, she was one of a kind," Boone said.

So was the bubonic plague, Russ thought.

"God, this town won't be the same. I'm just plain flabbergasted. Who'll we have to look down on us? Jesus Christ!" His remark brought a few smiles.

Again, Russ expected an admonition from his father, but it was his mama who said, "Take it down a notch, Boone. One day we'll be sitting in a kitchen remembering your mouth."

Russ had worked for Boone at the Sports Emporium ever since he came back from UT with a bum arm, his baseball career over. A few months ago, Boone had said, "This state needs a good ol' boy like me in the Legislature." Now that he was planning to run in the next election, he'd told Russ quietly that he was ready to get out of the business. He'd sell the store to Russ at a bargain, being that he was family. The idea had seemed like pie in the sky, until now. Lady's death might open up new possibilities.

All these people. All the faces that seemed to know what expression to wear. The lanky man in running clothes who was leaning against the counter, Mr. Brockman. He lived several streets over but ran by the parsonage at night after his kids were asleep. He'd probably seen the commotion, the cars, and like a good neighbor, stopped to see if something was wrong. Near him at the counter, a kind-faced woman they called Ruth Ann was making a fresh pot of coffee with such ease that this could have been her own kitchen. Old Mr. Hardaway, next door neighbor, and a couple of deacons were also there.

"Sorry, I just cain't wrap my mind around it," Boone said. He settled into a chair at one end of the table, the place marked by his coffee mug. The chair squeaked under his weight. He took a swig from the mug.

Russ noted how his daddy greeted all of them, one by one, before he took a seat at the other end of the table. Ivy sat down in the last vacant chair, beside Russ. He leaned toward her and asked what took them so long. She shrugged and said, "We had to talk to the sheriff."

His daddy told what happened. "And there she was at the bottom of the stairs. Didn't look like she suffered." He paused, gave a long sigh, and fixed his gaze on his hands, folded in front of him on the table, prayer-like. "From what I could tell, she just toppled down the stairs."

The room fell silent for a moment, and when the conversation resumed, the scene at the bottom of the stairs was left behind.

The wiry little deacon with thick glasses, Lowell Richey, had a pleasant manner about him, but Frank Steele, who might've been a linebacker in his youth, wore a scowl and said next to nothing. Russ knew most people called Frank "the Colonel." He was chairman of the deacons, a powerful position in the Baptist Church. But Lowell was the one who said, "Just tell us what you want for the funeral. The deacons will take care of everything. And don't worry about Sunday. We'll call the Association office tomorrow and get somebody good."

It came as no surprise to Russ that his daddy said, "I don't need a supply for Sunday, Lowell. I'll preach." His daddy was particular about his pulpit.

His mama, bringing a mug of fresh coffee, said, "Daniel, why don't you let them get somebody else to do it."

"You'll have enough on you these next few days, Brother Burdette," Lowell said.

"You'll need time with your family."

"Well... let's just say I'll let you know tomorrow if I need your help with that."

Russ knew that tone well. It was his daddy pretending he was still studying on it, but his mind was made up solid.

Knuckles rapped on the door, and the bony old man who came in was Don Petrie. Russ wasn't sure why his name had stuck with him, but he guessed it was because he'd heard Lady say so many times, "Don Petrie won't like it, but it's my money." He was Lady's lawyer, one of the professionals she called on out of necessity but whose advice she often rejected.

His daddy stood up and shook hands with the old man, who was profuse with apologies for arriving at such a late hour. Mr. Petrie had been at the country club, where he'd heard about Lady. How so soon? Russ wondered. But not surprising, the way news traveled in a small town.

"I thought it was worth driving by, to see if y'all were still up," Mr. Petrie said.

Russ offered his chair, but the old man refused. He wouldn't stay. He just couldn't resist stopping in to say how sorry he was. A few more words of condolence, a few more chuckles about what a hard time Lady always gave him.

Russ figured it was something about Lady's will when Mr. Petrie leaned in close to his daddy and whispered. But his daddy didn't make an effort to speak confidentially. "No hurry. Prob'ly best to wait till after the funeral," he said. "I'm glad she made you the Executor, Don. I expected as much. How about if I give you a call when things quiet down a bit."

The old attorney said something else in a low voice, a look in his eyes that said it was important.

Russ couldn't help but wonder, was it possible that Lady had something for him and Ivy in the will? Not likely. But if Lady left everything to her only son, and that was how it should be, Russ was thinking his daddy might back him in a business venture, might be glad to do that for him and Nikki and the boys. The Sports Emporium could be his. Lady, who had never lifted a finger for him, might wind up giving him a future, after all, him and his family.

Trouble and hope, Russ thought. Trouble and hope wander together.

Chapter 8

Daniel was on a first name basis with Death. He'd looked at it so often in the faces of his people. He'd seen it creeping into the eyes of the old in the pews, waiting patiently like a hungry dog. Death always had its way. And it was human nature for the grieving to seek out some balm in other living souls.

Grief comes in and rolls down on you like an ocean. And when the wave hits, it's like trying to empty the sea with a bucket. You think you can't carry it. But you do.

And grief shared breaks it up a little bit, fractures the pain, lets you carry it until the tears finally dry up, as they always do, when enough time passes by.

In the crowded kitchen, Daniel felt the grief around him and it made his own a little easier. The hum of voices, like a sad old hymn, so sad it has become sweet, a kind of music that people sing to each other without notes.

In small towns, the ritual of gathering to absorb the loss together, blood reaching out to blood beyond its own veins, started in somebody's kitchen as soon as the word got out.

Tonight it went on until ten o'clock, when Don Petrie left, and his departure seemed to signal others to leave, except for Russ and Boone. Daniel stood at the door, saying goodnight, shaking hands, thanking them for their offers to do anything, anything at all that he needed.

Frank Steele made no such offer. Frank. Daniel had never called him the Colonel, never could quite get the word out. Frank offered an obligatory handshake — limp, the kind that made you imagine he'd climbed into a cold freezer and turned blue and just now was pretending to defrost. "We need to talk after all of this is over," he said, and Daniel nodded.

Daniel was a little stooped on a good day. Living had climbed up into his shoulders, waiting there for the bend in his bones and then in his heart.

He went back to the table and slumped, and gave a heavy sigh.

"What was Frank Steele talking about?" Ivy asked.

Daniel waved her off. He couldn't get into it tonight. "Church business. It'll wait."

Russ said, "What's this Mama said about a call from Lady?" He frowned at Ivy. "She wanted you to go over there?"

Daniel heard the accusatory note in Russ's voice, but Ivy had always stood up to her brother, all five feet nine inches to his six foot two. She came back at him. "I don't know what she wanted. The car was gone. I assumed she was gone, too. Then she *was*... she was gone."

"What about her car?" Boone put in.

"Ivy just told you, the car wasn't there," Kitty said. All the company had worn her down, Daniel could tell from her terse reply to her brother when he didn't deserve it, not this time.

"Maybe her car's in the shop," Boone said. "Where's she get it serviced?"

A hush fell over the room. No one seemed to have considered that possibility. Daniel felt a little foolish. What a simple explanation if that's what they found to be true.

"She takes it to Dale Story," he said. "Over at the BP."

"One way to find out. The BP's open till eleven." Boone didn't know how to knot a tie but he knew how to get that Siri girl in his phone to do just about anything he asked. The BP was still open for business, but Dale, the mechanic, had gone home at six. Boone asked if Dale had been working on Lady Burdette's car. The teenager at the service station hadn't paid attention to what kind of cars were in the bay, and Dale had locked up before he left. The boy volunteered Dale's home number, and Boone punched in the number with his big log-like fingers.

Daniel hated to be calling anybody so late at night, but Dale must've answered on the first ring. Boone raised his hand to signal quiet. A moment later he called out, "Bingo!" and snapped his fingers. "Wait a minute, Dale. I'm gonna put you on the speaker phone!" He set the phone on the table for all to hear.

Dale's voice came through loud and excited. "She was out at the country club and her car died 'bout a hundred yards from the gate. I went out there with the tow truck, 'bout two o'clock. I b'lieve Ansel Brown's wife took Miz Lady home. My Lord, I cain't b'lieve she's dead!"

"The car's still at the BP?" Boone asked.

"Yep. It's the alternator. I cain't get the part till Monday."

Daniel wanted to get the timeline straight. "Dale, this is Daniel Burdette. Did you call Lady to tell her you had to order the part?"

"Yessir — I left a message. Said she should call me to authorize the order, but she didn't."

"What time was that?"

"Lemme think. Hm-m-m." Daniel imagined he was scratching his head. "I'd already told her when I picked up the car that it was prob'ly the alternator, the way she described how it acted. Losing power, the way it does, and all the electrical going haywire. But I called her, soon as I checked it out. Like I said, she didn't answer so I left a message."

Ivy chimed in at that point, sounding as impatient as Daniel was. "Was that maybe three thirty?" Daniel understood she wanted to believe there was nothing she could've done for Lady when she was at the door.

"Well — that sounds about right. I cain't pinpoint the time, exactly."

Daniel thanked the mechanic for his help and told him to go on and order what he needed. He said, "I'll come by and settle up soon as I can."

"I'll do it. I'm real sorry about Miz Lady," Dale said.

"See you around, Buddy," Boone said. He put away his phone, stood up, and puffed his chest out a bit. Rambled some more about how the town would not be the same without Lady Burdette. A pillar of the community, fallen but not forgotten. Daniel had never heard him try for eloquence. He guessed old Boone had heard it elsewhere, where Boone got all of his good ideas.

"I'd planned to go to Nashville tomorrow and meet up with some old boys about fundraising for my campaign," Boone said. "Don't know if I ought to cancel."

"Please don't cancel, Boone," Kitty said. "Anything you need to do for us, you can do the next day." Her frosty tone put an end to anything her brother might have wanted to say about his run for the state legislature. It was a sore spot all around, Boone a right-wing Republican, the Burdettes Democrats, but most times family took precedence over politics.

"Kitty's right. You go on and do what you need to do," Daniel was saying when the phone on the wall rang.

Kitty answered. "No, no, it's not too late," she said, then motioned for Daniel and handed him the phone. "It's the sheriff."

"Tell him we found the car," Boone said.

The car mystery they'd solved hardly seemed to matter in light of the sheriff's reason for calling. Daniel listened to a lengthy explanation, said, "All right" and "I see" and in the end, "I appreciate the call, Sonny. Keep us informed."

The kitchen had grown silent. Daniel took a moment to let what he'd heard sink in."They're sending her body to Nashville for an autopsy," he said. An announcement, unemotional, like announcing in church that the Men's Prayer Breakfast was rescheduled.

"An autopsy?" Kitty whispered.

"Sonny said they don't get second chances to do an autopsy, so it's best to go on with it when they have questions that need to be answered."

"What questions?" Kitty asked.

"About the way she died." Daniel was getting his rhythm back, the calm of his voice, the way he had of calming others. "We'll know in a day or two what's going on. It's probably nothing."

If any of them believed it was nothing, they didn't say so. Daniel wasn't sure, himself. Nothing had a way of becoming something. He looked at his wife. Wasn't that how it had been with Connor? Nothing, and then something that brought on more heartache.

Daniel felt the ocean of grief again. He would need more buckets.

Chapter 9

Old people died. The church was full of old people, and sometimes they fell like dominoes, Ivy had heard her daddy say. Neighbors, too, like Mr. Hardaway's wife. Ivy remembered coming home from school and seeing the ambulance, the paramedics rolling the gurney, the sheet covering her body. Old Mr. Hardaway in the yard, shaking his fist at the sky, crying, "Why? Why *her*? She was the best woman you ever made!"

Never had Ivy heard of an autopsy for anyone who died in Montpier, old or young. Until this one. Lady.

There was something about the tennis bracelet. That was the reason for the autopsy. Ivy had heard it in Sonny Bellingham's voice, as they'd stood in Lady's hotel-like bedroom the evening after she died. Decorator art on the wall. Not one photograph of Lady's grandchildren. Not even one of her son. You'd expect a photo of Daniel's graduation from seminary or a wedding photo of Lady and Jack. Nothing like that. Just those watercolors in gilded frames that you might see in a Marriott.

"Hard to see how it broke in a fall," the sheriff had said about the bracelet, "and wound up with her clutching it like that." His words didn't have the ring of a casual remark. They had the weight of a theory already taking shape, suspicion that this was more than an old woman losing her balance and toppling down the stairs.

Sonny Bellingham struck Ivy as someone who couldn't rest until he got to the bottom of things. She could hardly disapprove of that. If the sheriff Sonny had defeated in the last election had been more persistent, he might have found Connor. "He was lazy," Ivy's mama had said. From what Ivy had seen of Bellingham, she'd bet he was not lazy.

Ivy was fond of Boone, but she could take only so much of him. They all seemed to let out a breath when her uncle was gone. She sensed her daddy had been waiting to say something more, waiting for Boone to go, and she guessed

Russ did, too. Nikki called the second time, and Ivy heard her brother say, "Don't wait up."

More coffee all around, and her daddy sighed. "This business with the autopsy. Sonny mentioned something about Lady's tennis bracelet when we were at her house. How she was holding on to it, but it was broken. I thought she might've stumbled, fooling with the bracelet," he said. "But there's more to it."

Ivy crossed her arms and drew into herself, listening as her daddy said the sheriff had told him that two tiny diamonds were embedded in the carpet, next to the newel post at the top of the stairs. And there was a fresh scrape on her wrist. He couldn't say how it got there. The autopsy would shed more light on the matter.

The bracelet could've broken when Lady was taking it off, Ivy thought, but she could see why the sheriff was suspicious.

"Does he think somebody pushed her? Somebody tried to jerk the bracelet off of her wrist? Somebody's fingernail scraped her?" her mama asked.

Her daddy shook his head. "Sonny didn't speculate. And he cautioned me, wait for the autopsy. Don't go talking about this. So we need to keep a lid on what we know."

Russ said, "If somebody else was in the house, trying to grab her bracelet, how do you explain why she was still holding on to it? Diamonds from a broken bracelet are still valuable."

"There was no sign of a break-in at the house," Ivy put in.

"She could've let somebody in," her mama said. "But Lady sure wouldn't have had anybody upstairs with her. Probably not even family. It's been so long since I've seen her upstairs, I can't even remember when. It's been months since I was even in her house."

It may have been the memory of Lady's inaccessibility that rushed at them with the force of a fierce wind. A sudden stillness fell over them and for a moment they were silent, searching each other's faces. For what, Ivy couldn't have said. She rubbed her arms, aware of a chill, like the chill she'd felt at Lady's house. The broken tennis bracelet, the autopsy, the scenarios they had imagined — these things had grabbed their attention, but they were only peripheral matters.

At the heart of it all was the hole left now that Lady was dead. For all that Lady was *not,* her presence had meant something. In Montpier. In the Burdette family. Like a monument that was always *there.* You never paid it much attention, but if they took it down, you thought of it every time you passed by where it used to be.

Lady was gone. She was not coming back. Only now was it starting to sink in.

Chapter 10

He hardly ever got a good night's sleep. He would wake from troubling dreams, drenched in sweat, wandering once again through his dead-end decisions and runaway mistakes. Muscles aching, yearning for the end of the week. Watching the light in his eyes grow dimmer with each passing month. Scraping for the rent, like a chicken scratching at the dirt. Trying to scrape the dirt from his heart, too, hoping it might be clean enough for a good woman's love, and he might be satisfied.

But sometimes he dreamed of her.

In those dreams, he was drawing her tight against him, his face buried in her hair, the skin of her back as warm as the heat from a bonfire. Those dreams let him drift into that black, sweet nothingness where memory and dread can't reach.

One time, just once, he was with her like that. Such a long time ago. Too long for him to still be chasing something that would bring the feeling he'd had back then. God only knew how he'd tried, like a Greyhound that runs as hard as he can, time after time, but everybody knows he won't catch the metal rabbit, and even if he did, it wouldn't be what he thought it was.

Not too long ago, with one of Juan Luis's cousins, he thought he could be content. But she was the one that couldn't settle for what seemed like love to him, or as close as he could get to love. If only that could've been enough. But love meant something else to her. It meant getting closer. It meant questions he couldn't answer. It meant promises he couldn't make.

This is what his life had come to. Hanging drywall with the Mexicans. Living in a motel for weeklies, where the roaches rent for months, where a window AC only put out on cool days. Tonight he could not fall into even a restless sleep. The call he never expected had come that evening after he'd made his nightly pilgrimage to the taco joint and the convenience store for a six-pack of Colt 45. He'd shed his shirt, rank with sweat and drywall dust, when Baxter, who managed the apartments, banged on his door. "You gave somebody this number? We ain't your answering service." Baxter, red-faced and fat and mad at the world since he was twelve, handed him the cell phone. "Five minutes, and don't give this number out again."

He'd only given it for an emergency, because he kept buying burner phones. In a town where nothing much ever happened, it was a safe bet there would be no call. But here it was. He cradled the phone in his hand and turned away from Baxter who was listening too hard.

The voice, then, taking him back, back to all that he never wanted to remember and never wanted to forget. The word landed hard. He felt it in his chest. Dead. And the other word. Home. "Please. It's time. Come home." It took a moment to breathe. Memories came flooding in, and regret, and the hard truth that you may think you will have time, but Death makes sure you don't.

The Fourth of July always made him think of home. Made him wonder if he could ever find his way back. And now, through this endless night, he couldn't think about anything else.

Wouldn't Death think it was a fine joke if that's what brought him home?

The dark slid into gray dawn, and finally, giving up on sleep, he got out of bed. He had made up his mind.

When the rusty old van full of Mexicans came by to pick him up, as it did every morning at 6:35, he went to the driver's side. He hated to say it. Juan Luis had been good to him. But he told him he couldn't finish the job, he had to move on, and asked could they settle up.

Juan Luis didn't argue. He drew a wad of chalky bills from his dirty chinos and pulled off a few more than he owed. "I am sorry to see you go, Connor," he said. "Go with God, *amigo*."

Chapter 11

As first light streaked the sky, Ivy finally drifted into a deep slumber. Two hours at most, until sunbeams fell across her quilt.

There is a moment between sleeping and waking, when you don't remember. When all you know of life is your own breath. Then, in another heartbeat, a memory comes like a shadow, an uneasy feeling that something is not right.

And then comes the certainty. The knowing crashes into you.

Like remembering Preston is gone. Like remembering Connor has disappeared.

And this morning, remembering Lady is dead. Feeling the force of it all over again.

A minute passes and then another, and reality finds its way into you. The air has changed now, as you listen to the whisper at the back of you. This... is how... it is. This... is how... it will always be.

Fully awake now, Ivy heard the cough of a lawn mower. Mr. Hardaway on his old riding mower, mowing the yard around the parsonage. A good neighbor.

And then came the sound of voices from the kitchen. The church women had arrived with their casseroles and pies with flaky homemade crusts and fat yeast rolls.

Small towns grieve by feeding each other. Ivy had lived in small towns all of her life, and she had witnessed time and again that Death drew people together like nothing else, and food was at the heart of it all.

Ivy noted that Ruth Ann from last night was there again, making the list her mama would need to keep track of who brought what, return clean dishes to their proper owners, and write notes of thanks. Now her mama was bent over at the refrigerator, making room for a huge foil-covered platter Mrs. Hogan, the church organist, handed her, so carefully, so lovingly, the same way the wise men must have presented their gifts to the Christ Child.

Someone asked, “Do y’all know when the funeral will be?”

Ivy wondered how they should explain the delay, but her mama didn’t lose a beat. “Mr. Gerard is in there right now, talking with Daniel about arrangements,” she said.

Generally, the women just smiled at Ivy, polite enough, but there was something behind their smiles, like she didn’t quite belong in the parsonage’s kitchen. Ivy wasn’t sure why until one of them came toward her. Mrs. Pauley had led the cherub choir, little kids up through kindergarten that were nearly as tall as she was. “Ivy, I hope we’ll be seeing you at church sometime soon,” she said, her sugar-coated reproach delivered in that high-pitched voice she used with the cherubs.

I’ll be in church soon. I’ll be at Lady’s funeral, Ivy wanted to say. But Ivy had been brought up to be well-mannered and respectful. “Thank you,” she said, before excusing herself to join the men.

Mr. Gerard wore a black suit, white shirt, and a gray tie. Tired clothes that Ivy thought he might have worn twelve years ago when her grandfather died. But he was nearly bald now, with a combover that didn’t quite work. “I was just telling Brother Burdette what a great lady his mother was,” the funeral director said with such apparent sincerity, with such a desolate expression, that it would seem his sorrow over this death was much greater than over any of the hundreds whose bodies had passed through his funeral home.

Ivy took a seat beside her daddy, who said, “Mr. Gerard tells me Lady has already made arrangements.”

“That dear woman took care of everything that she could do up front,” Mr. Gerard said. “Wrote her own obituary after she lost Jack. That’s when she did her own pre-planning, pre-payment package. Paid in full, which saves money. Prices do go up, you know — but y’all don’t owe a penny! I showed Brother Burdette the casket and vault she picked out. Rosewood casket. Beautiful.” He patted the binder he was holding at his side. “Do you want to see the picture?”

“Not now, thanks,” Ivy said. She’d see the casket soon enough.

“Doesn’t look like there’s much for us to do,” her daddy said.

“Did she plan the service, too? The music and scriptures and everything?” Ivy asked.

"No, she left that part to us."

Mr. Gerard spoke barely above a whisper. "You let me know when you get the go-ahead from the sheriff. We'll be ready." So he knew about the autopsy. Ivy wondered how long before that would be all over town. Boone knew, so it wouldn't be long.

Her daddy brought her phone back that afternoon when he came home from delivering the basket of vegetables and fruits to Lonnie Briscoe's family. Just what you'd expect of her mama, Ivy thought. Death in her own family had taken a back seat. She'd told Ivy about the four little stairstep children whose mama had run off with a vinyl siding salesman.

Ivy took the phone from her daddy.

"Sonny Bellingham said I could pick it up. I knew you'd be missing it," he told her.

Ivy had, indeed, missed her phone. She had a bunch of emails and texts since she'd let the sheriff have it, though only a few looked personal. She hoped Sonny Bellingham hadn't gone through all of her saved messages. Surely he was too professional to do that.

"Sonny said the autopsy's scheduled for Monday. But they've finished whatever they had to do at the house. We can get in," her daddy said. "I'd like to go on over there."

Ivy thought it seemed too soon to tackle that chore, but her mama said, "We'll need to clean out the refrigerator. Other things can wait. It's all too raw right now."

And it did feel raw, later in the afternoon, as Ivy stood alone in Lady's kitchen. Her parents had gone to the foyer. Ivy heard her daddy's voice, as he told her mama how he'd found Lady at the foot of the stairs. Saying something over and over had some therapeutic value. Saying the same words and phrases until they lose their power to hurt.

Ivy tried to tune it out. Her daddy would need coffee. As she located the coffee and took cups from the cabinets, she felt like an interloper in Lady's kitchen. She'd never baked cookies with Lady or made hot chocolate, something girls did all the time with their grandmothers.

Her mama returned to the kitchen and said, "Let's get to it," and they cleaned out the refrigerator, filling sacks with milk, cheese, and condiments. "Lady would not want anything to go to waste that we could use," her mama said. They threw out leftovers and Ivy put the dishes in the dishwasher, along with a bowl and mug. Dishes from Lady's last breakfast, Ivy thought.

Her daddy came into the kitchen with a few file folders, and they sat at the table while he went through the paperwork, to the hum of the dishwasher.

"She kept her affairs in order," he said. "She did that. I thought I'd find her will, but Don Petrie told me last night he has a copy. Sounded like he wanted to get at it as soon as we can."

"Nothing in the will should be much of a surprise, Daniel," her mama said.

They lingered in the kitchen longer than they had to. Late afternoon shadows began to fall around them. No one seemed in a hurry to leave Lady's kitchen. They stayed until the coffee pot was empty. Ivy knew they would not be sitting around that table like that, ever again.

Chapter 12

That afternoon, the old Greyhound crawled into Montpier, coughing black smoke. The same bus that was brand new and shiny bright when it began to serve that route, decades before. The Four-Ten, they called it. It arrived weekdays at 4:10 p.m. and you could set your watch by it.

The rumbling died down and the brakes hissed as the bus pulled up to the Terminal Café, on the town's back side. The bus station was set among a desolate-looking laundromat, a thrift store, and a couple of abandoned buildings, across from a row of ramshackle houses whose occupants were out on their sagging porches trying to cool off. Passengers on the bus sometimes made jokes about the *Terminal* Café, but people in Montpier had never known any other name. It was just a place where you could get a snack and a cold drink or coffee or a final meal before leaving town.

That afternoon, when the Greyhound driver cranked open the squeaky door, only one passenger stepped down onto the hard concrete. He hoisted the strap of his duffle onto his shoulder and began to rub his palms together, hard, like he was rubbing away stains. He looked down at his hands then, rough and scarred like an old man's, and thought of all those hands had done in just twenty-nine years, and he knew he could never rub it all away.

He stepped into the Terminal Café to buy something cold and wet, something to take the dust from his throat. He'd been sweating in the air-conditioned bus and outside it had to be ninety degrees.

The cold drink was gone by the time he reached the square.

Everything seemed familiar, but tired. Everything looked worn out, like he was. Some storefronts were empty, and he could've sworn the courthouse used to be twice as big.

He took an out-of-the-way route to the parsonage. It wouldn't have been much more than a mile if he'd gone by the Back Home Market, but no. Not that it made any sense to avoid it, but he didn't even get close. He took the long way. That was about right, he guessed. Never been a short cut home. A few more minutes couldn't mean much after ten years.

He had dreamed it, imagined it, even prayed for it. Tried to pray, anyway. For ten years he had thought about coming home, walking into that kitchen with the smells that lived in the walls, smells of bread baking and coffee perking and chicken frying. He had dreaded it, too. He never could picture how it would be that first moment when they caught sight of him. Maybe they'd rush to him and throw joyful arms around him, like the father of the prodigal son in the Bible. You didn't grow up in Sunday School and hearing your daddy preach all those sermons without that story deep-rooted in you. But maybe their backs would stiffen and they would cross their arms and wait to hear a plea of forgiveness. *I'm no longer worthy to be called your son.*

Connor Burdette, the prodigal son.

He felt his steps growing slower, his thoughts weighing on him, like he was carrying everything he'd lost and hoped to regain, every mistake he'd made, every missed chance to make amends. There was a moment when it seemed all he had to do was step away from the past, forgive himself, and step into the arms of those who knew him before. Those with his blood. Those who understood his heart beat like theirs.

Here it was now before him. If he was just strong enough to step across, into forgiveness.

The sight of the brown brick bungalow made his heartbeat hammer in his ears, and for an instant, he was tempted to turn back. Back to dead end jobs and stomach gnawing when he had no work. Back to the careless glance of strangers and leaving someone's bed before she woke. Back to another bus taking him to nowhere.

He stopped, looked hard at the house, and took a long deep breath, thinking how little things had changed. The maple tree in the front yard had grown, but he was sure he knew which branch he fell from once. The rose bush that grew under the window of his bedroom looked the same. His mama would've kept it pruned. And the porch swing — he just knew it still squeaked.

And all of it made him think it was possible, just possible, that he might pick up where he'd left off.

He shifted the strap on his shoulder then and walked on, and felt something hopeful rise in him, rise with each step closer.

Closer to home.

Chapter 13

The air was cooler. Evening had a purplish cast to it when Ivy came in carrying one of the paper sacks from Lady's house.

Her daddy had wanted Lady to get an alarm, but he didn't even lock his own kitchen door. "What would anybody want from a parsonage?" he'd said.

Her parents were still a minute behind her, bringing their own loads from the car. Ivy left the door open, stepped into the kitchen, and stopped.

A feeling washed over her. Something was different, changed but familiar. She sensed a presence. The smell of sweat and worry in the air.

"Who's there?" she whispered.

Footsteps then, in the hall. Ivy dropped the sack on the table. "Who's there?" she called again, something uneasy in her voice, but not fear. Strange that she did not feel danger. Mostly what she felt was curiosity.

And there he stood. And the years fell away.

"Ivy," he said.

She formed the word, but there was little air behind it. "*Connor.*"

A powerful shockwave tore through Ivy and mixed up all of her feelings. Disbelief — relief — then a surge of red anger. She heard herself shriek and felt herself sway. Connor hurried to grab her, strong hands grasping her arms, holding her steady. And then rage consumed her. Ivy's hand shot up and delivered a hard slap to her brother's cheek.

He drew back a little, not much, scarcely more than a jerk of his head, and released her. "I'm sorry," he whispered. Sorry for leaving, for putting the family through hell, is what Ivy heard, thought she heard, wanted to hear, but no, what he said was, "I'm sorry I scared you."

Ivy felt words somewhere in her — *Scared? Is that what you thought? No! You can't begin to know* — but her throat was all closed up. Tears begin to push their way out from behind her eyes, tears that she'd held back for years.

And then she found herself throwing her arms around her brother's neck.

That brief moment, just enough for her to get the scent of cigarettes and sweat, was interrupted by their parents rushing in, calling, "What's the matter?"

Ivy pulled back, her breath still catching like a sobbing child, and her body found a chair to fall into.

She would remember her mama's hands flying to her mouth. Embraces, murmurings — words that were scarcely intelligible, just feelings — but her daddy's voice was clear: "You're home, son." *No apology or explanation necessary. You're home.*

Through the blur of tears, Ivy kept staring at this man who only resembled her little brother.

His eyes. So much older. A weight there, the shadow of hard years in his eyes.

He was taller now. At nineteen he'd been a twig of boy, with the geometry of boys. All angles. Sharp edges. Self-conscious that he was so much smaller than his brother. Still not as tall as Russ, not as powerfully built. Strong shoulders, but a little stooped, and something in the center of him had a hollow look, like a tree gone bad at its core. But he was not the scrawny kid Ivy had imagined living on the streets for ten years. Not what you'd see in a homeless shelter.

His jeans were so worn, they were shiny, but his plain blue shirt looked clean. Something about a fresh-washed shirt touched Ivy, that he hadn't wanted to come home dirty.

She was the only one crying. She felt foolish but couldn't stop. Tears for time lost, for the little brother lost, for all that was broken and could never be the same. All she really wanted to do was to strike Connor's chest again and again with her fists, to make his heart feel the bottomless, endless hurt that he'd caused his family. All of that was not out of her. But she just sat there feeling weak and helpless, until her daddy finally squeezed her shoulder and said, "It's all right, Ivy. Everything's gonna be all right now."

Even as she got hold of herself, Ivy wasn't having it. Everything couldn't be right, ever again.

The quiet of the kitchen was broken by humming. Ivy had forgotten how her mama used to hum as she worked in the kitchen. It had been so long.

Her daddy came through to refill his coffee mug and tilted his head to listen. An old tender smile came to his lips, full of love and hope.

What was that tune? It came to Ivy, from church, years ago. *Oh how He loves you and me.* Seemed her mama was on good terms with God again tonight.

At the supper table, Ivy was still ashamed of her tears. Wished she could pull them back. Connor didn't deserve them. But that hard slap, no, she was sure he'd earned that.

The calendar could have rolled back a decade. Someone who didn't know the Burdettes — hadn't heard her daddy cry out again and again for God to protect his boy, hadn't seen the longing in her mama's eyes as she stared at the empty chair — might think Connor had been at the table every night for these ten years.

Her parents' ease with it all made Ivy squirm. Maybe they were reluctant to put Connor on the spot for fear he'd take off again. But surely they had the same questions she had? Where had he been all this time? What had he been doing? Was it pure coincidence that he'd come back one day after Lady's death? Connor owed them answers.

But no one was asking, everyone talking about food as they filled their plates. Ivy knew her mama had a knack for throwing a meal together, but tonight she'd outdone herself, all so quickly. Connor's favorite meal, country fried steak, mashed potatoes, gravy and biscuits. Vegetables from the farmer's market — green beans, corn, and homegrown tomatoes.

Ivy waited till they all had their mouths full to ask Connor the first question of any substance. "Have you heard about Lady?"

"What about her?" Connor stared down at his plate, letting his fork play around with the mashed potatoes, smothered in gravy.

Ivy hesitated, and a beat was all it took. Her daddy said, "I'm afraid it's bad news, son." His pastor voice, resonant as a church bell, sounding just the right note of consolation. "Lady passed away. Just yesterday."

Connor looked up. A blank stare at first. Then he stammered, "Oh — Oh no."

The words convincing enough, but not the right emotion. Ivy couldn't explain, but she was certain somehow. He already knew.

Her daddy went into the story that he'd perfected after telling it so many times. How he found Lady, how she must have tripped, how he was confident she didn't suffer.

Connor set his fork down, touched his forehead, then shook his head. "I guess I thought she would always be here."

Ivy hoped regret was gnawing at him that he didn't come home before Lady was gone, but that was not what she heard in his voice.

Her daddy kept on. "They're doing an autopsy."

Connor blinked a couple of times. "Why? What happened?" This much sounded genuine.

Her daddy explained why the sheriff was suspicious, and her mama weighed in. "Nothing'll come of it. Just Sonny Bellingham being a sheriff. Good man, but he's looking too hard for trouble."

"Don't say anything about any of this, Connor," her daddy said. "People know they sent the body to Nashville. That's bound to be all over town, but nothing else. Sonny might not oughta told me the rest of it, but he did, as a courtesy. Keep it quiet."

Connor picked up his fork and speared a round slice of tomato as big as a saucer. Frowning, he said, "Like I'm gonna be looking up old friends to tell about it. Not hardly."

Ivy didn't know what to make of his remark, and from her parents' expressions, they didn't either. Coming home didn't mean staying. But if he was staying, maybe he was making a promise. No more contact with those old friends. Especially that one, Joe Ray Loomis.

Her mama brought in leftover peach cobbler, promising she'd make a chocolate pie for tomorrow night. "Russ'll be over with Nikki and the boys. They have two boys." She brightened. "Owen's eight, Drew's nine."

Connor took an oversized helping of peach cobbler. Ivy watched him eat, shoveling big forkfuls in his mouth the way someone does when he's been hungry for too long, washing it down with sweet tea, shoveling in more.

Her daddy said, “Russ woulda come over tonight but he had to close up the Sports Emporium. It was gonna be too late.”

“Yeah,” Connor said, his voice reminiscent of a sulky nineteen-year-old. “Too late.”

Ivy could feel a charge in the air, and she wondered if the years would have done anything to ease the strain between her brothers.

Chapter 14

The old phone hanging on the kitchen wall wouldn't quit ringing. Connor watched his mama as she answered each call and leaned against the kitchen counter, fooling with the curly cord. It took Connor back to the summer they moved into the parsonage when he was eight. The phone was already ancient, but his mama had never had a phone in the kitchen of any other parsonage. The kitchen was the heart of her homelife. You would've thought that phone was a priceless antique or the latest technological invention.

Visiting was what she called those conversations. All the news of the town passed through those phone wires before it ever came out in the *Gazette*. Deaths, marriages, babies born. Chitchat and gossip that never appeared in the *Gazette.* Sickness, scandals, and church politics. All part of the fabric of small town life.

Seeing his mama on that old relic took Connor back to all those nights, these past years, that he'd wanted to throw his voice into the dark and reach out to her.

Tonight she spoke about what was lost and what was found. Lady, lost forever, and Connor, found after so long. He felt an ache in his chest, hearing her speak in hushed tones: *He's home. Yes. Yes, answered prayers.*

He retreated to his room, unpacked his duffle, and put his meager belongings away. It took all of ten minutes, shifting some clothes from drawers full of who he was at nineteen, the smell of what used to be. He didn't know how he ought to feel. It made him want to burn those old clothes. It made him want to tell his mama, *I'm not him. I can't be him anymore.* But still that ache, that she wouldn't let go of the son she'd thought was lost to her forever.

He began to feel he couldn't breathe, like he would suffocate if he didn't get some air.

The front porch was not breezy, but the air stirred a little. Connor settled on the top step, leaning back against the rail, his long legs stretched out. Smoking a cigarette. Sometime later, the screen door flapped behind Ivy. Surprise in her voice.

"There you are. We were wondering where you were. I think Mama was afraid you'd disappeared again."

"You sure know how to make somebody feel welcome," he said.

"Just telling the truth." Ivy sat in the swing, gave a little push with her toes, and the swing began a gentle rocking, making that lazy, squeaky sound. Still squeaking, just as Connor had imagined.

After a while, he said, "Maybe I shouldn't have come back."

"Why do you say that?" Ivy asked. With the gray-dark around them, Connor couldn't get a fix on her face. He could only hear her voice. She sounded cross.

"Mama seems happy enough, but I don't know about everybody else."

"You don't think Daddy's happy?" Ivy said. Connor noticed she didn't mention herself.

His laugh was more of a bark. "That's just how Daddy is. You know what they say about home — they have to take you in. Daddy's always gonna do the right thing. You can't tell if his heart's in it or not."

"Robert Frost. 'Home is the place where, when you have to go there, they have to take you in,'" Ivy parroted, like she was reciting for school.

Connor finished his smoke and started to toss the butt but changed his mind. He didn't want to litter his mama's yard. Waited a minute and tucked it in his shirt pocket. A single firefly caught his attention, a flickering light coming from the grass like an S.O.S. Could be hurt or just lost, and all the other fireflies gone. Connor watched the drowsy blinking of that lonely phosphorescent light. That aloneness that he knew all too well. And he thought about the fireflies Ivy used to catch in Mason jars, remembered how he'd protested when he was maybe four. Mama had punched holes in the lid so they wouldn't die. But Connor bawled, "Let 'em go! They just want to carry a little light into the dark!" Repeating words he'd heard their mama say a thousand times. And he'd heard her say, "It's a blessing to free a firefly."

Though Connor eventually joined in chasing the lights, he never kept them in the mason jars too long. Something in him soared when he let them go free. Tonight maybe it was the little boy who still lived in him that made him smile when he saw the fragile light finally lift off into the night sky. *Go home,* his silent message. *Go home.*

"Why *did* you come back?" Ivy asked suddenly. "Why *now?* Ten-year anniversary, is that it?"

Connor hadn't expected that. Not right now. He'd been home three hours, tops. It took a minute to answer. "Seemed like the right time."

"I don't believe you," Ivy said. "I don't believe that's all there is to it."

"You calling me a liar?"

"Are you?"

Connor smiled to himself, remembering that line from childhood quarrels. *Liar, liar, pants on fire.* He said, "It's for me to know and you to find out."

"I will," Ivy said. "I'll find out."

He laughed. "I'm just messing with you, Ivy. Don't be so damned serious."

"It's too much of a coincidence. Lady died yesterday, and today, you show up."

More silence. Connor finally said, "I've been thinking about it. Maybe I just needed a reason to come back. Like I said, it seemed like the right time when I heard about Lady."

"I knew it! I knew you'd heard. Why'd you pretend you hadn't? And how'd you hear? Somebody had to call you. Who was it? Who knew how to reach you?"

"I'm not up for twenty questions, Ivy. Not tonight." Connor straightened himself, tried to get a better look at her face, but it was too dark. "Being from a preacher's family, I thought I might see forgiveness. Hell, I thought y'all might even be glad to see me."

"Forgiveness," Ivy repeated. "Now that's precious. Being a preacher's son, you ought to know all the sermons on forgiveness are big on repentance. You didn't come home saying you're sorry for all you put us through. You didn't ask for forgiveness." She was breathing harder. He could hear it, like she was struggling for air. "Where *were* you, Connor? What have you been doing for ten years? Ten years and *nothing* from you!"

Connor was sure she was close to crying. He didn't mind that she'd slapped him but he didn't think he could bear to see her cry again.

Was this what he could expect if he stayed?

"All these damned questions. You think you want to know, but you don't." Connor stared at something, somewhere in the distance. "You don't want to know about all the places I've been. Trust me."

And then they were quiet for a long time. The only sounds were the crickets chirping and the swing squeaking. After a while, Connor felt the tension ease. Time slid by, and when his sister spoke again, she sounded like the Ivy he remembered. Her words came out as soft as the darkness that kept them from seeing each other's expressions.

"It's just that we were all so worried. We weren't sure you were even alive."

He didn't say anything. What was there to say?

"You're going to stay, aren't you?"

It was a moment before he answered. "I hope so."

Connor left Ivy rocking in the porch swing. He could sure use a beer, but sweet tea would have to do. His parents' voices came from the kitchen, and he stopped, just to hear that familiar sound, like the harmony of an old tune. They were talking about a call from Don Petrie, Lady's lawyer. Connor remembered Lady would say, "Don Petrie won't like it, but it's my money."

"What's so urgent?" his mama said. "We know what's in the will."

"Maybe we don't," his daddy said. "I'll find out in the morning, first thing."

Chapter 15

Kitty woke to a sun-bright room. Eight-thirty was impossibly late for her. All these years, every morning before she was even fully awake, her first thought was Connor. But this morning her heart lifted — *He's home!* A surge of fear that it was just a dream, but then, *Yes! He's asleep in his bed!*

The kitchen was drenched with sunlight. Kitty poured herself a cup of coffee. Married forty years, and Daniel could still surprise her with his thoughtfulness. He'd made coffee, left a full pot, and let her sleep. Straight through the night! She had a vague memory of hearing him moving around, soft shuffling rattling noises, more like a dream. Her body must have been desperate for rest, as if some part of her had been awake for ten years. And her husband knew it.

Most mornings these past years Kitty was up before the sun. In the quiet moments before her house came to life, she would sit at the kitchen table, hands around a steaming cup of coffee, and think about her boy, her lost son. Always wondering where he was. And was he cold? Was he hungry? Was he hurt, somewhere, needing help? She would pray for him, a wordless prayer, a prayer every mother knows, even though she'd quit feeling that her prayers ever escaped the kitchen window. And then one day — it was March — his voice. *Mama. It's me.* No one would ever have to know that she'd kept that secret. So hard to do, but it was the right thing.

Connor had been such a sweet child. So tender-hearted. Even as he was growing up, he was easier than Russ. Russ with that temper of his.

The summer they moved to Montpier, when Connor was eight, Lady dislocated her shoulder. She fell off a stool, trying to reorganize the shelves in her walk-in closet. That evening, Daniel and Kitty took a meal for Lady and Jack. Connor, such a joyful child at that age, wanted to give his grandmother a gift and had settled on a jar full of fireflies.

They all went out on the portico, Lady's fancy word for the porch.

"Nobody ever gave me anything like this," Lady said, in a wistful voice, not at all like the commanding tone that came so naturally to her. And she bent down, touching her forehead to Connor's. A rare moment of tenderness that no one but Connor ever earned. And then Connor repeated what Kitty had said to him many times, "It's a blessing to free a firefly," and he removed the lid. And Kitty would never forget how they lifted off, rising past Connor's face, how all their dazzling lights seemed to mirror the light in his eyes.

In the after of her life, after part of her heart went missing, the before memories were all she cared about, the only comfort. As the sun seeped through the windows and filled her kitchen, those mornings, Kitty could see the light in her boy's eyes, as clear as if he were sitting across the table from her.

Kitty was humming, turning out pancakes, and minding the sizzling bacon when Connor made his way into the kitchen. Something she'd imagined so many times, just the simple image of her sleepy son coming to breakfast.

"What's that you were humming?" he asked.

Kitty laughed. "Some old song. I don't even know."

Connor came close and leaned in to inspect the pancakes. Kitty felt his tentative touch on her back, and then he slipped his hand around her waist and gave a little hug. She reached up but her fingers barely grazed his chest before he'd moved away.

He sniffed the air. "Nothing in the world like the smell of coffee and bacon."

Kitty's heart swelled. She knew it was his way of saying he'd missed this. He'd missed home.

She'd made his favorite breakfast. He helped himself to coffee, and she served up a stack of pancakes. Kitty was sure he'd known hunger, and cold, and God only knew what kind of hurt, but she wouldn't let that worry take away from the serenity she felt this morning. Here he was, in her kitchen, and he would never have to be hungry again.

And then Ivy was there, rubbing her eyes, bare feet, tousled hair — like something had taken her back to another time, too. "I don't know when I've slept straight through like that," she said.

"You missed the pancakes," Connor told her. "They're all gone."

"Oh, I wouldn't worry about that," Kitty said, and she went back to the stove and poured more batter onto the griddle.

A few minutes later she set another plate of fluffy pancakes and crisp bacon before them and joined her children at the table.

Just like last night at dinner, Connor had taken his old place, across from Ivy. Russ would be sitting next to Ivy, in the old days, Kitty was thinking when the phone rang. It was that plumber again. "No, Daniel's not at the church this morning, but I expect he'll be there later," she said. "I'll tell him to call you."

"Saturday morning and Daddy's not at the church?" Connor said.

It was true, Kitty knew. The church had always taken precedence over any of the kids' sports, any family activities. She could tell, from Connor's tone, that the memory had a little bruise for him, maybe for Ivy, too. She'd told Daniel, *The years are short.* There would always be a sermon to prepare, but the children would be gone. Yet she knew Daniel's love for them was as deep as hers, as deep as his love for the gospel. The children had to know it, too.

"Don Petrie wanted to see him about Lady's will," she said. "Don't know what that's all about. Daniel is Lady's heir, nothing complicated about that. But there was something Don Petrie thought Daniel ought to know."

"Maybe she left a chunk of money to some wacko organization," Ivy said, reaching for more maple syrup. "She told Boone once that she was addicted to the Psychic Network."

"She was just trying to get a rise out of him," Kitty said. She thought about First Baptist's plans for a Family Life Center. "It would sure please Daniel if she left something to the church."

"Whatever's in her will, I'll bet it's iron-clad. Lady would've made sure," Connor said. "Iron-clad like her."

Breakfast was unhurried, like holiday breakfasts, Kitty thought. The same special-day feeling. They were pushing bites of pancakes around in the syrup, soaking up the last bit of sweetness, when Daniel returned.

He headed straight to the coffeepot and brought his coffee to the table. He sat down at the table opposite Kitty, said, "Look at the time. Looks like breakfast is about to slide right into lunch." Joked that Kitty never fixed pancakes for him. But his manner didn't match his words. The humor didn't show in his eyes. For someone who put on his pastor face every day, his no-matter-what-goes-wrong face, Daniel was not hiding what was apparent to Kitty. Something must have come up in his meeting with Don Petrie that rattled him.

Kitty reminded Daniel that she would've made him a real breakfast if he hadn't needed to get out so early to meet with Don Petrie. "Out late and up early, that man," she said. "I guess you have to admire him. He must be pushing eighty, and still serving his clients."

"I don't know how much legal work he actually does," Daniel said. "He's always involved in some project in the Rotary Club, serves on a few Boards, goes out of town a lot. He puts in some time at the country club bar, I know that for a fact."

"Well, why was it so important to talk to you this morning?" Kitty asked.

Daniel leaned forward on his elbows. Kitty could almost feel the tension in his fingers, tight around the coffee mug. He tilted his head and frowned, as if he was trying to figure something out. "Don Petrie drew up a new will for Lady," he said. "She signed it just this past Monday."

An uncomfortable silence fell and no one spoke for what seemed like a full minute. Kitty felt unease creep into her joyful morning. Daniel drank more coffee. And then he fixed his tired eyes on Connor.

"Did Lady know where you've been, all this time?" he asked.

A dark shadow moved across Connor's face. He didn't answer at first. Kitty held her breath.

And then a sharp "*No!* How would Lady know where I was? I don't know why you'd ask me that. Why you'd even think that."

Daniel made a sound that was mostly bewilderment. He said, "Because, Son — she left everything to you."

Kitty covered her mouth, but her soft cry escaped. A cry of feeling, more than knowing. She didn't know yet the full measure of what Daniel's words meant or what they would come to mean, but she felt their weight. And when she looked across the table at her son, she saw that same weight in his eyes.

Chapter 16

Daniel Burdette was a praying man, a man who had decided long ago to put his life in God's hands. Like every other sinner, he'd failed many times. He had let doubts creep in. His faith had wavered. But he'd kept praying.

For ten years he had prayed for his lost son. Each morning, sometimes at dawn, he went to his office in the church, closed the door, and he would fall to his knees and pray. There in the quiet, he would beg God to protect his boy, to bring him home. And he would call out, "Forgive me, Lord — for anything I did that drove him away!" He had stopped making excuses to God. Stopped trying to justify the way he'd let his temper get the best of him with Connor, when the boy was struggling with right and wrong. Stopped trying to convince God that it was righteous anger, rooted in love and worry.

Earlier today, before his meeting with Don Petrie, he'd felt a powerful urge to go back to that spot in his office. The spot in the carpet that was showing wear from ten years of praying. This morning he'd knelt and whispered, "Thank you, God..." And choking back tears, "Thank you for bringing my son home."

Daniel was a man of simple needs. He never craved money. Not because the Bible said the love of money was the root of all evil. It was just how God made him.

Growing up, he mowed yards, as most boys did. "It'll build character," his daddy told him. Jack Burdette expected him to earn money, too, but the widows who hired him learned they could pay in sugar cookies and milk and stories on their front porches. And when he was old enough to work after school at the mill, Daniel did it to please his daddy, not to save for a dream car. When he finally did buy a car, it was a 1959 Buick, more dents than speed. A wrench in his hand, lying underneath the chassis, he realized he was made for fixing broken things.

His country was broken, he came to believe, as Vietnam began to divide the nation. Before he left home, looking beyond the tiny corner of the world where he had spent his eighteen years, Daniel would watch his daddy pause in front of the nightly news and shake in anger at protestors on college campuses. Jack Burdette's face turned purple, as boys burned draft cards. "No better than deserters, and they shoot deserters!" he bellowed.

Lady made excuses for the outbursts that erupted so suddenly from Daniel's father, most times so easygoing. "You know he was at Normandy," she said. Daniel thought if he could just explain his convictions to his daddy — but Jack Burdette always blew up, and Daniel began to feel rage, new and frightening, boiling in himself.

None too soon, Daniel left Montpier. Driving his old '59 Buick over the mountain, he felt like he was traveling at the speed of light. Breathing a clean breath at last. Heading toward the University of Tennessee, a place where he was sure he would find like-minded students.

Football was a religion at UT, with its enrollment of more than 25,000, and frat parties drew more attention than a war in remote jungles. But Daniel did find a small faction, a mix of intellectuals, long-haired pot smokers, and students like himself who looked more like the farm boys majoring in agriculture — all deeply committed to the idea that Vietnam was nothing like their fathers' war. As months went by, letters to *The Beacon* and speeches in front of the Student Center turned to nonviolent demonstrations. By the time Daniel was an upperclassman, something was taking hold. The war raged and increasingly militant protests across the nation fueled passions on the sleepy Tennessee campus. Daniel felt something taking hold of him, something fiery, intensifying as they marched and waved banners and chanted, "We won't go!"

He was never sure how the violence started at a protest on Cumberland Avenue that turned ugly. Amid screams of "Commies!" and Traitors!" came something slamming into Daniel's wrist, and his sign went flying. The angry mob on the sidelines hurled bottles, rocks, and bricks and someone with a baseball bat began to swing at the demonstrators. Daniel went after him. A small wisp of a girl carrying a sign that said, "No more killing" tried to grab him. "No Daniel! Remember, *peace*!" But his blood was running hot. He had never been in a fight his entire life, not even a playground scuffle, but from somewhere in him a storm emerged, fury that gave him the strength to wrestle the man down and wrench the bat away from him. And then he began to hit him. Over and over. Blind with rage, he kept hitting. Until police dragged him off.

Daniel went to jail, with others from both sides of the melee. Whenever Daniel remembered, knowing he would surely have killed the man if he hadn't been restrained, he was still amazed that he was released after twenty-four hours.

He left the jail, walked directly to a chapel on the campus, and began to pray.

Daniel did not stop believing that Vietnam was an immoral war. But in his prayers, he seemed to hear God's voice, telling him that even though the cause was just, his anger was not justified.

By the time he met Kitty, Daniel knew he could not fix brokenness in his country. He knew he could not mend broken people who came to him with their sins and sorrows. But he dedicated himself to preaching God's healing grace, knowing it would be the work of a lifetime to fix his own brokenness.

Nobody ever got rich as a preacher, but Daniel was satisfied to pay the bills. It was a great blessing that he'd found a woman who wanted a simple life, too. The sort of life that made a heart kind. Time and again, Kitty had saved him from himself, drawing him close to her and whispering love. Love more powerful than anger.

For some men, even too much is never enough. For Daniel Burdette, whatever he had was always plenty. Sometimes it gnawed at him that his mama had so much and cared so little for those who didn't. Daniel thought, if I ever have too much, I'll give most of it away to those who don't have enough. But whenever he told Lady about something the church was doing to help people, he watched her eyes glaze over. She would listen, but never offer a dime beyond her regular small contributions to the church.

He had prayed that generosity might someday touch her soul. And now Daniel had to admit, in his quietest moments, with all the talk about Lady's will, he'd been thinking that death might be able to do what living never could. Make her money do some good.

On the way home from Don Petrie's office, he'd prayed over Lady's change of heart. None of Daniel's good intentions mattered now. He wouldn't be the one to decide.

In the end, he turned to the prayer he'd been praying since he first heard God's whisper. "I trust you." Now he would try to put the money business in His hands.

Still, at the edge of his prayer, he'd felt a nagging worry. *What does Connor know about all of this?*

This morning, Daniel let the silence hang over the table for a minute, and then he had to ask. He'd had his boy home such a short time — he hadn't wanted to fire a barrage of questions that Connor would surely answer, given time and space, but that was before the will's contents came to light.

"If Lady didn't know where you were, didn't know if you were even alive — like the rest of us..." Daniel's voice broke as he remembered how Kitty kept insisting on keeping the landline, saying, *if he's alive, he knows this number.* He tried again. "Why did Lady leave everything to a grandson that might not even be alive?"

Connor slid back, his chair scraping the floor, making that sound that sets teeth on edge. Daniel thought he was about to get up and leave, but he just gripped the table with white knuckles, like he might be hanging onto something... his father's last thread of belief in him.

"I don't know! I don't know what the hell she was thinking!" he said. "All I know is, I never talked to her, not once. I'll swear it on the Bible."

Daniel raised his hand, the settle-down gesture that he'd used with all his children, and it seemed to work. Connor was calmer after a minute. He said, "Maybe she did it to get back at you for something. Did *you* do something to get on Lady's bad side?"

"No," Daniel said.

"None of us did," Ivy said. "Not her grandchildren — the ones who didn't run away. Or her great-grandchildren. She just didn't care that much about us."

Daniel wanted to say no, that wasn't true, but truth was, Lady never paid that much attention to Ivy and Russ. She was always partial to Connor. And maybe now, he thought, she'd just cared most for the lost sheep.

Connor took a long breath, looked down and shook his head. A note in his voice made him sound more like the boy Daniel remembered. "I don't know what else I can tell you. I didn't know anything about the will, not till you told me. I wish you could believe me."

Daniel gazed at Kitty, who had closed her eyes, like she was trying to squeeze out what she was hearing. He turned to Connor. "I believe you. I do. Still, the way it looks..."

It took a moment, but Daniel could see his words struck a chord. Connor left the table then, only to take a few long strides to the counter. He stood at the refrigerator, filled a tall glass with orange juice, and gulped down most of it.

"I get it. Lady dies, and the sheriff has his suspicions. And here comes Connor Burdette, that prodigal son showing up after ten years. So it looks like he knew he was coming into some money. A lowlife that wouldn't wait. That's why he came back." He finished off the orange juice, set the glass on the counter with a thud, and returned to the table. "Everybody thinks I'm a criminal, anyway, so, hell, why not just cuff me now and haul me off to prison."

"Don't say things like that, Connor! Don't think those kinds of thoughts," Kitty cried. "Nobody's accusing you of anything."

Daniel knew his wife would never admit she'd had some doubts of her own.

"I believe you, Son," Daniel said again, "But if it turns out that Lady's death wasn't an accident, the first thing Sonny's gonna want to know is who benefits from her will. It wouldn't raise questions if I inherited, as expected. Or if it was all of us. But you can see how this looks."

Ivy spoke up, her voice suddenly ringing with authority, a teacher's demand. "Can you prove you weren't back in town before Lady died?"

Daniel looked at his son, long and tenderly, the seconds ticking off.

Connor said, "I came in on the Four-Ten yesterday. I may still have the bus ticket, if I didn't toss it." He shook his head and smiled a sarcastic smile. "What was I thinking, coming back? I'm not the same. I'm not that boy. I've paid for my mistakes, but nobody" — he glared at Daniel, then Kitty, then Ivy — "nobody in this town is gonna let me forget. Much less forgive."

Daniel had no doubt that Connor had paid, paid dearly, in his own way.

Connor rubbed his palms together, that habit Daniel had noticed since he was back, like he never could feel his hands were clean. He said, "What is it you want from me?"

Daniel whispered, "All I ever wanted, Son. The truth. Just the truth."

Chapter 17

Where do I find the truth? Connor thought. And when I do, God help me, how can I ever say it? How can my family ever hear it? The truth meant digging through all the layers of lies that he'd piled on top of each other. Stories he'd made up. Years of being somebody else — or nobody. Living the lies he'd told himself. The truth had always been so far away, as far away as home. Connor didn't know how he could ever start to tell the truth about that kind of life.

"I'm gonna see if I can find that ticket," he said, and he went to his room.

He knew where the crumpled bus ticket was. It was in the pocket of the jeans he was wearing, the same ones he'd worn yesterday. He could've shown it, but he had to get out of that kitchen just to breathe for a minute, out from under their suffocating judgment. I shouldn't have to prove myself, he thought. Maybe I'll just tear it into shreds. But he didn't.

Instead, he went to the bathroom, stared in the mirror at the eyes that looked so old, and washed his face. He walked back to the kitchen and tossed the ticket on the table. His mama and Ivy looked at him with what seemed like hope, but his daddy was still slumped over his coffee, staring into the cup as if he might find wisdom at the bottom of it.

"I was living in this place, not far from Nashville, the kind of place where you can get lost," Connor said. "I felt safe there, safe enough, with a bunch of Mexicans. Illegals, but nobody bothered them, and nobody bothered me." He didn't sit down. This wouldn't take long. "Here's the truth. I didn't know anything about Lady's will, and I didn't know anything about that robbery until Joe Ray Loomis pulled a gun. I still blame myself, though. I was young and stupid and shouldn't have been there."

"I knew it," his mama said. Ivy's expression seemed to soften, too. His daddy — all Connor could see in his daddy's eyes was sorrow. Sorrow for how the world is.

"It was all Joe Ray. The clerk at the cash register — Raleigh — he'd sold beer to Joe Ray before. I just went along to buy beer. I didn't have a gun. And I sure didn't shoot Raleigh."

Daniel straightened up. "You know they blamed it all on you, Son. We didn't believe it, but you weren't here to deny it." Connor guessed his father just couldn't resist the little dig, a little scolding. And yes, he guessed he deserved it.

The scene at the Back Home Market flashed through his mind like a movie, as it had a thousand times. The moment he saw the gun and realized everything in his life was about to go south. The crack of the gunshot. Raleigh's cry as he toppled to the floor, the blood gushing.

"Raleigh looked like he was dying, and I just left him there. Left him to die. I didn't do a damn thing to help him." It was a long stretch of time before Connor could go on, and when he did, his voice sounded far away. "Joe Ray drove me to the by-pass, and I started hitchhiking."

His daddy said, "You didn't have to go away, Connor." This time, his voice was gentle.

And then Ivy chimed in. "They never found the gun, and Raleigh said the same thing as Joe Ray. He said you were the one with the gun. You shot him."

"They put it all on you, Connor," his mama said. Connor had always imagined she was hurt, but it seemed so much worse, hearing the pain in her voice.

"That's why I couldn't come back," he said. "Raleigh was in on it."

He looked from one to the other, trying to see if there was any faith in him left in their eyes. "Joe Ray and Raleigh set it all up, and Joe Ray was supposed to shoot, to prove the robbery was for real. But I didn't know. So I yelled at him when I saw the gun. That had to be why his aim was off and he hit Raleigh instead of the wall. I figured it all out right away. And when I found out Raleigh had lived, it was like a miracle. I'd thought Raleigh was a dead man. Maybe God had heard my prayer. But I knew I was still in trouble. I waited for the years to tick off, so I wouldn't be arrested, but then..." He looked at this hands, not sure he could ever explain why he still didn't come back, why facing his past seemed like a mountain he couldn't climb.

A moment passed, not a sound. And then Ivy asked, "How'd you figure out what Joe Ray and Raleigh had done?"

"Libraries have computers. Even the homeless can use them." Connor felt a catch in his throat, like he'd said too much. "That's the truth," he said.

Chapter 18

All morning in the kitchen, the memory kept flashing through Ivy's mind. She'd thought about that summer when so many fireflies filled the yard every evening, unlike any year before or after, and she captured them in mason jars. Connor would chase her, begging, *Let 'em go!* She promised they wouldn't die. Mama had made holes in the lid. But one night she left a jar outside and forgot about it. Connor found it, with its clump of lifeless fireflies, their lights extinguished, and he began to wail, *You killed them! You're evil!* A word only a preacher's son would use. Their mama had to pull him into her lap and give him a stern talking to about that word. And about another word — forgiveness. Ivy had said she was sorry, but Connor had to cry for a while, before he came to her with a tear-streaked face and said, *I forgive you.*

Ivy was ashamed. She'd never meant to leave the fireflies to die. Her brother's tears, the sweet innocence in his words — all of it — she remembered how something crumpled inside her.

As Ivy ran through the town, the same course she followed most every day, the music on her headphones swelled and drowned the labor of her breath and the beat of her heart, but she was thinking of the shadow that hung in her brother's eyes. Eyes of a grown man now, but she could still see that little boy. Trying to be brave. Trying to be tough. And she knew she would forgive him in a heartbeat if he'd just say why, *why* he'd felt like he had to shut them out of his life for so long. Or if he'd say, *I'm sorry. Sorry for these ten years. Please forgive me.*

Ivy had started running in high school. In those days and for a long time, it felt like she was running toward something. Toward the life she wanted. Lately it seemed like she was running away. Running from the past.

She always took the back streets and made a wide loop around the town square. Past the bus station, past the Back Home Market, and finally past the church. That put her back on Grand Avenue, a broad, quiet street with a fair amount of shade. Not far from home, Boone's shiny Lincoln passed her and pulled off to the side.

Ivy jogged up to his window. Boone powered it down and said, "You look like you need a ride, girl. The bank sign says it's ninety-nine."

The fumes from his cigar smoke kept her from getting too close. "I'm just fine, thank you," she said, "and that old bank sign has never been right." She pulled off her headphones and squeezed the sweat out of her ponytail. "Where're you going?"

"I thought I'd head over to the parsonage." He kept the engine running. "I hear your no-good brother's come home."

If he was making a joke, it was a bad joke. Ivy's voice turned cool. "Word gets around."

"Why in Christ's name did he come back?"

Ivy hadn't expected that. Not from her uncle, who'd had such a close relationship with their family. He'd taken Russ and Connor camping and fishing. He'd taken them to UT football games. Russ was always his favorite. Ivy knew that. But Connor was family, too. And you don't throw away your own blood.

"For ten years, it's what we've all prayed for. Thought you did, too, Boone."

"Ten years he put his family through hell. Your mama's heart broke every time the phone rang."

"Maybe Connor wants to clear his name," Ivy said. "He says he didn't shoot that clerk."

"Or maybe he heard about Lady and hurried back so he wouldn't miss out."

Ivy watched him puff on his cigar, wondering if Boone knew something about the will. She couldn't see how. The thought skittered through her mind that he might've heard from her mama, but no. She wouldn't have done that. Russ didn't even know about the will yet.

"What do you mean, miss out?" she asked.

"Shoot, Ivy. You're supposed to be a smart girl. Don't know how your brother found out Lady was dead, but there's no such thing as coincidence. He gets the first bus from down-and-out back to forgive-me-please. Gets home before Daniel divides the spoils." Boone leaned closer to the window, and Ivy got a whiff of him. Smelled like cheap aftershave and sweat mixed with whiskey. Starting Saturday night early. "Your daddy's a saint. We all agree on that. The kind of daddy that would share with his kids when he inherited a big sum. You didn't think about that? Seems to me Connor came back to make sure you and Russ didn't get his part."

Ivy stared at her uncle, seeing him through a new lens. "You think it's all about money."

"It always comes down to two things, honey. Blood and money." Boone let out a stream of cigar smoke. "Depends on how bad off your brother was. Might be he came home *before* she died. To hurry everything along, if you know what I mean."

Ivy took a step back, feeling like she'd been slapped. "You can't really believe Connor had something to do with Lady's death."

"Whether he did or not, he's gonna drag your family through the mud, just like before."

Ivy heard the edge in her voice, but she didn't care. "I don't see what Lady's money has to do with you, Boone."

Drops of sweat pooled on his craggy forehead. He turned and adjusted the air-conditioner. "If Russ can take the Sports Emporium off my hands, it'll free me up to run for the State House. That's the most important thing to me right now. We have to hold on, here in Tennessee. We gotta hold on to our values. For our state, and our country. If we start electing godless liberals, we're doomed. That's why I'm running for this seat. And a campaign takes the kind of money you wouldn't believe."

Ivy had heard her uncle spout political views before, but not like this.

"What if Lady was still alive? Nobody would be getting an inheritance."

"I imagine she would've backed Russ. I'd already given that some thought."

"You might've been surprised if you were counting on Lady's generosity," Ivy said.

Boone shrugged. "Lady knew a good bet. But we'll never know. Anyway, it's a damn shame she died."

He wasn't looking at Ivy now. The cigar smoke made him squint as he stared off into the distance. And then he began to ramble about Joe Ray Loomis. "I've been in church with that boy ever since he came back from juvie. I can testify he's a good Christian. Just seventeen when he took the heat for something Connor ran away from. Joe Ray went to the altar and repented of all the sins of his young life. He was changed. He'd made mistakes, but he never shot anybody."

Ivy could hardly take it all in. She really didn't know her uncle at all. "You believe Joe Ray Loomis? Connor is your nephew, Boone!" she yelled.

He turned back to her and raised his voice, too. "And Kitty's my sister, and no boy worth his salt would ever hurt his mama like Connor's done!" He punched the air with his fat forefinger. "Your brother needs to go to the altar, too. Repent for what he did ten years ago. Take responsibility. He won't be arrested. Too much time's gone by."

A car passed, the first they'd seen. Boone threw up his hand, and the jolly face he put on made it seem he knew the driver. But it was just a face. A moment later he was glaring at Ivy again. "I hear they sent Lady's body up to Nashville for an autopsy. Things could get nasty." He shook his head. "It's a cryin' shame, all this trouble. If your brother had just stayed gone..."

The sun beat down on Ivy's shoulders. Her running clothes were soaked through, and all at once she felt drained. "Connor didn't shoot anyone. I believe him. I believe everything he told us," she said. Hearing her own words was a revelation. She hadn't realized until this moment that it was true. "And you can go straight to hell, Boone," she said.

Another car passed. This time Boone didn't look to see who it was. He was studying Ivy. Maybe he was thinking he didn't really know her either. And that was just fine with her.

He grunted. "Get in. I'm still your uncle and it's hot as sin."

"No!" Ivy said.

"Suit yourself." He sucked on his cigar a little. "Maybe I oughta catch your folks later."

"Maybe you should," she said.

Ivy watched the Lincoln pull away and glide down the street. If this was how Boone felt about his own nephew, how could Connor expect the town to welcome him? She remembered what he'd said: *Nobody in this town is gonna let me forget, much less forgive.*

But now Ivy was sure. Her brother didn't have to say he was sorry. He didn't have to ask. She had already forgiven him.

Chapter 19

"You'd think Mama was entertaining Jesus," Russ said, first thing after Boone had finally found his way to the store that morning.

"Sounds about right." Boone said.

"Me and Nikki and the kids are supposed to be at the parsonage at six," Russ told him.

"Sure, take your two fine boys. Show your brother what *you've* been up to while he's been missing," his uncle said. "I'll close."

But then, middle of the afternoon, Boone just left the store, a few belts into the Jim Beam he kept in his desk drawer. Russ knew his uncle wouldn't be back, knew it the minute he got a whiff of the whiskey. Not the first time Boone had pulled a stunt like that.

He put off calling Nikki, put off hearing her grumble about Boone. Though he agreed with her complaints about his uncle, his boss, he had no control. Didn't she realize? He could always hear in Nikki's voice that she was thinking, *no backbone.*

As time came to close and it was clear he'd be staying, he had no choice but to call.

Nikki's sigh came through the phone loud and clear. "The boys are driving me crazy. They can't wait to see this uncle they've never met." She added, "Kitty's built him up like he's some kind of superhero."

"Take 'em on over there. I'll be along later," Russ said.

"You sure?" she said, and he knew she'd caught something beneath his words.

Part of it was wishing he could show up with his wife and kids. Like Boone said, let his brother know he had something to show. He'd been building a family.

But he told Nikki, "I'm just pissed at Boone."

Russ was sick and tired of being dependable.

Everybody knew what he did for the Sports Emporium. Everybody knew how Boone depended on him. He was the one the coaches called anytime they had a question. He kept up with the latest equipment. Hell, he was the one out marketing to all the sports teams in the district when Boone was sitting on his fat ass waiting on some daddy to come in wanting a soccer ball for junior.

Russ was the one who convinced Boone they needed a website, *had to* have a website these days, and he found the tech guy that put them in the online ordering business.

Most of their revenue now came through online sales, but Russ still called on the high schools. Watched the young athletes practicing with the same devotion, the same certainty, he'd had back in his glory days, before he tore up his shoulder. Swapped stories with the coaches. Kept them buying from the Sports Emporium when they could order from anywhere. Boone had no clue about that kind of marketing.

In the store, Boone came and went when he pleased. Treated Russ like the teenage help. But when it came to closing, Boone trusted Russ not to leave the kids in charge. Especially tonight, the one named Dewey who called himself Diablo.

And it wasn't only Boone.

When his mama's washer broke down, Russ was the one who took her to Home Depot in Durbin Falls to pick out a new one, and he installed it. His daddy had not one speck of handyman in him. When the pipes froze at the parsonage, Russ crawled under the house with a hair dryer. The foundation of that old place had cracks and crumbles, and somebody had given an estimate of fifteen thousand to repair it, but his daddy had said, "I watched this video. Can't take on something like that by myself, but you and I can fix it, Son."

So they worked on it, cementing some of the deepest cracks. Russ knew the foundation would require more before it was solid, and it would be up to him.

There was always something at the parsonage. Like that goddamned hot water heater that decided to fill his parents' utility room with water on his birthday, and he had to go over there with a shop vac. And when he'd cleared out the water and promised to install a new water heater the next day, he'd told his parents that Nikki and the boys had a birthday cake waiting for him. "It's your birthday, Son?" his daddy said. "I didn't realize!" Which only made it worse.

And yet here was Connor, back after ten years of God knows what, and from the way his daddy had talked on the phone, Russ would bet his parents expected nothing of his brother. No accounting for those years. No justification for the hurt he'd caused his family. No remorse.

Just stay. That was all they would ask.

Like the prodigal son story Russ had heard all his life. The father making such a fuss over the son who came home when his money ran out. Nobody cared that the son who had always been there got a raw deal.

Russ had always been there.

It was just not right.

Chapter 20

"Be careful with those," Connor heard his mama call as he lifted a flat of marigolds from the trunk of her car. Her Ford Escape, the same car she'd been driving back then. Seemed like everything these days had to bring back that Fourth of July.

That day — so clear still — his parents loading picnic leftovers into the trunk of her car. His daddy glancing up, tilting his head the way he did sometimes. Not like he recognized who was riding shotgun in Joe Ray's old truck as it took off from the City Park, tires throwing gravel. Not even like a lament for the reckless ways of Montpier's young people. More like he was curious, wondering, What's the emergency, with the fireworks about to start?

Connor balanced the flat and did the same with another.

"Over there," his mama said, from the kitchen door.

He set the plants beside her gardening tools and watering can. Eighteen small pots in each flat. Grower's pots, she called them. "A lot of flowers," he said, heading back for the others.

"My garden needs sprucing up," she said. "The spring blooms have lost their pizzazz."

Connor wouldn't have thought she'd be buying new flowers today. But no one seemed to be thinking about Lady's death hanging over them, her funeral, or her body about to be cut up in an autopsy. Even his daddy took time this morning for a meeting with Don Petrie. All Connor could figure was that his parents had seen enough death to know how you were supposed to find your way through. The only way, maybe. Go on with your life, best you can. Plant flowers.

A white Highlander pulled into the yard. Car doors slammed. Two boys came running, then put the brakes on in front of him.

"Are you Uncle Connor?" the bigger boy said.

"Just Connor," he said. "How about you?"

"I'm Drew."

The other held a soccer ball against his hip. "And who are you?" Connor asked.

"Owen." Nearly as big as his brother but he had a younger face, a younger voice.

The driver's door opened, finally. Even before he saw her, Connor could feel her. The air suddenly felt like it was full, about to rain, as she came down the driveway. That fluid motion, like water rushing toward him. She had a kind of sway, changing the air as she walked through it. Looking like she always did, like she'd stepped off a movie screen. Not dressed up, though. Faded jeans, a sleeveless gauzy-looking top of some kind that fit loose, and flip-flops. It wouldn't have mattered if she'd been wearing a burlap sack.

The boys looked like *What do we do now?* and Connor felt the same way: *What do I do now?* He half heard them say something, then they ran off into the back yard.

Nikki came closer, no hurry. And then she was there, right there. Close enough that he could have reached out to her. Touched her. And something in him wanted to, but anything would be too much, and anything would never be enough.

She let her mouth make an almost-smile. "You're back," she said.

"Looks like I am," he said.

He could've been meeting his brother's girlfriend for the first time. The same old spark flared up, and the ache that came with it. Heartache buried beneath ten years. Nights he'd held her in his dreams, when he could feel her arms and smell her skin.

"You look like you're all right," she said. "Everybody was worried, afraid you were dead. I didn't think you were dead. I always believed you were out there. I could feel it." The almost-smile had vanished, and her eyes looked like the past had risen in her, about to break. The same ocean wave that Connor felt washing over him.

He took in some air. "I'm all right," he said. Not knowing how to go on from here, he turned to the open trunk and reached for more trays of marigolds. "Mama brought home a bunch of flowers from the farmer's market. I don't get why she wanted them today."

"Her flowers are Kitty's way of putting things out of her mind that she doesn't want to think about," Nikki said. "Wish I had the knack."

Connor picked up both flats. The tray in his left hand tipped, and trying to right it, he dropped the other one. Both hit the pavement, plants spilled all around.

Nikki was quick to kneel on the ground and reach for one of the flowers. Connor bent over the damage and muttered a quiet curse. "Looks like I made a mess of things."

"I know just what you mean," she said, without looking at him. She examined the flower, its roots still intact, and set it back in the little pot. Connor scooped up some dirt and pressed it around the plant. And his hand brushed hers.

It felt like lightning. Lightning burning them to the ground, leaving only strangers staring at what used to be. What never could be again.

"You'll get dirty. I can finish this," Connor said.

Nikki waited, her gaze fixed on his for a minute, then stood up. "As long as they have their roots, they'll be all right."

"Don't tell mama what I did," he said.

"I won't."

He looked back down at the dirt and felt her move away from him. Felt the air change.

Not his brother's girlfriend. His brother's wife.

Chapter 21

Late but not yet sundown, Russ heard the commotion in the backyard. Kid noise, his boys. *His.* And a musical phrase that could only be Nikki's laugh.

He walked around the side of the house. At the corner, before the backyard came into view, he stood still for a minute and just listened. A cheer rose up, Nikki again, and then he heard it. "Good play, Owen!" Connor's voice. Russ would know it anywhere, and the sound brought something that felt like relief, even when all he wanted to feel was resentment.

Had to be soccer. Owen was the one who'd be the star athlete, not his year-older brother. And Owen was crazy for soccer. Soccer hadn't caught on in Montpier when baseball was Russ's game, but now kids started soccer by the time they were three.

He rounded the corner, and sure enough, his boys were kicking the ball around with Connor, and Nikki was watching, sitting on the picnic table. Russ put on the face they expected, like he was so glad to see everybody, but only Nikki seemed to notice him.

She jumped down from the picnic table, met him and threw her arms around him. She looked like she wanted to say something but didn't know what, so she just held onto his arm, leaning against him. Russ wondered why the sudden affection. Not like she greeted him that way every night. Was she putting on a show for Connor? The kids and Connor finished a play, then Russ caught his brother's eye. Connor tossed the ball to Drew and started walking toward him.

It couldn't be anything but awkward, those first moments, brothers meeting for the first time in ten years. In the few seconds that it took for Connor to cross the yard, Russ took his measure. Six feet or so, lean. Kind of bent over like their daddy, but broad shoulders that made Russ think he finally knew what work was. Maybe he wasn't strung out on drugs or anything like that. Russ blinked. In the man approaching, Russ had a vision of the boy they'd feared was dead.

He moved away from Nikki and took a step forward.

Connor's hand went out first, and Russ took it. Strong grip that Russ returned. He said the words he hadn't planned to say. "Welcome home."

"It's good to be here."

Russ punched his brother on the shoulder, maybe just a little too hard.

"Ouch. You're stronger than I remember," Connor said. All of it friendly enough. No bear hugs or anything that spoke of love and blood and time lost, but it was a start. Then Russ saw something in his brother's eyes that he had not counted on from the boy who'd caused so much pain. He saw eyes that were older than they ought to be. Like he'd seen too much and was haunted by it. And for the first time Russ had a glimpse of what all the time away from home might have demanded of his brother.

"You got some fine boys there," Connor said, and then he turned away, as if he didn't want Russ looking too hard at him.

Nikki stepped up beside them. "Most of the time they're good boys. Fuss and fight sometimes, like brothers do."

Russ nodded. It was all he could manage right then. All those feelings tangled up in him wouldn't shape into words.

But one thought came out clear. Maybe. Just maybe. Maybe it'll be all right.

Chapter 22

Daniel had been praying all afternoon. "*Give me the right words, Lord. Help me know when it's time.*" Not like there was a *right* time or even a *good* time. But no question he had to do it, had to tell Russ about the will before it came out some other way. It felt like he had a match in his hand, about to light fireworks, and he feared they would blow up his family.

The time came. And when it did, Daniel knew the Lord had provided.

It came at the end of the meal. Tonight, Kitty had brought out the good china. Handing the dishes to Ivy, to set the table in the dining room, she had dropped a plate, and it broke into smithereens, but Kitty wouldn't let that spoil the mood. "Glad I have a set of twelve," she said.

Everybody knew what it meant to eat in the dining room. Daniel thought he should've said something to Kitty. It might've eased the strain if they'd just gathered in the kitchen, with their old sunflower dishes.

All evening the little boys' chatter had tempered the chill in the air.

Finally, Drew asked, "Can we be excused? We didn't get to finish our soccer game."

"Connor never played soccer," Owen said.

"Not *never*," Drew said. "He just didn't play on a team."

"I'll need a lot a practice," Connor said. "A lot of coaching. You up for that?"

"Are you staying here?" Drew asked.

"That's my plan."

Daniel felt something like a balloon leaking air. Seemed they all had waited to hear that announcement, but it took a child to ask.

Owen said, "Mom told us not to count on you to stay. You might be on a visit is all."

Nikki moaned, "I didn't... It wasn't like that..."

Connor let it pass. "I'm not planning to go anywhere anytime soon." He caught his brother's eye. "You OK with that, Rusty?"

"Rusty?" Owen and Drew said at the same time.

"I used to call him Rusty."

The little boys laughed out loud, too loud, but Russ's full-of-daggers look said what he thought of Connor's joke.

And then, the doorbell. A welcome interruption.

Kitty answered and came back to the table carrying a sack. "That was Mr. Hardaway. He'd bought some fireworks for his grandsons, but they aren't coming into town for the Fourth after all. He wanted our kids to have them."

The little boys cheered. Connor, it seemed to Daniel, knew his comment about Rusty had gone flat and saw an opportunity to leave the table. He patted his belly and said, "I'm stuffed. Thanks, Mama." He scooted his chair back and took the sack from his mother. "C'mon, boys. Let's take a look at those fireworks."

And Daniel thought it was time, but it wasn't yet.

The rest of the family left the table, too, carrying their plates. As they headed into the kitchen, he heard Ivy asking Nikki, "What have you told Drew and Owen about Lady?"

Russ might not have heard, his eyes so full of something else Daniel could only imagine.

Nikki said, "We told them she went to heaven. What else?"

"How did they take it?" Ivy wanted to know.

Nikki shrugged. "They had a few questions, but they didn't cry. Maybe I shouldn't say it, but I think they were always a little afraid of Lady. She didn't pay much attention to them."

Ivy said, "What questions?"

"Oh, I don't know. They asked how she died. I told them she fell down the stairs. They wanted to know if it hurt, and I said probably she didn't feel a thing, it happened so fast. Drew asked if Grandpa cried because his mother was dead. I told him people don't always cry, but that doesn't mean they're not sad."

Daniel smiled at his daughter-in-law, and she smiled back.

Then Russ said, “Owen wanted to know who would live in Lady’s house now.”

And that was the moment Daniel knew the good Lord had given him. It was time.

He said, “I met with Don Petrie this morning. He told me he’d drawn up a new will for Lady a few days ago.”

Daniel took his fresh coffee over to the sink, where Russ was standing. The window framed a sweet picture. Connor and the boys, having a good time. Daniel wasn’t sure Russ was hearing him. Really hearing.

So he said it, straight out. “Lady’s new will made Connor her sole beneficiary.”

That got his son’s attention. Shock, more than Daniel had even expected. Russ looked like he’d grabbed hold of a live wire.

A beat of silence. Two beats. Three. And finally, “I don’t think I heard right.” Russ’s tone said he damn well knew he’d heard right, and he was not taking it well.

The room fell silent. The women stopped clearing the table, putting away food, filling the dishwasher. Like Russ, they stood motionless. Daniel knew what they were waiting for, same as he was. Knowing Russ was holding in something powerful, something that might explode any time. That was the way anger showed itself with Russ, the way it had always been, a controlled burn, slow like rust, and then watch out.

And Daniel knew how that kind of anger could take over, take you to a place you never wanted to be. With the Lord’s help, he had wrestled down his own anger that was so fierce when he was young, but the memory was raw, and his heart ached for his son.

After the longest time, Russ pressed his hands on the edge of the sink, so hard, his knuckles went white. “She left everything to Connor,” he said. Not a question. A statement full of indignation. And without waiting for an answer, he raised his voice. “She knew where he was all along, didn’t she? So Connor must have known about the will. That’s why he came back!”

“Don’t go there, Son,” Daniel raised his hand. Trying to keep his voice level. Trying to keep the situation from running off the rails. “Connor didn’t know anything about it until today, after I found out.”

"He *says* he didn't know." Leaning forward, Russ looked like he could charge right through the glass, to where his brother was setting up fireworks, with his sons looking on.

Maybe Nikki believed she could calm him. Maybe she was the one who could, Daniel thought, as she came over to the sink, crowded in between them and slid her arm around her husband's waist. But her words were not calming, even as she whispered to no one in particular, "What was that crazy old woman trying to prove?"

Daniel shook his head. "I don't know what was in Lady's mind, but God works in mysterious ways." He glanced at the scene in the backyard. Connor seemed happier than any time since he'd come home. Daniel looked back at Russ, all that anger on his face. Hurt, too, but not what you could see. Daniel knew how deep the hurt was buried. He didn't know which of his sons deserved his pity more. And maybe he ought to feel sorry for himself. Lady could've made it possible for him to share with his children, make their lives easier. Instead, her decision was about to tear the Burdette family apart.

"How much is her estate worth?" Russ asked. A reasonable question but sharp-edged.

"Millions. At least ten but probably more." Daniel hadn't mentioned that to anyone, not even Connor. He could feel the women draw in their breaths, Russ not so much. How much didn't even matter, Daniel knew. What mattered was that she gave it to Connor.

"Lady named Don Petrie the Executor," Daniel said. "He'll give Connor good advice when the time comes. After the funeral."

"Did Don Petrie go along with changing the will?" Russ asked.

"He had to. It's what his client wanted. But when I asked him Lady's reason, he said, 'She never explained her reason to my satisfaction.'"

Russ slammed his fist on the counter. "Goddammit! How could Lady treat her family this way? Nobody does that to her own blood, nobody with a heart." He turned to Daniel, his eyes full of hurt now. "And you know something? Soon as Connor's got money in the bank, he'll be outa here because that's what he does. He runs. And God only knows what he'll do with it."

Kitty spoke up before Daniel could. The mother's voice. "You need to settle down, Russ. This is not doing anybody any good. Your daddy's right. It can all wait till after the funeral."

Her words hung in the air for a minute. Russ pounded the counter again, but it barely made a sound, an echo of desperation.

Another moment passed, as Daniel watched Connor light a bunch of firecrackers.

And then Russ gave Nikki a look. "Tell the boys it's time to go. You need to take them home."

Nikki glanced at the backyard. Russ didn't give her time to protest. "Get 'em right now," he said.

Daniel sent up another prayer, but the fireworks were already exploding. The little boys squealing. Connor yelling, "Watch out!" And the firecrackers pop pop popping.

Chapter 23

A mother never stops being a mother. Never stops feeling that maternal pull, as strong as the moon on the tides. Kitty had been a mother for thirty-four years and she knew that pull was not just love pure and simple. It was love and worry and fear for what the world can do. It was hope and hurt and more. Tonight, she was mad as a hornet at Russ, but in the deepest part of her heart, she felt that mother's ache for her firstborn.

Lady had managed to split Kitty's family apart. And that was the one thing Kitty could not, would not forgive. If her mother-in-law were alive, she'd tell her, *You're a mother but don't pretend you know anything about a mother's love.* And she would have some un-Christian things to say to the old fool, too. Things you don't find in any version of the Bible.

Russ had gone to the car with Nikki and the boys, but he was not leaving. Kitty wished he'd go with them, take some time to cool down. But no. He had something to say to Connor. Something hard and sharp, Kitty knew. Like the edge of a broken plate.

Connor, her lost son, her found son — he did not deserve his brother's contempt. He'd only wanted to come home. He had not wanted ten million dollars. He only wanted to be forgiven, and to forgive himself.

Kitty watched from the kitchen window, her arms crossed. She had loaded the dishes in the dishwasher and scrubbed her hands. She'd told Ivy, "Go on. I'll finish up." Kitty hadn't wanted to talk to anyone. Not even Daniel. He'd gone to his study. Fathers don't know their children's hearts like mothers do, Kitty thought. Even before her baby comes into the world, a mother feels that beating heart, and she never stops feeling it.

Connor took a seat at the picnic table and lit a cigarette. Kitty would say something to him about smoking, but not now. So much else to worry about. And all she wanted for Connor was for him to stay, and be happy staying. Be happy again.

As Russ appeared in the backyard, Kitty felt her breath quicken and she held her arms tighter around herself. He spoke to Connor, not too loud, but Kitty could make it out.

"So you get it all, little brother. Shithead. Now we know why you came back."

Connor got down from the picnic table, tossed his cigarette, and crushed the butt. "Slow down, Rusty," he said. "That's not why I came back."

Kitty cracked the window to catch every word, and Russ's anger came through loud and clear. "Liar! Lady wouldn't leave ten million to somebody she thought was dead."

He moved in closer, and Kitty saw him clench and unclench his fist. Connor raised a hand, palm out. "Whoa! Ten million? You're full of shit!"

"Don't say you didn't know. Tell the truth, dammit. Just tell the truth for once!" He punched Connor's chest with his finger.

Connor pushed back. And then Russ swung. A quick punch that caught Connor on the jaw and staggered him.

Kitty yelped and hurried out the kitchen door. "Stop it! Stop it right now!" she called.

Connor, smaller than his brother but just as fired up, regained his balance and tore into Russ. And then Russ landed a blow that sent him sprawling backwards.

Kitty ran to her sons and stepped between them. "Lord, Lord!" she cried. "Stop!"

Russ finally seemed to hear her. He stepped back. Connor sat up in the grass, rubbing his jaw.

Kitty saw Ivy come running, and behind her, Daniel, walking fast at first, then slower, his face full of disgust and beneath it something she recognized as disappointment.

"So it's come to this?" he said. "This is what it's come to, boys?"

Russ looked hard at his daddy and said, "It's not right. You know it's not right, what he's done."

"Right's got nothing to do with what I see here. What I see is wrong," Daniel said.

Connor made no move to stand up. "All I did was get on a Greyhound and try to come home."

"That's not all. Not by a long shot," Russ growled. "You knew Lady was dead. You had to know about the money. What else are you holding back?"

"Enough!" Kitty shouted, her palms pressing her temples as her head began to throb. The air grew still for a long silent moment. And then in a quieter voice, Kitty said, "That's enough. Get up, Connor."

Connor exchanged a look with his mother. He was shaking his head, just barely, as he got to his feet. She knew he was saying, *No. Don't.*

"It's all right," Kitty told him, and then she turned to her husband. "I'm sorry, Daniel. I was the one that called Connor when Lady died. He gave me a number once."

She had never seen such a lost expression on her husband's face.

Chapter 24

Connor felt the burn of shame, seeing his parents this way. He saw his mama move to the picnic table and let herself sink onto the bench, and it looked like something had crumpled in her. He saw his daddy's eyes fixed on her as she moved, like he was trying to find something of the woman he knew, trying to see the woman he had loved and trusted for forty years. What he'd done to them, Connor thought, might be worse than all the other mistakes he'd made these past ten years.

Dusk had settled around them. A few fireflies had come out, and a sudden cool breeze gave some relief from the stifling heat.

Ivy said, "You want some ice?" For a moment, Connor had forgotten his jaw. Seemed like he deserved the ache. He shook his head.

And then Russ spoke, something cautious in his voice now. "Mama, are you saying you knew where Connor was all along?"

She shook her head. "Not all along. He called once. Just one time. March eighteenth this year."

Connor went over to the bench and sat down by her. He started to say something, he didn't know what, but she kept speaking. "I always said I'd keep the landline. These i-phones are fine and lots of our friends are giving up their landlines. But that's the number Connor knew."

"Why didn't you tell us?" Russ said. Still trying not to be harsh with her, Connor could see, but the edge was there. "We were all wondering if he was even alive, and you knew, Mama!"

She nodded, looking down at her hands, folded prayer-like. "It was wrong." She raised her eyes to Daniel then. "I knew you'd think you could convince him to come home. Connor knew it. You'd think that was the right thing. And you'd try. I was afraid we wouldn't ever hear anything again."

Connor had to make this right somehow.

"None of it is Mama's fault." And he began to tell them how he'd wanted to call many times before, but he'd always imagine they'd find him. "I wasn't ready to be found," he said. "I had burner phones, so I gave Mama the number where I was staying. Made her promise she'd use it only for something like a death in the family. Made her promise she wouldn't tell." The look he gave her said he was so much sorrier than he'd ever be able to say. "I shouldn't have asked you to keep it from Daddy," he said.

She looked up at him, all mother's love.

His daddy hadn't said a word through all of this. He hadn't moved from the spot in the yard where he was standing when he'd heard his wife say, "I was the one." Connor thought he seemed more stooped than usual, his shoulders carrying a weight he could hardly bear.

"I'm sorry, Daddy," Connor said.

His father gave a slight nod. Connor wasn't sure what it meant.

And then his mama surprised him. She sat up straighter, more like she'd reclaimed herself, her rock-solid certainty, and she spoke in her mother's voice. "So that's the end of any talk that Connor knew about Lady's death before I called him, the night she died. Whatever anybody else in Montpier might think, we" — she made a big circle with her forefinger that included all of them — "*we* know the truth, and we have to act like a family."

She gave Russ a piercing look.

"We still don't know why Lady changed her will," Russ said. "Why she gave everything to a grandson that could've been dead."

Connor said, "And if you figure that out, you be sure to let me know."

Russ grunted. After a minute, he said, "I need to get home." He darted a look at Connor that was not unkind. "Better put some ice on your face. It'll be all right. I've had worse."

And then their daddy spoke, finally. "Good it's all out in the open," he said.

Sounded to Connor like he was just saying words.

Chapter 25

There were a few things that Ivy always believed she could count on. Like the Four-Ten bus that would never be a minute late or the sign outside the Farmers and Merchants Bank that always showed the temperature too high. Like Sunday mornings at the parsonage.

Sunday meant her daddy left for church an hour before Sunday School started, brushing lint from his dark suit. Sunday meant her mama would rush around, late for Sunday School, long after she had no children to gather up and strap into car seats. That Sunday feeling tinted the air, the restless anticipation as sure as the promise of a summer storm.

And all her life Ivy had counted on her parents' absolute honesty, as unfailing as daylight and dark.

But this morning as Ivy poured a steaming cup of strong coffee, she saw the broken plate that her mama had set aside. And she thought of something else, something about her family that had been shattered.

She heard the urgency of high heels, as her mama came into the kitchen, purse hanging on her arm. Pale green dress belted at the waist, a look that not many women in their sixties could carry off. Her mama was a slender woman with a smattering of gray in her dark hair. She didn't often look sixty. But this morning the years showed. She'd tried too hard to conceal the dark circles and sagging skin around her eyes. Her make-up was chalky, blush too pink.

Ivy said, "I like your dress."

Her mama didn't acknowledge the compliment. She gathered up her Bible and Sunday School book from the kitchen table and looked around. "I thought my glasses..." she said, then spotting them, took a few quick steps to the counter where they lay beside the broken plate.

It was the plate that held her attention for a moment. She hadn't seemed troubled when the plate broke last night, Ivy thought, but now her brow wrinkled. She set the five pieces in order like working a puzzle and ran her fingers over the edges that fit together loosely.

And then, as if shaking herself from a dream, she said, "I'm running late." She picked up her glasses. Her three-inch heels clicked against the linoleum as she hurried to the kitchen door.

Ivy heard her whisper, "Maybe I can put it back together again."

It's the humidity that gets you. You feel like you're swimming through the air, muggy and thick and steamy. That's July in Montpier, as in most of Tennessee.

Ivy felt the sweat drench her the minute she stepped onto the front porch with her coffee. The screen door slapped behind her, and Connor came out.

"Already shaping up to be that kind of day," he said.

"A scorcher."

"Heavy. Something heavy in the air." He leaned on the rail and took a long breath. "Thought you'd be going to church."

"Did you really?"

"Nah. Preacher's kids — we have church crammed down our throats until we get to decide, and we say we've had enough."

"But then there's Russ."

Connor's laugh had no mirth in it. He winced as he rubbed his jaw, but Ivy could tell he didn't want to talk about his brother or last night.

"Want to go to Ben and Lynn's for breakfast?" he said. "If they're still in business."

"They are. Big crowds at lunch, but I've never been there for breakfast."

"Our family never ate breakfast out. Time for a change, don't you think?"

Things had already changed. Changed too much. But Ivy didn't say it.

"Give me fifteen minutes," she said.

Though the heat was bearing down, they walked to the square, taking zig-zag streets and short cuts through alleys, as they'd always done. Never thought of driving the five blocks and paying to park at a meter. The leafy maples of Grand Avenue were welcoming, offering some shade and a slight breeze. The Griddle, known by most as Ben and Lynn's, was the only eatery on the square, and though there were a few other restaurants in Montpier, none were open on Sunday morning except the Blue Ribbon, a glorified bar near the bypass.

"Wonder if they've cleaned the grill," Connor said. "The greasy grill was the secret of their success."

Ivy remembered. The Griddle was not your typical teenage hangout. No music. No video games. But their hamburgers were legendary.

"There was an old sour-puss waitress with cat-eye glasses," Connor said. "She used to get after me and my friends when we were too loud." He mimicked her nasal voice: "'You boys need to settle down now.' She'd poke my chest with her long red fingernail. Looked like a claw."

Ivy listened to Connor as he recalled those days. Reaching back to a simple time, the *before* time. She wondered if he believed he could take up where he left off.

"You think Ben and Lynn have come out of the closet?" Connor asked.

That took Ivy by surprise. Everybody knew the owners were gay, but nobody ever spoke of it. Ivy had heard they came from Atlanta and bought the café from a man heading into bankruptcy, before her family moved to Montpier. They lived in an apartment above the café.

"That's the kind of thing you shouldn't say out loud," Ivy said.

Connor's eyebrows lifted. "Has my sister been drinking the Kool-Aid?"

"No Kool-Aid, but think about it. Everyone likes Ben and Lynn but the minute *that word* comes up, you might as well nail a "Closed" sign on their front door. There're too many Boones in this town."

Connor shook his head. "Don't seem right."

They had reached the door of The Griddle with its hospitable sign, big script on a chalkboard, a smiley face in the corner: "Welcome! Have a nice day!"

Ivy looked around the wooden tables and chairs in the middle and the red booths on the side, and her first impression was that not much had changed, except the waitresses who now were all twenty-something or younger, fresh-faced and smiling. The décor was the same. Framed black and white photographs featured highlights of the town's history, including the hotel — elegant for a small town — that had burned sometime around 1950. Ceiling fans stirred the air, thick with the comforting smells of coffee and bacon.

A couple in church clothes with a toddler girl, all ribbons and petticoats, had come in ahead of them. Probably Methodists. The Methodists had an early contemporary service that would have finished by now. Older customers in their Sunday finest would likely be heading out to the eleven o'clock services in one of Montpier's four downtown churches.

As Ivy and Connor stood in front of the counter, waiting for a table, Lynn, at the cash register, called out, "Connor Burdette? Can't believe my eyes! Is that really you?"

Connor raised his hand in a silent greeting. People looked up from their scrambled eggs and biscuits and pancakes.

"Heard you were back, Bud."

"Yep," Connor said. "That's one piece of gossip that's true."

And then Lynn's attention turned to an elderly black man who had hobbled up to pay. One of the young waitresses in jeans and tee shirt motioned Ivy and Connor to a table.

Ivy picked up the big vinyl-covered menu, glanced at the special, "Brains, eggs, and grits, $5.95," then noticed that both Lynn and the old man at the cash register were darting quick glances at Connor. Funny look on Lynn's face. The sullen customer shoved his wallet into his back pocket. His scowl deepened, and then he came their way, walking with the uneven gait of an old man half-crippled from long years of hard work.

"Connor," Ivy said, in a wary voice.

"What?" He turned to follow her gaze.

"Connor Burdette?" the man called out before he reached them.

"Yes, sir?"

"Whatever slimy rock you crawled out from under, you shoulda stayed there," the old man said, and with a powerful shove, he sent Connor's chair toppling over.

Ivy stood up. "Who *are* you?" she said, as Connor scrambled to his feet. But the man turned away and limped to the door, into the street.

The café had grown so quiet, the only noises were the rattle of dishes and low voices from the kitchen. Someone back there was saying, "Two over easy. One brains and eggs."

Lynn hurried to Connor. He was short, pear-shaped, carrying too much weight, and the short dash or the excitement had left him breathless. Setting the chair upright, he said, "Oh my goodness, I shoulda seen that coming when he asked me if you were really Connor Burdette."

"What's his problem?" Connor said, rubbing his jaw.

Lynn's eyes were fixed on the bruised jaw. "Oh my goodness, you're hurt!"

Connor touched his face again. "The old man didn't do this. Who *is* he?"

People were going back to eating, flatware clinking against plates, a rising hum as conversations started up again. Lynn lowered his voice. "That's Henry Dalton."

"Who's Henry Dalton to me?" Connor said.

"Dalton," Ivy echoed. *Dalton. The clerk that was shot at the Back Home Market.*

She saw the sudden memory in Connor's eyes, too. Saw it before Lynn said the words: "His grandson was Raleigh Dalton."

Chapter 26

"No, Connor!"

Connor heard Ivy's voice, but it was a faint noise that seemed to come from far away. His thoughts had flown to another time, a gunshot, a young black man's shrieks, his own cry — *No-o-o-o-o!* — sounds more real to him than anything coming from the café. All he wanted was to catch up with the old man and tell him, *I did not shoot your grandson.*

He rushed out the door and into the edge of the street and could not believe that the old man who could hardly walk was nowhere in sight. He looked one way and the other. And then he heard his sister behind him. "C'mon, Connor. Please! Let's go home."

But an ancient faded-black work-horse kind of pick-up rounded the corner and turned into the street. Connor didn't waste a second thinking about it. He ran into the street in front of the old Ford Ranger and stood there, waving his arms, his feet planted wide apart.

He heard Ivy scream his name, but the only sound that mattered was the screech of brakes. It hadn't worried him that the old man might run over him. Only now did he even consider that the brakes could have been bad. But they weren't.

As Connor walked over to the driver, Ivy came running behind him, yelling. "Have you lost your mind?"

The window crawled down, and Mr. Dalton said, "You're one lucky fool."

"I want to talk to you," Connor said.

"I don't have no more to say," the old man muttered, looking straight ahead, his grip tight on the steering wheel.

"I do," Connor said. "You think I shot your grandson. I didn't. I didn't shoot Raleigh."

It took a moment, but Mr. Dalton let his eyes meet Connor's. He glared at him, squinted, studied him, and Connor could tell the instant the old man decided he might want to believe him.

"You want to talk to me, get in," Mr. Dalton said.

"Connor, I don't think — " Ivy whispered.

"Shut up," he told her.

It had been twenty years or more since he'd told his sister to shut up. He imagined she'd still shrink back, but she followed him around the front of the cab to the passenger side and said, "If you're going, I'm going with you."

"Ivy, you can't — "

"Shut up," she said.

The worn-out pick-up turned into a short driveway at a simple white clapboard house, with a yard in bad need of mowing and tangles of flowers that needed weeding. Flowers given back to the order of God's care, exploding with colors the way He had made them.

Connor couldn't remember that he'd ever been to this side of town before. The law that was supposed to let all kinds of folks live in harmony with each other hadn't found its way yet into the hearts of Montpier. But this black community on the south side was not so different from other older neighborhoods in town, Connor thought. Small houses interspersed with new, stylish upscale houses here and once-stately homes there. Across the street, a young black woman sat on her porch, working on a laptop. Next door to Mr. Dalton's house, an old black woman on her porch busied herself shucking corn.

Mr. Dalton unlocked the door and went in. He didn't tell them to follow, but Connor was sure they were supposed to. Something about the tidy room spoke of a woman's touch. The crocheted afghan on the back of the couch, the knick-knacks, photographs all over the walls.

Mr. Dalton said, "If my wife was here, she'd offer you lemonade."

"Is your wife at church?" Ivy asked.

A pause before he answered. "You could say so. She's buried in the church yard."

Ivy gave a little moan. Connor managed a feeble "I'm sorry."

The old man finally made a gesture for them to sit on the couch. He said, "I don't drink lemonade no more. The way Jane made it, bad for my sugar. I drink water is all. Nearly seven months, she's been gone. She passed just before Christmas."

Connor was thinking maybe losing his wife had affected the old man's mind, like this morning at Ben and Lynn's.

He couldn't keep his eyes off the photographs. They covered the walls and filled the surfaces of side tables. A bookshelf that contained only a few books was full of framed photos. Pictures for a church directory had a certain look, Connor knew. Mr. Dalton and his wife posed with a girl in some, with a boy in others. Photos of the girl everywhere, from child to woman. In a couple of glamour photos, she was stunning. Hanging prominently above the mantle was the picture of a handsome young man in cap and gown. Connor pointed to it. "That's Raleigh."

Mr. Dalton nodded. "Graduated high school out in Los Angeles."

Connor rubbed his palms together, let the old man settle with some groaning into a recliner, and then began what he had been rehearsing in his mind. "I've spent a lot of time thinking about what I did and what I could've done. I'm sorry about all of it, especially Raleigh, and I know he said it was me, but it wasn't. Joe Ray was the one with the gun. I don't think he meant to hit Raleigh's leg." He felt his heartbeat speed up, as memories came into focus. "It looked bad. Real bad."

Mr. Dalton blinked, like he was remembering, too. "It was bad, all right. That shooting's what started all the bad. All downhill from there."

"I swear, I didn't shoot him," Connor said. "I didn't even know Joe Ray had that gun."

Mr. Dalton shook his head and scowled like something had suddenly soured in him. "Why would Raleigh say it was you if it wasn't?"

Connor thought, *this old man won't like hearing the truth about his grandson.* He said, "If I could just talk to him..."

"Well... They ain't invented that kind of telephone. Raleigh's over in the graveyard by the church, next to his grandma."

Connor felt the air leave his lungs. Raleigh, dead? No! All these years, Connor had wrung some comfort from knowing that Raleigh lived. Not because of anything he'd done. He had not lifted a finger, and that would haunt him forever. But the gunshot had not killed Raleigh.

When he spoke, his words came in a rush. "My God, what happened?"

The answer took a minute coming. "Out in Los Angeles. Overdose."

The room filled with that kind of silence that only death can bring. Long, long silence. Connor looked at Ivy, her eyes full of the kind of sorrow he so often saw in his daddy's eyes.

Finally, he said, "Why'd you want us to come out here, Mr. Dalton?"

The old man looked him in the eye. "So you could *see*."

"See?"

"See that Raleigh didn't come from trash. A black boy gets shot, and people think he was just some thug that nobody ever loved. No sir! I loved that boy!" His voice cracked. "I still do." He shifted to the edge of the recliner and reached for a small photo on the side table, a child with that first-fish kind of grin, holding up his catch. Then he pulled himself up in his chair, as straight as he could. "He was smart, too." His old eyes shone. "I could tell you stories."

Mr. Dalton put the photo back in its place. He looked around the walls, and Connor believed the old man was seeing all he'd lost. "His mama left him with Jane and me when he was a baby. Keisha thought Hollywood was just waitin' on her. Didn't work out like that. Nothing ever does. Wherever you go there's back of the tracks, and that's where she wound up." A grunt. "Raleigh was better off with Jane and me. We raised him up right. But time came, he wanted to live with his mama, go to high school out there."

The old man managed to stand up, sounding like his old pick-up truck trying to start. He hobbled over to the fireplace and fixed his gaze on the boy in cap and gown. "He did all right in high school. Tried college off and on. He coulda done it. I know he coulda. Keisha said he was lazy. He'd work at something and quit, try something else and quit. Couldn't stick with nothin'."

Connor let his gaze rest for a minute on the graduation picture, thinking, You and me, Raleigh. Both of us too far from home, trying to find our way back.

"Then him and Keisha had a falling out, and one day he showed up on our doorstep again. Stayed here two years." The old man was bent, his legs splayed. But he stood as still as a tree weathered with age, bracing himself with one hand against the fireplace.

It seemed he'd lost his train of thought, so Connor spoke up. "That's why he was in Montpier, working at the market."

Mr. Dalton picked up the thread. "After a while I got a notion that he oughta take a job at the Back Home. The manager went to our church. I always believed work gave a man pride." A little snort. "I still wake up nights wondering what if I'd just kept my mouth shut."

The old man's eyes were shiny now, his voice full of enough blame to go around. "He nearly died at that market, you know. Somehow, he called 9-1-1 and they got to him and saved his leg. Saved him, but not really. Soon as he was able to leave, he didn't want no part of Montpier. Or me. All he wanted from me was a ride to Nashville, to the airport. He went back to Los Angeles. It wasn't long... he was in awful pain from that leg. Went to the streets for something stronger than the doctors gave him."

A long, long silence. Connor couldn't listen to any more of this. He stood up, trying to rub the stains off his hands one more time. "I'm sorry about it all. I am. But I wish you'd believe me. I didn't shoot him."

All at once the old weak eyes flamed. Mr. Dalton pointed a crooked finger at Connor and came toward him. He seemed even more crippled, struggling to stay upright, like grief, more than his knees, was bringing him down. "It shouldn't oughta been that way!" he said as he stumbled forward.

Connor made a quick move to catch the old man. He grabbed the big arms that he was sure were once powerful and helped the feeble man to stand. Mr. Dalton didn't resist the help, but he wouldn't meet Connor's eyes.

"I wish I'd never set foot in that store," Connor said. "I'd change it all if I could."

The old man looked around the room once more and finally seemed to come to himself. After a minute he said, "I'll take you home."

The ride was quiet, until they came to a little church, with a cemetery at its side. The pick-up slowed to barely creeping, then came to a stop. "Jane's buried there," he said, pointing. "See that double rock? And Raleigh's that shorter stone. Big cities ain't got a lick of mercy. We brought him home." Connor couldn't tell which tombstones the old man meant, but he nodded.

Mr. Dalton lowered his head to the steering wheel and spoke to no one. "Living's a sorrowful business. You walk behind every mistake you ever make." He raised his head then and looked at Connor. "There's a lot of death in this town. Even dead men like me, walking around, using up air, waiting for my time to run out so I can rest over there, by my wife." Then he let his boot lay heavy on the accelerator, and they moved forward. "There's no forgiving in me for you. Not yet. Maybe someday."

Connor said, "That don't mean I'll stop trying."

Chapter 27

Daniel had a glimpse of Frank Steele holding back as the rest of the congregation fell in line to shake hands with their pastor, tell him what an inspiration the sermon was, and remind him of their prayer requests. And, this Sunday, three days after the death of his mother, they were offering words of comfort. *So sorry about Lady. Praying for you. Bless your heart.*

But nothing like that from the Colonel, who stepped up at the end of the line, without offering his hand, and said, "We need to talk."

Daniel said, "Come to my office in five minutes." Five minutes, not to visit the bathroom or even get a glass of water. Five minutes in his office, to kneel where he always prayed, as if it was a holy spot on the carpet, the threadbare place where he felt the spirit most deeply. Daniel knew from the hard glint in Frank Steele's eyes that whatever the reason the Chair of the Deacons wanted to talk, it was bound to be trouble, and Daniel wasn't sure he was up to it. Not without strength that only the Almighty could give. And so he prayed until he heard a demanding knock on the door.

Daniel meant to direct Frank to the big wingback chairs that provided a more comfortable place to talk, but the Colonel didn't wait to be directed. Not much taller than Daniel but back as straight as a board, he had the air of a man who had always been in charge. He came in saying, "I'll keep this short. Would put it off, considering your mother's death, but fact is, we've put off too much too long already." Four swift steps took him to the chair in front of Daniel's desk before Daniel could get in a word.

"What's on your mind, Frank?" Daniel settled in the chair behind his desk that gave him some height over the chair across from him. Not intentional. Just something he'd noticed.

The Colonel straightened in his seat, pulling on the lapels of his sport coat. Windowpane design. No tie. Frank never wore a tie. Daniel had heard him remark that First Baptist was too "high church" for his liking, but it was the only Baptist church in town.

What seemed it might be a smile turned into a smirk. Frank said, "Expected you to preach on the prodigal son today."

Daniel felt the jab, but he kept his voice level. "As you know — I hope you've been keeping up — I'm in the middle of a series. Sermon on the Mount." He stopped short of asking Frank if he'd paid any attention to the sermon today on the light of the world.

"Your boy came home. Prodigal son, people say. Seemed like that woulda been a good sermon. Appropriate for the time."

"Maybe in the future."

"He wasn't in church today." No mistaking the edge in Frank's voice.

Daniel said, "Connor's a grown man. Time comes when parents can't tell their children what to do. He's twenty-nine, and he makes his own decisions."

"Seems to me Connor's made some bad decisions," Frank said.

Daniel felt his hands clench. This man knew how to push his buttons. Truth was, he'd struggled for years with his feelings about Frank Steele, who ran the Radisson Tree Harvesting Company. Jack Burdette had never wanted his lumber company to go that way, the business that he'd built into one of Mercer County's biggest employers. When his health failed and he needed to sell, Radisson had made a generous offer, but he'd accepted far less from a smaller outfit that promised to respect the land as he had done. Promised not to follow Radisson's example, taking down all the hardwoods and planting fast-growing pines. Raping the land, Jack Burdette called it. As ugly as strip mining in coal country.

Daniel could hear his father now: "I'd rather burn 'em than do what Radisson does."

But just five years after Jack Burdette's death, ownership changed hands again, and Radisson wound up with the company that Daniel's father had founded. And Frank Steele, who used to be Jack's right-hand man, now ran the operation in Montpier.

Daniel had prayed about it. *Help me not to hold this against Frank. He's just a businessman. Help me, Lord, to act like his pastor.*

It would have been easier if Frank were not such a hard man.

"Is Connor what you came to talk about?" Daniel asked.

Frank shifted again in his seat and straightened himself. Daniel had noticed a habit the Colonel had, pulling himself up as tall as he could, a way of demonstrating authority. "I came to talk about your sermons. You don't come down hard enough on sin, Daniel. That's a problem."

Younger people in the church called him Daniel, but the Colonel was a traditional man, who'd always said Brother Burdette, until now.

Daniel nodded, signaling that he was listening, not that he was agreeing. After a moment he said, "Do you have some particular sins in mind?" He regretted saying it the moment the words left his mouth. He refused to get into an argument with Frank about the hot-button issues that would split the church down the middle. Church was not the place for politics.

The Colonel squinted at him. "No preacher worth his salt would need a list."

Daniel leaned forward and looked Frank in the eye. "You got me there. Yes, I could find enough sin in the world to condemn, if that's what the Lord put on my heart." He felt a rise in his voice that he hadn't intended. "Tell me, Frank, you call it a problem that I preach about a God of forgiveness and mercy? You want fire and brimstone, a God of justice and retribution?"

Frank let the question pass. Once again, he straightened himself, and this time Daniel believed this was what he'd come to say. "We — the deacons — we just don't know if you have the spirit anymore."

It was a long moment before Daniel said, "I see." And an even longer moment before he said, "I'll meet with the deacons and hear what they have to say. After I bury my mother."

The Colonel stood up, hiked his chin and said, "You couldn't even get your mama to church. You can't get your children to church. And now the autopsy — yes, everybody knows! Raises questions. Too many questions about your family. Not what the church needs."

The charged air did not leave the room with him. Daniel closed his eyes, overcome with a sudden weariness that he felt deep in his bones. His family split apart, his mama's doing. Even Kitty — something broken between them. And now, this. His church, about to be lost.

All Daniel knew to do when life got so heavy was to pray. He asked to be raised up above the heaviness. He asked for mercy and healing for his family, and finally he managed to thank God that the Colonel didn't know about the will. Not yet.

Chapter 28

Kitty wanted to pretend she wasn't there when she heard Boone pounding at the kitchen door, the booming voice: "Anybody home?"

"It's open," she called, sounding like she had to drag up the welcome to some place it didn't want to go.

Boone must have come from church. Not First Baptist. His church. Extreme in their views, serving an angry God, was how Kitty thought of The Gospel Fellowship.

His thin hair was slicked back. He wore red suspenders over a white shirt and smelled like he'd bathed in after-shave. He helped himself to a chair, across the table from Kitty, and glanced at her half-eaten sausage and biscuit. The chair squeaked under his weight.

"Where's your family?" Boone asked.

Kitty had wondered the same thing. Daniel was meeting with Deacon Steele after church, but she didn't know about Ivy and Connor. "Out and about," she said.

"Thought you'd be fixing a big Sunday dinner."

"Not today. People have brought in plenty of food."

Her brother had a way of looking at her, head tilted, glint in his eye, like he was so sure of something about her. Boone was sure about a lot of things that weren't so, but being wrong never stopped him from being certain.

"Thought I'd say hey to your boy... the lost one," he said. "And see about you."

Kitty frowned. "What about me?"

"Well — " Boone leaned back a little, lacing his thick fingers, setting his hands on his belly. The chair groaned. "I know it's been terrible on you, how he's done his family."

It was terrible, she thought, the not knowing.

"Came in dragging his tail, I expect, like they do when there's no place else to go."

Kitty's voice took on a sharp edge. "Don't know why you'd think that. Where'd you get your information?"

As soon as she asked, she knew. Even before Boone said, "Russ tells me things. The good son he is. He's been hurt by it all, Kitty. Getting pushed to the back pew, after all he's done. It ain't easy for that boy."

Kitty stood up and whisked her coffee mug away. At the sink, she looked out on the yard and thought about her boys out there fighting. Sadness swelled in her. Russ was a good son. Maybe she hadn't given him enough of something he needed from her. But Connor was the son that needed more from her.

"Saw Joe Ray Loomis at church. Everbody knows Connor's back." Boone's words jolted Kitty. She turned and glared at him, but he went on. "When Joe Ray got out of juvie, he repented at the altar. Confessed to it all, how he went along with the robbery. People might forgive Connor if he'd go to the altar, too. Own up to the shooting."

Kitty's cheeks flamed. "If you came here to beat your nephew with a Bible, you can go."

"Aw, Kitty, now don't be like that..."

"Boone, you listen now and listen good," Kitty said, staring him down. "Joe Ray Loomis lied. And you're a fool if you believe him."

Boone shook his head. He placed his big hands flat on the table and pushed, groaning a little — whether from the effort of standing or from despair that his sister was so willing to say what she saw in him. At the door, he stopped and looked at Kitty with a hangdog expression, but she turned back to the sink, and the window. Until she heard the door closing and felt something closing inside her, too.

Chapter 29

The sound of gunshots woke Ivy.

She thought she heard her brother's voice, crying out, a sound that seemed to come from somewhere far away.

The digital clock at Ivy's bedside showed it was 12:35 a.m.

The shots came from Connor's room.

Ivy and her parents nearly collided in the hall, all of them shouting Connor's name. Her daddy reached the door first, threw it open, and flipped on the light. Connor was gone.

"Oh no, not again," her mama whispered.

Two panes of the old window were blown out, fragments of glass scattered across the floor.

Ivy heard her daddy calling 9-1-1, while her mama rushed through the house, her voice anxious and irritated. "Where *are* you, Connor?" — as if he were still that small boy who used to hide when they were trying to leave for church. Ivy went out the front door, which was unlocked, nothing unusual about that. The porch swing was rocking a little. The air was still, silent now.

A squad car brought two young patrolmen who looked like boys playing cops. A little lost, they stood in the doorway of Connor's room eyeing the shattered window. City Police on night duty. While the beefy guy was on his phone, the skinny one made an apology of sorts. He'd been on the force less than six months. "Mostly we pull in drunk drivers. Sometimes get called on a domestic, but nothing like this," his eyes wide.

Probably doesn't even shave yet, Ivy thought.

The other finished his call and said, "Somebody from the Sheriff's Office is gonna be along d'rectly." The parsonage was within the city limits, but according to the patrolman, the chief sometimes handed off a case to the sheriff if it was going to involve an investigation.

Deputy Harlan Stokes arrived a few minutes later. Ivy met him on the porch steps, asking, "Where's Sheriff Bellingham?"

"I imagine he's with his family, Miss," the deputy said, with a little snort, like anybody should know you didn't always get the sheriff every time you called.

Still, Ivy couldn't help wishing Sonny Bellingham had shown up tonight. This red-headed deputy with big ears, who was trying without much success to grow a mustache, didn't inspire confidence. She'd felt like asking, *How old are you, anyway? Where are the grown-ups?*

But she let her father do the talking. He told about the gunshot, and Deputy Stokes called for an investigator. Sooner than Ivy would have expected, the investigator she remembered from Lady's house arrived. J.D., she recalled. The deputy took him to Connor's bedroom. Ivy wondered what J.D. was thinking about the Burdettes' troubles. All in the last three days.

She was at the coffee pot when she heard noise on the front porch.

Connor was there, breathing hard.

Chapter 30

"Joe Ray," Connor said, still trying to get his breath. "It was Joe Ray Loomis."

His parents had hurried to the front porch, his mama clasping her hands, his daddy taking a moment to close his eyes. Praying, Connor figured. *Thank you, Lord, that my son didn't run off again.* Because that's what they'd always be expecting. Connor knew it, and he didn't know how he'd ever earn back their trust.

He could feel his parents' unasked questions: *Where'd you go? Why, son? Why can't you just let the past fold away and remember who you were, who we all were, before any of that business with Joe Ray Loomis?*

"I chased him all the way to the BP station." As soon as he said it, Connor thought it was just like he'd been chasing that mistake. Trying to catch up to it and unmake it.

"He got in a truck that was parked there and drove away," he said.

His mama came to him and put her arms around his waist, pressed her cheek against his chest and murmured, "Oh Lord." Connor smelled that shampoo he remembered from his childhood, that comforting smell of home and hope and what used to be. After a moment, she looked up into his face like she was searching for the boy she lost, then turned away and went into the house.

"Can't you see what you're doing to your mama?" his daddy said.

Connor felt the force of the words, like a hard slap, and the shadow of shame began to creep up in him. Like he was a kid again, and he'd done something stupid, and his daddy acted like he'd committed a capital crime.

He couldn't defend himself. Part of him wanted to rise up and say he never meant to hurt anybody. But here we are, he thought. Hurt was what he did best.

And then Deputy Stokes was back out there with his own questions, everything a cop was supposed to ask about what Connor had seen.

"I can tell you who it was. It was Joe Ray Loomis," Connor said.

The deputy cocked his head, like he had to think about that. "Where were you?"

I was between nowhere and wannabe, Connor could've said. Halfway down toward forget, almost to don't give a damn. But he answered, "Here in the swing. The shots woke me up."

"Don't you have a bed? Fine house like this, why were you sleeping on the porch?"

"I wasn't expecting Joe Ray Loomis, if that's what you're getting at."

"Just seems like — " the deputy scratched behind his ear — "anybody would expect you to be there in your bed when they shot your window out."

"Not *anybody.* It was Joe Ray Loomis." Connor took a step closer to him. "You got a problem with me? Cause it sounds like you're accusing me of something."

The deputy puffed up. "Just doing my job is all."

Connor was spitting mad. He'd been furious enough at Joe Ray, coming to this house, this parsonage, and breaking what little peace his family had in sleep. Angry at the guilt his daddy heaped on him, as if he didn't already carry guilt like a rucksack on his back. It wasn't this self-important deputy that riled him so much. Mostly he was full of dismay for thinking he could ever fit in here again. That he could ever feel anything but helpless. That he could ever be forgiven.

Deputy Stokes grunted. "I expect the sheriff will want to talk to you tomorrow."

"Fine," Connor said. "I'll talk to the sheriff. You and me are done here." He turned away into the house and listened as the screen door flapped against its frame.

"I thought I was in pretty good shape," he said, taking a bottle of water from the refrigerator, "but I couldn't catch him."

All of them, his parents and sister, were in the kitchen now, while the investigator was at work in his bedroom.

"Are you sure it was Joe Ray?" his daddy asked.

"Yes. *Yes.*" Connor felt his voice rising. He was still hot from his daddy's scolding on the porch, so this didn't set well. "I'm not making it up!"

"Nobody's accusing you of making anything up, Connor," Ivy said. "We just want to know what happened. What were we supposed to think when we couldn't find you?"

Connor sat down in the chair next to his mama and gave his account again. "I saw somebody running toward the street. I yelled at him, and it surprised him, I guess. He stopped, for just a second." Connor snapped his fingers. "He looked straight at me, there under the streetlight. No doubt about who he was. Then he took off, and I went after him." He remembered thinking about what he might do if he caught Joe Ray, what he'd like to do but knew he couldn't.

"I guess Joe Ray heard you were back, and he doesn't want you to be telling your side of the story. About the shooting at the Back Home," his daddy said.

"Bet you anything the bullets they find in my room came from the same gun Joe Ray used," Connor said. "He's dumber than a stump. And prob'ly high on meth courage. He was already gettin' into that stuff back then. And no, I wasn't, in case that's what you're thinking."

Connor saw the streaks of dawn before he finally fell into a deep sleep. When he woke around eight and went to the kitchen, he glanced at his family and knew they hadn't slept much either. All of them had that worn-out frazzled look. And he couldn't help thinking how he'd brought so much trouble into this house. That's what his daddy had meant last night. Morning had made him see how the quiet that defined the parsonage, like a calm sea, had turned stormy since he'd been home. He hadn't meant for it to happen, but he couldn't deny it.

"Don Petrie called," his daddy said. "He wants us to go to his office, soon as we can, so he can show you the will. Or I can drop you off if you want to go by yourself."

Connor made a face, like that was ridiculous. "I don't want to go by myself. I don't know anything about legal stuff."

His daddy nodded. "Don Petrie said we could start getting the financial records together from Lady's house. Thought we might get into it today."

The phone rang, and his mama answered.

"It's Sonny Bellingham," she said, holding the receiver out for Connor.

He took a breath, wondering what now, before he said hello.

But Bellingham sounded downright chatty, asking how he was doing after last night, how the family was doing. The sheriff even said, "I hated to hear it. Thankful no one was hurt." He said they had a warrant out for Joe Ray Loomis.

"Your family might want to know," the sheriff said. "They're doing Lady's autopsy this morning in Nashville. I ought to get preliminary results by the end of the day." Then he said, "Why I'm calling — can you come to the station and give a statement?"

Lawyer's office, sheriff's office. As Connor hung up, he thought how much simpler life was when all he had to do was wring eight hours of sweat out of himself, pour in a few beers after work, and try to sleep without dreams.

Chapter 31

Daniel had studied his son while the old lawyer went over the will, paragraph by paragraph. The hard look in Connor's eyes said he was pondering every word.

And then Don Petrie adjusted his glasses and asked, "Any idea why Lady chose you, Son?"

Connor's answer was sharp. Almost angry. "*No.*" But he caught himself and said, "Believe me. I wish I knew."

Don Petrie sat low in his chair, with a wall of musty smelling lawbooks behind him. He let out a low whistle. "Sole beneficiary." He exchanged a look with Daniel, then turned back to Connor and let his gaze settle. "It's quite a sum."

"I said no," Connor repeated. "I don't have a clue why she left it to me."

Daniel had heard enough confessions to recognize the truth when he heard it. Something ringing up from his son told him all he needed to know. The boy had never been able to tell a lie, any more than a nun could wear red.

Daniel had remained silent, had let this be between lawyer and client. But now he spoke.

"You're one of my mother's oldest friends, Don. Didn't she give you some reason why she changed her mind?"

The lawyer took a long breath, laid his gnarled fingers on the pages of Lady's last documents. "I did question her some," he said. "She knew what she was doing. That woman carried more sense in her little finger than most people learn in a lifetime. But she didn't always explain herself." He glanced at Daniel. "You know."

"I do," Daniel said. "I sure do."

The lines in Don Petrie's face deepened and his voice grew thin. "I remember she looked at me like grim death. 'You're my executor. I trust you to find Connor,' she said. 'Bring him home when it's time.' The last words I ever heard from her mouth."

Outside the wind was kicking up. A branch scraped against the window.

Don Petrie didn't seem to notice. He raised his crooked forefinger, taking up where he left off. "And when she died, the minute I heard, the weight came down heavy — Lord! What if I couldn't ever prove you were alive or dead?" He fixed his eyes on Connor and said, just above a whisper, "But here you are. Just like that. Like an answered prayer."

Daniel heard thunder rumbling in the distance, a storm coming, and he heard something in Don Petrie's voice that he didn't like. Not an accusation. More the shadow of it.

Connor rubbed his knees, then stood up like he couldn't take much more of this. "If there's nothing else — "

Daniel could almost hear the old lawyer's bones creaking as he pushed himself to his feet. He remained at his desk, straightening somewhat as he said, "Several times, toward the last, Lady talked about her twin brother. The way she put it, he *died tragically in his youth*."

"Name of Landon," Daniel said. "He was gone long before I was born."

"Seemed like he was on her mind lately." Don Petrie squinted, eyeing Connor. "Said you were the spittin' image of that lost brother. I suppose you were lost, too. Lost to her."

The sky had turned slate gray, clouds like billowing smoke. In the edge of memory was something else Daniel had heard about the boy, but the wind kicked up, and Don Petrie seemed to notice the weather for the first time. "Y'all might not oughta go out there till this blows over," he said.

Connor said, "The sheriff's expecting me," and headed on to the door.

The boy's used to rough weather, Daniel thought. Just plows on through it.

Chapter 32

The rainstorm had turned into a steady downpour.

Connor jumped out of the patrol car and jogged through the rain to the kitchen door.

"There you are!" his mama said when he came in, shaking off the wet. "I couldn't imagine what was taking so long." Relief rose from her voice, into her eyes. Like she'd been afraid the sheriff had locked him away. Or afraid he'd left again.

He glanced at the clock. Twenty past one. "It took longer than it should have."

"You must be starved. Let me fix something." She was already at the refrigerator.

"I'm OK. Bellingham ordered in some sandwiches." Connor stared at his hands. He didn't know why they felt so dirty. "I need to wash up," he muttered to himself. The sheriff's office was downright sterile, compared to the rooms he'd lived in these past ten years. But the deputies glanced at him like he was dirt, and all that digging up the old business with Joe Ray made him want to roll up his sleeves and scrub. Like he could ever get clean.

Growing up, Connor didn't spend much time in his father's study. That was reserved for serious talks, some offense that his daddy was sure was going to lead to the damnation of his soul. The memory of his daddy's disappointment seemed to live in the walls and in the upholstered chair with frayed arms.

It was Ivy who sat at their father's desk. The legal-size document in her hands had to be a copy of the will.

"Does Daddy know you're prying?" Connor asked, leaning inside the door.

"He told me I could read it."

"Where is he?"

"Lady's house. He went to pack up some files and bring them here," she said. "Guess you'll have your work cut out, deciding what's personal and what goes to Don Petrie."

Connor stepped inside the office. "Did you find any loopholes? If you do, I'll be the first to jump through them. I'm sick of all this."

"I wasn't looking for loopholes." Ivy laid the will on a short stack of pages. Her frown meant she had something on her mind, and she'd have to say it. He refused to give her the satisfaction of asking. He waited.

Finally, Ivy said, "I guess I thought she'd at least mention us. But no. Not even a 'Good luck' or a 'God bless.' And here's what burns me up. Daddy had her Power of Attorney. He had her POA for healthcare. And if Don Petrie was unable to act as her personal representative, she named Daddy for that role. She always knew Daddy would do whatever she needed, whatever she asked, whatever was right. All the workhorse stuff. And how did she reward him?"

Connor was tired of defending what was in the will, but he couldn't disagree with her point. "She left him nothing," he said. "*Nothing* is what I wish she'd left to me."

Ivy's frown deepened. "How could Lady do that to her only son?"

Connor blew out a long breath. "Like I've said more'n a dozen times, I don't know what was in her mind. Why are you asking me?"

Ivy pushed back from the desk and swiveled in the chair. Staring out the window, into the rain, she said, "You were her favorite. We were just taking up space in your shadow. When we moved to Montpier, you were eight years old, a cute little boy who thought it was fun to visit Lady. Russ and I had our friends, sports, things to do. We didn't pay much attention to Lady." Her face still turned away from him, Ivy said, "You were really her darling, Connor."

Connor rubbed the stubble on his chin. He said, "You know, Ivy, you've always got it all figured out. You think you know every damn thing about everybody, but if you tried to wade through all you don't know, you just might drown." And he left the room.

Ivy had been right about having his work cut out for him. His daddy unloaded two banker boxes, packed with files, and parked them in the middle of the living room.

"You don't expect us to get into this right now, do you?" Connor asked.

"No. Thought we could work a little at a time if we had some of the files here."

Connor turned to leave, but his daddy asked, "Everything go all right at the sheriff's office?"

"He asked and I answered," Connor said. "He kept poking at me, looking for holes in my story, but it was the truth so I'm not worried."

"You were gone a long time."

All the family watching the clock, wondering if I'd be on the Four-Ten, Connor thought.

"I wrote my statement, and a woman had to type it up so I could sign. She typed about 20 words a minute. Me and Bellingham got to talking about the Back Home," he said. "I told him what really happened. I got the impression he didn't care much for the sheriff back then. Said he'd always had questions about that investigation."

Something changed in Connor's voice. "The bullet last night — it didn't match. The gun Joe Ray used here was a 9mm. The gun from the Back Home was a .38."

"I didn't think they ever found that gun," his daddy said.

"No, but they recovered the bullet from Raleigh's leg."

His daddy nodded, like he knew how much Connor had counted on the bullets to match, how he'd needed it. Proof, finally, that the .38 was Joe Ray's. Proof *his* version was the truth.

The rain didn't stop but it had turned soft and steady. A soaking rain, Daniel called it. Good for the farmers. The kind of rain that could make the world feel clean for a little while.

Connor had gone to the refrigerator when the phone rang. Sonny Bellingham had received the preliminary findings from the autopsy. Connor was not surprised when he said, "Guess I ought to talk to your daddy." Maybe Bellingham didn't know who Lady had named as her heir. Connor called for his daddy. Probably it was his stubborn streak, but he saw no reason why he ought to leave the room to give privacy.

His daddy picked up a pen and note pad, and after the call, he turned and said, "Let me see if I can read my scribblings. '*Multiple contusions and abrasions, fractured left wrist. Cause of death, acute intracranial hemorrhage due to blunt trauma.*' Sonny said the scrape on her wrist came from her tennis bracelet, but nothing in the report suggests how it broke."

Connor said, "Sounds to me like she fell down the stairs and hit her head."

His daddy nodded. "Also, the path report showed Lady had a heart problem. Aortic stenosis. She was on blood thinner. Sonny asked if we knew about the heart trouble."

Connor couldn't help thinking she did have heart trouble but not the kind an autopsy would pick up.

"She never said a word. Not one word." His daddy shook his head. "Aortic stenosis is a serious condition. Maybe she passed out, and that's what caused her to fall."

"Woulda been nice if the report said straight out, *It was an accident,*" Connor said.

So many maybes, he thought. Maybe Joe Ray got rid of the gun. Maybe I was a fool to try to come home. He listened to the rain. And maybe I ought to be on that Four-Ten bus.

Chapter 33

Russ knelt on the cool ground at the back of the parsonage and ran his hands over the foundation, trying to find the crack. The crack he'd felt in his dream.

What is it that makes a man dream about a cracked foundation? What kind of worry pulls him from a warm bed on the Fourth of July, sure that the cracks he and his daddy cemented are failing, that something down deep is about to let go? And makes him drive through the silent streets at dawn to prove it was just a dream?

There is always a kind of crack you can feel before you can see it.

The repairs he'd made last summer, with his daddy looking over his shoulder, held fast. There were small splits and crumbles, minor problems, but other fractures were new and looked like they could be serious, the kind that left unattended could in time pull everything down.

A light went on in the house. His parents were early risers, and he figured they'd seen him prowling around, so he went to the kitchen door. Sure enough, his mama was making coffee. He told her why he was there, told her about the dream, and she gave a gentle laugh. "I believe in dreams, Son," she said. "I believe they're messages from God."

And then the first distant *pop pop pop* of firecrackers went off. A familiar early morning Fourth of July annoyance. But this morning Russ saw his mama startle at the sound. Something in her eyes told him she was hearing gunshots, not firecrackers. Imagining, and remembering.

Every Fourth of July morning, the Burdettes gathered for pancakes.

This year the boys rode their bikes from their house in Holly Hills. The forty-year-old neighborhood had a solid feel to it. Old and reliable. A neighborly place where it was safe for children to ride bikes in the streets. Russ hated all the new pretentious McMansions, thrown up in three months, that Nikki admired. The out-doing-it part of town. Sprawling yards, private pools, but eerily quiet, never the sweet sound of children chasing each other in the yard.

Holly Hills was just beyond the city limits, about three miles from the parsonage. Drew and Owen had begged their parents. *We're old enough! Please! Please!* There was only one intersection that Russ worried about, but it had a light, and the boys had promised up and down, they'd get off their bikes and walk them across the street on the green light. Good boys. Good sons. Careful. Just like me, Russ thought.

His daddy met Russ's family at the kitchen door. "Your mama told me you were here early this morning about the foundation."

"Looks like the basement could start taking on water," Russ said. "I'll check it today."

"It rained hard yesterday."

His daddy turned away, and Nikki shook her head, whispering, "Always the good son."

Russ tried to pretend it didn't gnaw at him when his boys kept pleading with Connor to come out in the back yard with them and shoot off the last of the poppers Mr. Hardaway had brought over on Saturday. But he couldn't help it. It annoyed him.

"Come on, Connor!" Drew begged.

"Ten minutes, OK?" Connor said.

Russ finally had enough. He pointed to the back door. "You guys can be excused," he said, glaring at one and then the other. "Go! Get outa here."

He hadn't meant to sound that harsh. Not the voice the boys were used to hearing from him. He was not the parent who laid down the law. That was Nikki.

Russ saw the hurt in Drew's wide eyes. But Owen was not so easily wounded. "Promise, Connor?" he said. Did not even look at his daddy.

"Ten minutes. Promise," Connor said.

And that was all it took to satisfy the boys. *My* boys, not his, Russ thought, as he watched them race off to the backyard.

Russ made his way to the living room with the others, all except his mama who said, "I'll clear things away. It won't take me a minute."

His daddy took a seat in the overstuffed armchair that everyone knew was his. "Gerard's Funeral Home called late last night about the body," he said. "I asked Tim Briggs to officiate with me. Tim's a good friend, a good man. The one I want up there to help me carry the weight."

Russ sat with Nikki and Ivy on the sofa. He knew Reverend Briggs, minister at First Presbyterian. Had nothing against him. But he said, "How will that go over at church? Him being an outsider and all?"

His daddy said, "It's my mother, my pulpit, my call." As confident as Russ had ever heard him. And then, "I wondered if y'all wanted to say anything about your grandmother at the funeral. You know, sometimes the family members speak."

Russ didn't hesitate. "Got nothing to say."

"No thanks," Connor said, his words just as blunt.

Ivy said, "Daddy, whatever you decide will be better than anything we could say." Trying to smooth things over, Russ guessed, and his daddy nodded, like he was satisfied.

Connor, sitting next to the door, said, "Looks like company."

Russ could've guessed Boone, from the two knocks that sounded like the door was coming off its hinges. It flew open and his uncle stumbled in, maybe already a little tipsy. Red pants, blue suspenders and a stars-and-stripes shirt. "Glad you weren't in that bed th' other night, boy." Boone took two long strides toward him and clapped Connor on the shoulder.

"Not as glad as I am," Connor said.

"I just can't believe Joe Ray Loomis would do such a thing," Boone said. "The boy's got the spirit in him now. Turned away from sin."

Connor stood, stepped away. "I think my ten minutes are up."

As Connor left the room, Russ thought about all the times Boone had declared how things absolutely were, when they were not. And all the times Russ wished he could just walk away when his uncle was showing the true down-to-the-studs jerk he'd always been.

His mama came in and told her brother if he was there for breakfast, he'd missed the bus. Boone gave a hearty laugh and said, "I know my sister loves me."

She said, "Well, don't just stand there. Sit down," pointing to the chair Connor had left.

"Nope. I'm goin' on over to the square," he said. "Thought I might oughta pass out some campaign flyers before the parade. Y'all are going, aren't you?"

Russ said, "With our two boys? Got no choice."

Ivy said, "It doesn't start till noon. We've got plenty of time."

"People come into town early to get a good spot." Boone paced a little. He said, "The VFW guys always make me teary-eyed. You know Artie Logan, fought in Korea? Still marches, dragging that bad leg. And there's that Bryson fella from down on Banjo Branch. Vietnam vet. He's never been right since the war. But he's always carrying the flag."

Russ was wondering if Boone had come by just to talk about the parade when he switched gears. "Gotta run, but I was wondering about the funeral. Nothing on the Obituary Line yet. I've been calling. Heard the body's back at Gerard's."

Russ noted the sharp edge in his daddy's voice as he said, "We'll be making the arrangements today, Boone. I expect it'll be on the Obituary Line tonight." It was no surprise that Boone knew about Lady's body. Probably news about the autopsy was getting around town, too. Small town, big ears.

"I'll keep calling." Boone stopped at the door. "Maybe Connor won't have such pressing business next time I stop by. I was hoping to give him a talking to."

Russ thought, Like Connor would ever listen.

"We prob'ly ought to head out, too," he said. "Are y'all going?" he asked his parents.

"I don't feel much like celebrating," his daddy said. "There's enough fireworks around here anyway."

His mama pointed out that they'd need to take Lady's funeral clothes to Mr. Gerard.

All of it a little schizophrenic, Russ thought. A big celebration and a funeral, side by side.

Ivy said, "I'll go to the parade with Connor if he wants to go."

Russ realized he'd heard nothing from the back yard. He went out through the kitchen and looked around. "Where's Connor?" he asked the boys.

"He left," Owen said.

"He just said we'd have to set off the poppers later." Drew's voice was not as sure as his words.

Russ walked over to the crack in the foundation, knelt down, and examined it again. He felt a rise of anger, so familiar lately. One broken promise already to his boys. He imagined his parents' worried looks when they heard Connor had left so suddenly. Imagined Ivy looking like she could bite nails. No consideration for anyone else. That was Connor. Independence Day.

Chapter 34

The July heat was heavy with competing scents when Ivy arrived on the square with Russ's family. Cigarette smoke, whiff of a woman's perfume, a man's sweat. There was an electricity in the air, a familiar feeling of anticipation. Kids fidgeting, neighbors chatting, newcomers crowding in for a good spot, all packed in, as Boone had predicted.

After a long wait, Ivy heard the first faint drumbeats of the marching band, far off down Mercer Avenue, where the parade had assembled at the high school. Drew and Owen complained that they couldn't see, so Russ moved them back and let them climb on the ice machine in front of Edelson's Bi-Rite. Ivy and Nikki kept their places until Ivy got it in her mind that she needed to look for Connor. She began to work her way around the square.

Aggravated at first, she kept imagining how she might heap guilt on her brother, once she found him, but worry began to take over. And she wondered if it would always be this way, if she'd always fear that at any time, Connor could just vanish.

As she moved through the crowd, someone called, "Ivy! Over here!" It was Gwenna Wallis from the college, Dean Keller's secretary.

Gwenna was so short that she surely had trouble seeing over the heads in front of her. She was standing beside a slim man of medium height with unremarkable features. Wire-rimmed glasses. Golf shirt and khakis. Gwenna didn't introduce him, but it was clear enough to Ivy that they were together. "I'm Ivy Burdette," she said. Only then did Gwenna say, "My husband."

He offered his hand, somewhat timidly, and said, "Chuck Wallis."

Ivy couldn't help wondering if this man knew about Gwenna and Dr. Keller. Maybe those were just rumors, she reminded herself, but smoke could mean fire, too, she'd learned. She pictured Dr. Keller, with his stomach hanging over his belt, his scraggly beard, and bottle-thick glasses. Still, he was an outgoing, effusive man who laughed easily. He'd impressed Ivy as someone who was kind, not as egotistical as some administrators in higher education. Looks weren't everything. Ivy had loved a movie-star-handsome man and see how that turned out.

Gwenna lowered her voice. "That position I talked to you about?" She raised her heavily penciled eyebrows. "I'll be sending out a call for applications next week. *Journal of Higher Education* and some other print and web sites."

"You should get a huge response," Ivy said, keeping her voice low.

"Oh, we will, and we'll have to conduct a search. Protocol." Gwenna was whispering now, and as the drumbeats and the crowd noise grew louder, it was nearly impossible to hear her.

"Why are you telling me this, Gwenna? Not that I don't appreciate it."

"Because Dr. Keller would like it if *you* applied. He'd like it very much, Ivy. He's very impressed with what you've done in the lit course."

"I'm flattered. I am," Ivy said, her voice strained. "I just don't know."

Now the Grand Marshal led the parade onto the square, the mayor and his wife waving to the crowd from his expertly restored Mustang convertible. Gwenna stood on tiptoe and craned her neck. The band began to play "You're a Grand Old Flag," and the majorettes came into sight. So young! Ivy thought. Fresh-faced baton twirlers with their big perfect orthodontist-enhanced smiles. Their heads full of dreams that they believed with all their hearts would come true.

"You need to let him know you're interested," Gwenna said. "I realize you have Lady's funeral this week. I'm so sorry about her death, but you need to make time to talk to Dr. Keller."

"I'll try," Ivy said.

Gwenna leaned close. "Someone already has his ear. A certain deacon at First Baptist." Her whispers were hard to follow. "I believe he was the one who told Brother Burdette about the opening this summer. But let's just say he has some concerns now. And he's very influential."

Ivy didn't have to ask if that was the Colonel. "What's he got against me?"

"He's afraid your world view might be too liberal for our innocent college students."

Ivy couldn't resist a soft laugh at the idea that she and her father might turn the young people's morals upside down. Thank goodness she wasn't pining for the position at CRCC.

The band paused on the square and finished their first rendition. For a minute they marched on to the drumbeat, circling the courthouse, and then they took up "America the Beautiful" — so many flat notes that it set Ivy's teeth on edge, but somehow you could tell the musicians put their hearts into it.

A handful of amateurish floats appeared now, lovingly put together by the Methodist Youth, the Senior Citizens Center, and a few local businesses. Ivy said, "I remember working on a float for First Baptist Youth Group. It took a thousand boxes of tissues."

"You know I go to First Baptist," Gwenna said. "I'm a member anyway. Chuck's there every Sunday. His dad's a deacon." She glanced at her husband. His eyes met hers, and he quickly turned away. Wasn't hard to imagine trouble in paradise.

"OK," Ivy said. "I can't go out to the college till after the funeral. It'll probably be Thursday. I'll have to cancel my class."

"I'll get a sub for you, Ivy." Her voice merry now, Gwenna said. "Wouldn't it be nice if we could act like a real institute of higher learning? Our students are supposed to be adults. We should be able to tell them class is cancelled and it's on them to make up the work." Gwenna patted Ivy's arm. "Let me know what you want the sub to cover."

Behind the last float, the VFW men brought up the tail end. The parade was moving onto Church Street where Ivy knew it would thread back to Mercer Avenue, back to the high school. The strains of music grew sweeter from a distance.

All of this, so familiar. But Ivy had never noticed before how the shadow of battle hung in the eyes of the old soldiers, these many years later. The Vietnam soldier Boone mentioned had help carrying the flag this year, a stronger young man clearly supporting most of the weight. Ivy tried to guess who the Korean veteran with a bad leg was because so many were old, so many seemed to be dragging themselves along. Still trying to carry themselves with dignity, hold their heads high. Beside one of them, a crippled hound, panting, also struggled to keep up, slowing down the old soldier. And then when it looked like man and dog could not go on, one of the younger vets broke rank, scooped up the hound, and carried him.

All of it touched Ivy more deeply than she would have imagined. These men who were wounded by the world and somehow found their way home. Connor was not so different, she thought. Wounded, still trying to find his way home, back to what he'd left. And maybe she was not so different, either. She thought that it might not be so bad to come back to this place, these good people, most of them, and the sweetness found only in small towns, as sweet as the scent of the flowers in her mama's garden.

Chapter 35

The cloying, too-sweet fragrance of funeral flowers lived in the walls and carpets of Gerard's.

It was a rough morning at the funeral parlor. Not that Daniel had to make many decisions. Lady had taken care of most everything in her pre-payment package. But the finality of it all! The tomb-like room where the coffins were lined up, where Mr. Gerard took Daniel and Kitty to see Lady's rosewood casket, top of the line. Lady's burial clothes. The deep rose suit she had picked out for herself. Along with the contents of the paper bag Kitty handed to Mr. Gerard.

"Undergarments," she told him. "Down to nylons and shoes, like she said."

Like she might need to get up and go, Daniel thought. Go dancing in heaven.

How many times had Daniel accompanied bereaved families when they met with Mr. Gerard? He had not expected such tightness in his throat.

On the way to the car he heard, coming from the direction of the high school, strains of "My Country 'Tis of Thee." He paused at the car door, listening as the music built, and at the end of the song, he found himself joining in.

His voice broke as he sang, "From every mountainside *let free-dom ring...*"

Kitty gave him her sweet smile, like she read his thoughts, like she understood that a freedom celebration and a funeral might not be so different. And again — it had happened so many times since Kitty said, *I was the one* — he pushed his hurt to the back of his mind and let himself remember that he had made mistakes, too. Especially with Connor.

On to the church. Talking to the custodian about setting up folding chairs anywhere there was extra room to accommodate the expected crowd. Going over the music with the church secretary so she could contact the First Baptist choir members. No matter that it was a holiday. They were there for him.

Daniel was rocking in the porch swing when Russ's family and Ivy returned from the parade. "Your grandma's made peanut butter balls," he told the little boys.

They turned their crumpled faces up to him, and Daniel saw why they were sulking. Russ was loading the bikes on the bike rack of the old Suburban that had belonged to his grandfather. And then Nikki was herding them inside, telling them, "Too much traffic!" but they weren't having it. "If you can't straighten up, we might just miss the picnic," she said.

Daniel smiled. He was thinking how grandparents could just dole out the peanut butter balls and let the parents pay for the dentist.

Ivy paused at the door. "I didn't see Connor at the parade."

Daniel's smile faded. He checked his watch, and said, "He hasn't been gone that long."

"He could've been on one of the side streets." Her voice trailed off, and she went inside.

Daniel gave the swing a push. The squeak as it swayed back and forth gave a kind of comfort, one of the few things you could count on, he thought.

Russ came onto porch. "Think my brother has pulled another disappearing act?"

"Don't jump to conclusions," Daniel said.

"I wouldn't worry," Russ said. "He'll be back, with all that money coming to him."

"It hasn't been that long," Daniel said again. But it felt like a long time.

The afternoon heated up. Daniel was heading inside when Sonny Bellingham pulled into the edge of the yard. He took his time making his way to the porch. Daniel thought he always walked with that unhurried gait like whatever he was going to, he knew it would wait for him.

"Good afternoon, Sheriff," Daniel said, a formality that suggested his discomfort with the visit. Sonny gave a little salute. Something uneasy in his manner, as well. Daniel said, "I have a feeling this isn't a social call."

"I wish," Sonny said, taking each step deliberately, up to the porch. "Is Connor here?"

Daniel felt the surge of dread that seemed to happen so frequently now. "No," he said.

"Do you know where he is?"

"No."

He might have to tell how Connor had wandered off from the backyard without saying where he was going. But not until he had to.

"When did you see him last?" Sonny asked.

"Before the parade. Sheriff — Sonny — why are you looking for Connor?"

The screen door slapped, and Ivy was there. "What's going on?" she said.

Sonny Bellingham shifted his position, maybe giving himself a minute to choose his words. Frowning a little, he took a stance with his feet wide apart, his arms crossed. Daniel hung on to the thought that if something had happened to Connor, if Sonny was there to say he'd been harmed, he would not be asking where Connor was.

"A call came in from a fella that lives in the trailer park where Joe Ray Loomis lives," Sonny said. "Not a model citizen, mind you. He's got a record, served some time in county on meth charges. Still dealing, probably, but a complaint's a complaint. It's my job to check it out."

"A complaint about Connor?" Daniel said.

"Connor was out there at the trailer park looking for Joe Ray."

Ivy groaned. Daniel took a deep breath.

"Yeah," Sonny said, like he knew what they were feeling. "I guess Connor got pretty revved up and said some things. Threatened him — that's what the fine citizen said."

"Threatened him? Why?" Daniel said.

"I guess Connor believed the man knew where Joe Ray was," Sonny said.

Daniel caught something in Ivy's expression, and he knew she'd decided to be up front with the sheriff. He didn't stop her.

"Connor left here about eleven o'clock," she said. "Didn't tell anyone where he was going. He'd been — quiet. All morning. I just thought it was what he's remembering about the Fourth. All that Back Home business."

Sonny nodded. "When you see him, tell him I need to talk to him."

"After I've ripped into him," Ivy said.

Now Sonny laughed. "I bet you know how to do that."

At the bottom of the steps, he turned around to Ivy. "You planning to take in the rest of the festivities?"

"I don't know. The day's not shaping up exactly like I thought it might," she said.

"Maybe I'll catch up with you later," Sonny said. And to Daniel, "Keep me posted."

"We will," Daniel said.

The day wasn't shaping up the way he'd thought it would, either.

Chapter 36

Connor had been missing for a solid five hours when Ivy went back to the city park. Missing. That's how Ivy thought of it. But he wasn't a minor. His family couldn't very well make a missing person's report on him.

He'd been missing for five hours — but he had vanished for ten years. This is not the same, she told herself. He'll be back.

She didn't care about the picnic, but she might run into Connor. Maybe he was just out wandering around town. Looking for Joe Ray. Trying to drag up the past.

The park was a couple of miles from the parsonage, and it was a sweltering afternoon, but Ivy walked briskly, even jogged a little, and it felt like she was sweating out some of her worry.

Like the parade, the picnic was reminiscent of every hometown picnic Ivy could remember. Kids running around, squealing and shrieking. Old men throwing horseshoes, trying for the clang that made them feel young again, and teenagers in the parking lot listening to their music, sneaking smokes, sure they were all grown up. People snacking and drinking. Mercer County was dry, even beer was prohibited in the City Park, so the drinks were soft.

Food was a religion in every small Southern town, and six o'clock on the Fourth of July was like Sunday morning church. Nikki had brought fried chicken, the kind that was like air in the South. Sometimes Ivy had to remind herself that Nikki came up the hard way, not as a little princess, like some of her country club friends. Nikki had said she fixed supper from the time she was twelve because her mama was working overtime at the factory.

After the fried chicken and the trimmings, Russ and the boys scattered, and someone asked Nikki to be a judge at a face painting contest. Ivy slipped away and ran into several old classmates who had settled in Montpier after high school or who had gone away and returned. Found their way home.

"Heard you were back," they said.

"Just for the summer," she said. But not with certainty.

She kept an eye out for Connor until it seemed useless. She told Nikki she was heading back to the parsonage to watch the fireworks with her parents. Leaving the celebration, she heard someone call her name.

"Going home?" Sonny asked, catching up to her.

"Trying to," she said.

"I'm headed your way," he said, "Come on."

"Aren't you on duty?"

He shrugged. "I'm always on duty. Doesn't mean I can't give a citizen a ride home."

His car was parked in a No Parking zone. Ivy hesitated, then stepped forward. He opened the door for her and said, "I promise, I won't arrest you."

She smiled, warming to him.

"Any word from your brother?"

"Connor? No."

Ivy settled in the passenger seat and Sonny pulled away from the curb. He drove to the next block before he said, "I was thinking, maybe sometime you might want to get a cup of coffee. Or maybe something to eat. With me." He let out a long breath, like he'd just pushed a heavy weight off his chest.

"Don't you have a family?" Ivy asked, and suddenly wished she hadn't sounded so cross.

"Yes. You have a family, too," Sonny said. "I don't see that's a problem."

"I mean, a wife," Ivy said, now trying too hard to sound matter-of-fact.

He let the words linger in the air a moment. "I had a wife. Paula died eighteen months ago."

The catch in Ivy's breath was audible. A little gasp. "I'm sorry... I didn't know."

Sonny took one hand off the steering wheel and raised it like a traffic cop. "No reason you should know."

"Still, I'm sorry," she said. "Really, Sheriff."

"I wish you'd call me Sonny," he said. "I don't want to have to call you Miss Burdette."

She was finally able to laugh a little. "OK."

"People never know what to say. I understand. Paula had cancer. Ovarian cancer that came up all of a sudden. Like a summer storm," he said. "Four months and she was gone."

Ivy could tell he was trying hard not to show his hurt, but she saw a line in his forehead that she hadn't noticed before. How had she missed it? Now, she could see the shadow of loss in his eyes.

"I have a son, too. Michael's just five. He has nightmares. Sometimes he calls out for his mama at night. I don't really know what to say."

Ivy thought how hard it was to find the right words sometimes. Like now. The right words were flying around somewhere in the air, but she couldn't catch them. She managed to say, "A child's a treasure."

"Yes, he is." Just a hint of a smile. "I hope he'll be all right someday. Hope we both will."

Silence then. He was driving like he was in a school zone. Ivy could feel something coming from him, a need to talk, a need to be heard. So she just listened.

"He lives with my parents over in Durbin Falls," Sonny said. "Just makes sense because of my hours. I go there when I'm not working. I'm heading there now to be with him when the fireworks go off and make a lot of noise. He gets scared."

Ivy thought of her mama, the worried look in her mama's eyes each year at the sound of fireworks. Like they always brought back the memory of that other Fourth of July.

They came to a four-way stop, and Sonny waited for another car to go, and then he waited some more before he moved forward. He kept talking like he had so much to say and such a little time. "Michael's autistic. Not a severe case, but I don't know what I'd do without my parents. They're getting up in years, though." His voice softened. "He draws circles, fills a page with perfect circles."

"Someday he'll tell you what's that's all about," Ivy said. "And you'll wonder why you didn't figure it out."

They both laughed a little.

The parsonage was in sight. The car slowed to a crawl. "I know you've been away, and I know you might be leaving again. But you might find home is not such a bad place." He glanced at her. "It's nice talking to somebody like you, Ivy."

She smiled back. She started to reply but saw that Sonny's attention had turned to the front porch of the parsonage. "Would you look at that?" he said.

Ivy's parents were sitting on the porch. Her daddy in one of the Adirondack chairs. Her mama in the swing, and beside her, Connor.

Chapter 37

Kitty was a careful gardener.

Flowers, like babies, had to be watched over. And as they grew, some needed more attention than others.

On her birthday in the spring, Daniel had given her an orchid. The orchid was one of the hardest of flowers to raise, and Daniel knew it, but he'd told her, "You'll find a way." And she knew in her heart it was true. Her houseplants flourished and her flower beds were the talk of the neighborhood.

At first, Kitty kept the orchid on the porch in the sun, but it needed more. More warmth, more love. She'd brought it inside and provided everything the needy plant ought to require. But she wasn't sure it was enough.

The house was filled with her thriving flowers, but the one that soaked up her attention was the one that seemed to be failing.

She was watering it, checking around the roots, when she'd heard voices on the front porch. Daniel — and there was Connor. She set down her watering can, closed her eyes, and felt some of her worry drain away. She touched her orchid and fretted over it a bit more before she went to the porch.

A careful gardener never gave up.

Now, in the swing beside Connor, Kitty watched the sheriff come across the yard. That deliberate look, something on his mind, and she knew what. Connor rubbed his palms together. A nervous gesture, but the hard glint in his eyes was what troubled Kitty. Don't borrow trouble, she thought. Mind your tongue. No sense spitting in the wind. It'll blow right back in your face.

"Daniel. Miz Kitty," Sonny greeted them, standing at the foot of the steps. "I guess this calls for another visit." Then he fixed his gaze on Connor.

"You're always welcome here, Sonny," Kitty said. Daniel would know she was slanting the truth, but sugar was better than salt.

"Wish you'd called me, Connor, to let me know you're back," Sonny said. Ivy stood slightly behind him. Kitty figured Ivy was not ready to join her family on the porch until she could decide whether she wanted to embrace her brother or punch him.

"Did I miss something? I'm supposed to call you every time I stretch my legs?" Connor said.

Kitty kicked at his foot. "That's uncalled for, Connor," she whispered.

"Smart mouth you got on you," Sonny said.

Daniel stood up from the Adirondack chair. "It's my fault, Sonny. I hadn't got around to telling him to call you. Don't blame the boy."

Sonny remained professional, but his words had an edge. "You didn't hear about the complaint against you?"

"Yeah. Daddy told me." Connor got up from the swing and walked toward the steps. Stood a minute, like he was pondering. Kitty felt a surge of relief when he spoke kindly. "Sorry for your trouble," he said. "I guess it wasn't such a smart move, going to the trailer park."

"You're right about that. Why'd you do such a fool thing?" Sonny scolded.

"I was pretty sure that lowlife knows where Joe Ray was, and I guess I got in his face a little too much," Connor said. Kitty believed he was trying to come around now, his expression earnest. "But I didn't lay a hand on him. Just put a scare in him. I don't know what he told you, but I knew better than to try to beat the truth out of him. There's no truth in him anyway."

Sonny touched the side of his face, rubbing up and down as if checking whether he needed a shave. "Yeah, that old boy served time in county, sent up on meth."

Kitty guessed the complaint was just a call, a gripe, nothing official. Somebody like that wouldn't come within a country mile of the Sheriff's office to fill out a form unless he had bruises to show.

"Your family was worried," Sonny said. Kitty started to say that wasn't law enforcement's business. But she didn't. She heard something true in the sheriff's voice.

Connor's voice flooded with sarcasm. "I thought you and me were on the same side. The right side. My mistake. Any kind of wrong happens, my name goes to the head of the list. But I can swear on the Bible, Sheriff, I haven't done anything illegal today or kicked a hornet's nest." He added, "Except the one that needed kicking at the trailer park."

"You've been gone since morning." Sonny narrowed his eyes, as if taking a yardstick to the truth to see if it would measure up.

Connor blew out a long breath. "I dropped in at the Back Home. Not sure why I wanted to. I must've walked into that place a thousand times while I was gone. Maybe I just wanted to see what it felt like, stepping into the past again." He looked away, pushed his hands into his pockets. "No one there knew me, and I didn't know anyone. I bought a Dr. Pepper and a Moon Pie and walked out."

Kitty said, "Tell him where else you've been, Connor."

He looked at her, and she nodded at him. "Tell him."

"I mowed Mr. Dalton's yard," he said.

"Raleigh Dalton's grandfather?" Sonny said. "The old man that lit into you at the cafe?"

"That's the one." Connor went down the steps and joined Ivy and Sonny. "I walked all over town today," he said. "Wondering if I'll ever fit in here again. Feeling like a piece of a puzzle that's already put together. Nothing much has changed here in this town. It's me that's changed."

He looked down at his shoes, kicked something that might've been a bug or a leaf. "He was out there, that crippled old man, sweating behind a fifty-year-old push-mower. His yard was about as grown up as a hay field. So I walked over. We both stood there a while. Then he stepped away and I went to work. He sat on the porch watching. Staring at me, like he was trying to see something. When I finished, I pushed the mower over near the porch. He stood up and said, 'Why'd you do something like that?' And I said, 'Maybe I owe you for something.' He looked hard at me, but his voice turned soft. 'I reckon you do,' he said. 'I reckon we all owe for something.'"

Kitty felt a pull at her heart. The son she'd been missing was suddenly close again.

Sonny was looking at the ground, too, kicking at the same bug or leaf or wisdom as Connor. Finally, he said, "Well," and let that settle. Then, "I'd better head to Durbin Falls. My little boy's waiting on me."

"To watch the fireworks," Ivy added.

"We'll prob'ly be holding up in his room, playing some music he likes," Sonny said, his gaze set on Ivy. Kitty thought there must be some meaning there that the rest of them didn't get. Something between the two of them.

Then, in a tone that was almost confidential, though all could hear, he said to Connor, "Stay away from the trailer park. Stop looking for Joe Ray. We'll find him." Connor nodded, but Sonny shook his finger at him. "Stop looking for trouble. There's enough of it looking for you."

The air seemed suddenly hot and thick and silent. Kitty thought of that old man, struggling behind a push-mower. Every time Connor said something that sounded like the boy she remembered, she thought, *This is the end of it.* He's finally home for good.

In the front window, the orchid seemed like it might finally be ready to thrive.

A careful gardener never gave up. Neither did a mother.

Chapter 38

Nikki wondered if she'd ever be able to remove the stain from her white linen dress.

The private lounge at the funeral home, where food was laid out for the family, was empty except for the stranger who had stepped inside the room as Nikki began to slice cheese. Something, anything to settle her stomach. Cheese and crackers and Coke. She hardly felt the cut to her finger, barely noticed until she turned toward the sudden voice.

"Oh Lord!" the man said. "I didn't mean to — Miss, are you all right?"

Nikki looked at her finger, looked down at her skirt, and saw the streak of blood.

"That'll be a bad stain. Blood's awful hard to get out," the man said. He came forward, grabbed a paper towel and handed it to her, then wet some more paper towels and waited for her to take them from him. "I didn't mean to startle you, Miss."

Nikki wrapped her finger. She looked up, wondering if she knew this man. Fifty-something, square jaw, big neck, built like someone who'd once played football, but his muscles had turned soft, his middle hanging over his belt. Hair cut in a flat top, which Nikki hadn't seen in years. He hadn't come through the line to speak to the family. She would've remembered the low-hanging khaki pants and the wrinkled, frayed-at-the-collar white shirt.

"I should know better," she said.

The man offered the wet paper towels. "Here."

Her finger wasn't bleeding through the wrapping, but the streak on her skirt spoke of a deeper cut. She took the wet paper towels, started in on her skirt, and tried to blot the worst of it away.

The first whiff of funeral flowers, Nikki had thought she'd be sick. That pungent, overpowering fragrance. But she'd managed to put on her game face and do what she was supposed to do. Stand with the Burdettes as visitors passed by the open casket.

The viewing room was crowded with funeral flowers, overflowing into the adjacent chapel. Most funerals were held in the chapel nowadays, but Lady's funeral would be at the big First Baptist Church. Room for a big crowd. Lady had put it in writing. She might as well have carved it in stone.

Visitation had started at four o'clock and was scheduled to continue until eight. Too much time, Nikki thought, but the line was long. "People just getting off from work," Mr. Gerard had said. "There'll be another wave after supper." He had come by to see if the family needed anything. What Nikki needed was for it to be over.

Only Connor looked as uncomfortable as she felt. He kept rubbing at his hands. Some of the townspeople conspicuously ignored him. Some looked at him with contempt, like he didn't belong and never would. He stood a little apart. Nikki would like to have done the same.

After a while, a tennis friend from the club started up a conversation with her, and she moved away from the family, away from the sweaty hands and strong perfume, from the "I'm so sorry" and "She looks so natural."

Dead was not a natural look, Nikki thought. But Lady would've been pleased. Deep rose suit that hid any evidence of the autopsy. Hair and make-up by Jillian Adair from Durbin Falls who, besides being Lady's regular hairdresser, worked on country music stars. Some of their careers had already died but their hair was perfect.

Nikki's friend asked where the little boys were.

"Playing with the neighbor kids. I couldn't make them do this. It's too much."

She and Russ had argued last night. Russ had followed his parents to visitations, funerals, and burials for years, until he was old enough to stay at home by himself. Russ always did the right thing. But he'd been a preacher's kid. Their boys were not. Finally, Russ had given in — but he'd had the last word. "They're going to the funeral! They're *going!*"

"You OK, Nikki?" her friend asked. "You look a little pale."

"Just these flowers," she said. "That too-sweet scent. About to make me sick."

The townspeople kept coming. After Connor took a break and came back smelling like Marlboros, Nikki decided it was her turn.

"You *are* the granddaughter, I believe," the man in the lounge said.

"I'm Russ's wife." Nikki stopped rubbing at her skirt and looked up. "Who are you?"

"Hank Royster. Private investigator from Nashville. I had business with the deceased."

Nikki caught her breath. Why on earth would Lady hire a private detective? And what was he doing here at the funeral home? Had to be money. Wasn't it always money?

"I was hoping to catch the Reverend. But he hasn't left his station, and I get the feeling he's there till the bitter end." A smile, then, "Maybe I could have a word with you."

"You really should talk to Daniel. Or my husband. But tell me, what was your business with Lady, Mr. Royster?" Nikki said.

"She hired me to find a missing person," he said, "and I did."

Nikki met his gaze for a moment. "I see," she murmured. Going back to the stain on her skirt, she whispered, "Connor."

She rubbed and rubbed at the blood, but she knew some stains never come out.

Chapter 39

"Must be a hundred degrees out there," the stranger said.

Daniel opened the door that led from the private lounge to a little patio, a table with an umbrella and some outdoor chairs. Like stepping into a steam bath.

The man followed him onto the patio. "Doctor says I'm supposed to watch the heat."

Daniel, impatient to get back to the mourners, ignored his complaint. He pointed to the chairs shaded by the umbrella. "We won't be long," he said.

"Yessir, I'll make it short." The man struggled for his wallet and showed his ID.

"You're a private investigator," Daniel said, examining the license.

"Did twenty in the sheriff's department up in Putnam County. Big meth problem up there. Retired, got a place near Center Hill Lake. But it felt like waiting around to die. Too much peace and quiet can kill a man." He was breathing hard. "Decided to get my PI license."

"This is not a good time, Mr. Royster," Daniel said. "But Nikki thought I ought to hear you out."

"I appreciate it, Reverend. And I'm real sorry about your mama."

Daniel thanked him. "Now tell me, what's this all about?"

Royster pulled out a handkerchief and wiped his face. "I had this client over near Shiloh. Country club type. Her husband started staying late at work. Clients, he said. But she knew something smelled funny. A woman always knows. Anyhow, she said she had a friend, tennis player in Montpier, that needed somebody like me. My client recommended me to Lady." He paused. "Please don't think I mean any disrespect, calling her 'Lady.' That's what she told me to call her. She said she had some trouble." He paused, then like a punch line, "Trouble's what keeps my bills paid."

"What kind of trouble did my mother want you to fix?"

"There's only one kind of trouble, Reverend. The losing kind. Shiloh lady lost her husband, little bit at a time. Your mama said her grandson was missing. Everybody's always trying to get back what they've lost."

"Connor," Daniel whispered.

"Yessir. She asked me to track him down. Said time was short. Time's always short in my line of work." Royster mopped his face again. "I did the job. Found him 'bout thirty miles west of Nashville working with some Mexicans, hanging drywall. Sticking out like a piece of white bread in a pumpernickel loaf. Working hard, looked like."

Daniel didn't say anything. Connor hadn't told them much about that life. He didn't need to. A father could see it in his eyes.

"Anyhow, I typed what Lady needed to know and mailed it to her." Royster crossed his legs. He wore wingtips and white cotton socks.

"I had to pick up a check from the Shiloh client today, and she hit me with the bad news. 'Did you know Lady Burdette died?' She showed me a copy of the *Gazette.* I read that big splash about Lady, saw her visitation was today. Said to myself, I need to pay my respects."

Daniel knew the *Gazette* had come out a day early, just because of Lady's visitation.

"She was a formidable woman," Royster said.

Yes, Daniel thought. Formidable. That was as good a word as any.

"Had you seen my mother lately?" he asked.

"No. Just the once. One face to face, and she hired me on the spot."

Daniel touched his forehead, felt beads of sweat. "And why was it you wanted to talk to me, Mr. Royster? Other than to offer your sympathy."

An uneasy silence drifted between them. "This is not the easiest thing to say, Reverend. But, here's the thing. I never got paid for my work."

Right. Money. Always the thing. "When did you do the investigation?" Daniel asked.

Royster leaned forward in his seat, put both feet on the ground, his hands on his knees. He closed one eye, like he was thinking hard. "June. Middle of June."

Just before Lady changed her will, Daniel thought. "I know this about Lady," he said. "She paid her bills."

"Don't mean to give the wrong impression," Royster said. "My secretary's out on maternity leave, and I'm a little late on last month's billing. But I can get Lady's invoice figured up in the next few days."

Daniel saw that the man understood his skepticism.

Royster laughed, a good-natured laugh. "You're a preacher man. Used to reading people. Like I do. I know you can see I'm on the up-and-up. I'm about as straight a shooter as a Winchester rifle. Lady was awful anxious to find out about her grandson." His expression turned reflective. A smile that seemed to remember some particular thing played on his lips. "I liked the old bird. No offense. She was hard as a redwood, but true. I liked her. So I went ahead and sent my report before I'd figured her bill. Somewhere in Lady's things, you'll find it."

Daniel pushed his chair back and stood. "I don't mean to be discourteous, Mr. Royster, but I need to get to my family. Send the invoice. You'll get paid."

As he walked away, Royster called after him, "Sorry for your trouble. God bless."

Daniel paused and turned to face the P.I. Maybe he was too quick to judge. "You know, my son's back," he said. "God bless you, too."

Chapter 40

"What'd you find?" Russ asked.

In a blinding-white shirt, blue-and-white striped tie, and black suit, his daddy stood straight as a two-by-ten board, like he was already about to start preaching. "Let's wait on everybody," he said, dropping the big manilla envelope from the bank on the kitchen table.

"Is Nikki coming?" Ivy asked.

Russ shook his head. "She took the boys to swim, so they could work off all that energy before the long afternoon."

He tried to push away the notion that there could be something in that fat envelope for his family. It wasn't smart to hope. He was here because his daddy asked him. That was all.

"The good son," Nikki had said. Always an edge to her voice when she said that.

It was a long fifteen minutes before they could get down to business. His mama had been in the backyard with her flowers. Seemed that was what comforted her. She finally joined them at the table after she'd poured coffee all around. His daddy finally took a seat beside her, and Connor finally came in, a tie stuffed in the pocket of khaki pants, a crisp white shirt that Russ figured their daddy had let him borrow.

"Don't know why I didn't think about her lock box before Mr. Royster showed up, and I tried to imagine where she'd keep a report like that," his daddy said. A slight tremble came into his voice. "Evidence of a life, recorded in a few legal documents. Marriage license, passports — remember that trip they took to Switzerland? Insurance papers. A long-term-care policy that Lady never had to use, thank God. Living on her terms to the end. I believe she departed this world exactly the way she wanted to go."

"Unless it could've happened on the tennis court," Ivy said.

"After she'd aced her serve," Russ said.

That brought smiles all around. Even to his daddy, who immediately turned serious again. "We'll get to Mr. Royster's report, but there's something else." He reached for the large envelope, upended it, and the contents spilled out. A couple of jewelry boxes tumbled onto the table. He picked up the smaller one, opened the velvety box, and turned it for all to see.

Lady's rings. A stunning bridal set, engagement ring and wedding band in a white gold setting with an elegant design. Russ remembered when his grandfather gave them to Lady on their fiftieth anniversary. Remembered wishing he could afford the likes for Nikki. Lady had put them away after his grandfather died. She'd kept wearing her own simple gold band.

His daddy fumbled, taking care as he removed the ring set from its cushioned resting place. "It's yours, Kit," he said, turning to her.

Her hands flew to her heart, like she was afraid it would leap out of her chest.

"When I asked you to marry me, I told you I was a poor man and always would be," he said. "You don't know how long I've wanted to put a diamond on your finger. If I was a smarter, better man, this would've happened long ago." He held out the rings, with a little flourish.

She took a moment to wipe her eyes with the back of her hand. "Hush now. You've given me all I ever wanted. I've had a rich life," she said, starting to remove her gold band. Then, "I don't think I want to let go of this. Maybe I'm a little like Lady, that way." She held out her right hand instead, and he slipped the rings on her fourth finger.

Russ had never heard his parents speak from the heart like that. Like there was nobody else in the room. He couldn't know what had passed between them since that day in the back yard when his mama said, "I'm sorry, Daniel. I was the one that called Connor." Russ wondered if it had been him and Nikki, what would she have to do to earn his forgiveness for keeping a secret like that? Or if a marriage was solid enough, did you just forgive, because not forgiving would tear down everything you'd built together?

Ivy interrupted his thoughts. She reached over and squeezed her mama's arm. "Fits perfectly," she said.

"Looks like it was made for you, Mama," Connor said.

Russ pointed to the other jewelry box. "What's in that one?"

His daddy picked it up and flipped it open, showing a gold watch. Russ knew it had belonged to Jack Burdette. A fine watch. His grandfather had bought it in Switzerland.

"Lady left this note," his daddy said, and he opened a little envelope. His voice had turned whispery, but he cleared his throat. *"Daniel, I want you to have my wedding ring set to give to Kitty. She's gone too long without a diamond,"* he read. *"Your daddy would want you to have his watch. I can just hear Jack saying, Time is all any of us have. Remember that, Daniel."*

He looked up. "I will remember." A pause, and he said, "She dated this note the same day she signed her new will. Like she knew her time was running out."

For the morning of a funeral, the mood was downright festive as they all admired the rings and watch. Russ was not about to spoil the moment. His parents deserved their gifts. All at once Lady was so generous, so thoughtful.

Just not to her grandchildren. Except for Connor. Connor had got his.

A fresh pot of coffee later, his daddy unfolded two pages from a white business envelope. "Here's Mr. Royster's report. Dated June 18. Lady got the report, decided to change her will, and contacted Don Petrie. The timing fits."

"Have you read it?" Russ asked.

"I did." He held the pages out to Connor. "Thought you might want to take a look first."

"You can read it," Connor said. "Read it out loud. Y'all are dying to know. If he's got something wrong, I'll say so."

Russ reached across the table. "I'll read it." His words flew into the air before he could think about it. His mama cut her eyes at him, like she was surprised that he spoke up like that.

He glanced over the pages, then began. "*Investigation Summary: Connor Burdette. Age 29. Subject located living in Dickson County in the Chestnut Hills efficiency apartments, converted from a Motel 6. Thirty-seven miles from Nashville. Going by the name of Connor Burgess.*"

"All true," Connor said.

"Subject worked construction with a crew of Mexicans," the report stated. *"He did not frequent churches or bars. He was not seen in the company of a female companion during the investigation."* Next to the apartments was a truck stop where Connor took most of his meals, the report said, except for fast-food meals he ate when he was on the job. His drivers' license, issued to Connor Burdette, had expired, and he had not applied for a new one.

Russ didn't know what he'd expected, but it sounded like his brother had led the most mind-numbing life you could imagine.

"On Saturday, Subject went to the public library," he kept reading, *"where he stayed for approximately thirty minutes. He was driving a 1998 GMC Sierra that may have belonged to one Juan Luis Vasquez."*

Russ looked up. "Driving with an expired license. Not too bright."

Connor shrugged. "The library wasn't five miles away."

"You used the computer," Ivy said.

"Every Saturday," Connor said. "I could read the *Gazette* on line."

"No arrest record was found," Russ read on, *"but the Dickson County Sheriff reported that once the manager of the apartments called him to break up a fight between Subject and one Miguel Morales. Subject had bloody nose and knuckles, but Morales took the worst of it."*

Russ saw his brother looking down at his hands, rubbing his palms like he was trying to get them clean. Maybe he didn't want to hear this, but he'd asked.

The P.I. had started sounding like a good ole boy talking at that point. "*Sheriff said Morales was a no-good wife-beater, married to Juan Luis Vasquez's sister, and he lit into her every time he got loaded. Sheriff had gone out several times on a domestic, but the woman never would press charges, even though she had a dislocated shoulder once. Vasquez had urged them all to lay low, since they were illegals, but they all knew what Morales was doing. After Subject saw the woman with a broken arm, cleaning the apartments, he confronted the wife-beater. Sheriff gave both men a warning but said to me that Morales got what was coming to him.*"

Russ looked around at his daddy, his mama, his sister, all of them staring at his brother.

"Busted him up pretty good," Connor said. "I prob'ly deserved to be charged but he deserved the beating."

"Did he leave his wife alone after that?" Ivy asked.

"He skipped the county. She's better off without him."

Russ read the rest. Words. Facts. But something else, beneath it all. He finished with a picture of his brother's life he hadn't had before, able to see who Connor had become. Befriended by strangers, but living as an outsider, living on a shoestring, living without a woman in his life, without family. Living with the fear that if he went too far from that out-of-the-way place, he might run into someone who'd recognize him. Trying to live down his past.

At the end of the report, in block letters, except for his scrawl of a signature, Hank Royster had written, "A pleasure working on this case. If you decide you want me to contact your grandson on your behalf, please let me know. I wouldn't worry about him. I believe his compass points true north."

Russ folded the pages and stared at Connor with a grudging admiration. "Guess you did a good deed, setting that wife-beater straight."

His mama pushed back her chair, went to Connor and put her hands on his shoulders. "I don't hold with fighting," she said, leaning close, "but it sounds like you saved that woman."'

Connor said. "Don't make me out as some kind of do-gooder. It wasn't like that. I lost my temper and couldn't stop. I could've killed him. All I did was beat at the world like I've been doing for a long time."

Russ knew that kind of red rage. He'd felt it time and again. Connor used to be different. Wouldn't hurt a firefly. But that was *before.*

"Don't be so hard on yourself," his daddy said.

Words Russ thought but could not speak.

Chapter 41

"In the sweet by and by...we shall meet on that beautiful shore."

Kitty let her gaze fall to the rings on her right hand as the First Baptist Church choir sang a heartfelt rendering of the old song, with piano and harp accompaniment. So familiar, melancholy, yet comforting.

Kitty and her mother-in-law were never close. But here in the church, overflowing with mourners, here with the music filling the sanctuary and then rising beyond, she touched the rings and felt Lady was there. Right there.

Reverend Timothy Briggs of First Presbyterian, who was sharing the pulpit with Daniel, had voiced a prayer and read Lady's obituary. Following the hymn, he read the "virtuous woman" chapter in Proverbs. Kitty wouldn't have thought to describe her mother-in-law as "virtuous," but the woman in the scripture had commanded respect, and so had Lady.

Then the organ swelled into "It Is Well With My Soul," and the congregation, more than six hundred, stood to sing. Four-part harmony, singing as one voice. A small-town voice, one that knew the old ritual of loss and grief giving way finally to some unshakable faith. The music surrounded Kitty, filled the very air she breathed and hit her with a force she had not expected.

Seated then, the congregation quieted, and Daniel stepped to the pulpit for his homily.

That's what he called it. Homily. Daniel never passed up an opportunity to preach.

"We're here today to celebrate the life of a woman who wouldn't want to be described as saintly," he said, stopping to let a little wave of soft laughter move through the crowd. "She's been described as colorful, flamboyant, sometimes outrageous. As her son, I had plenty of occasions to say she was exasperating. Some of you would agree. But your presence today is proof that you knew she was one of you. And you loved her. I know you did, hard as that was sometimes. That's why you're here. And you should know — that in her own way, Lady loved you, too. Loved you as only someone who spent every day of her life among you could."

He opened his Bible and read his text, Micah 6:8: "And what doth the Lord require of thee, but to do justly, and to love mercy, and to walk humbly with thy God."

Kitty had told Daniel that funerals were always too long and tedious, and he'd promised to make it short. She listened as her husband spoke in a gentle, teaching voice, which was his way, about justice, mercy, and humility. At the end of fifteen minutes, he said, "You know Lady liked to write letters that our fine newspaper liked to print. I want to read another letter. One she wrote to me, many years ago, after I announced to my parents that I wanted to go to the seminary and preach the word of God." He unfolded one page.

Kitty felt the warmth of memory. She was there the day Daniel had received that letter.

Lady had written with a mix of humor and wisdom. "I pray you won't acquire that pompous demeanor, that condescending tone of a TV preacher," she'd said. "If you must holler in the pulpit, holler against hypocrites. They're the worst. Jesus had no patience with hypocrites. Nor do I. Nor should you."

Lady had signed off exhorting him to remember Micah 6:8. "It's all the Lord requires, Daniel. The Bible says so. Notice it doesn't say a word about sitting on a hard pew."

Kitty caught Daniel's gaze. Like he wanted something from her. She had hurt him, keeping Connor's secret, and she might never forgive herself. But Daniel would forgive her because that was the kind of man he was.

It was the finest sermon Daniel had ever preached. Kitty nodded and smiled at her husband. She touched the diamond rings that had belonged to her mother-in-law. Lady's spirit was all around. What a complicated woman, Kitty thought.

Chapter 42

The quiet shuffling settled into silence, and Daniel took his place beside the coffin. "Let us pray," he said, and he asked God to take Lady into His arms. When he raised his head and looked at the deep hole into which the remains of his mother would go, for a moment he felt weak. He touched the casket to steady himself. The heat, he guessed. Ninety-five or more.

Mercifully, a tent gave some protection to his family, seated in the first row. The back two rows were occupied by women Daniel sometimes called the old darlings, all from First Baptist except for Lady's tennis partner, Audrey Brown. The other mourners kept trying to crowd under the edges of the tent. The funeral procession of more than fifty cars had come from the church, headlights on, ten miles per hour, through the center of town. It wound its way to the Montpier Memorial Gardens, the final resting place for generations of Burdettes.

Daniel read the Twenty-Third Psalm and made a few remarks about Lady's walk through the valley of the shadow of death. "Fearing no evil, if I know my mother," he said. And then a tiny woman with a big voice — Daniel knew she was pushing eighty — began to sing: *"There's a land beyond the river... that we call the sweet forever... When they ring those golden bells for you and me."* A moving rendition that pierced the silence of that somber place and left the air charged with hope and even, somehow, joy.

And then a young woman with a pretty face framed in wild black curls that fell to her waist came forward from behind the tent. She set a cage on the ground and pulled away a white sheet. A quiet murmur ran through the crowd at the sight of several white doves. Her raspy voice was lyrical, oddly comforting, as she explained, "The white dove release represents the release of the departed spirit. Like every soul is finally freed from life, we free the doves to rise into the sky." From the cage, she removed all but one dove, placing each in the hands of a family member, Daniel included. He'd been skeptical, but it was what Lady specified. Even now, he was uneasy. He exchanged a glance with Kitty and saw that she wasn't sure about this, either.

The little boys looked confused. Drew raised his face to Nikki. "Mama, what do we do with them?" he whispered, but his whisper carried, and the young woman smiled at him.

"Your family will release all the doves at the same time," she said.

Drew wasn't silenced. "Where will they go?" he asked, not whispering now.

"Home," she said.

"How do they know the way? What if they get lost?"

A soft murmur rippled through the crowd. The innocence of a child.

"The doves will follow the angel dove to our home," the young woman said.

Daniel felt his worry ease now, seeing the beauty of this ritual. He bent his head and let his cheek touch the soft feathers of the dove he'd been given, and he felt an unexpected comfort.

The young woman took the last dove from the cage. "Go home," she said, releasing it.

And then, at her instruction, the Burdettes released their doves. As the doves flew, Daniel heard the sweet strains of "Beyond the Sunset," coming from somewhere — the woman must've brought the music. A chorus of "Ah-h-h's" rose from the crowd. The angel dove, followed by a formation of eight pure white doves, flew into the bright blue, cloudless, western sky.

All except one. One dove veered off from the group, heading south.

"Sometimes one forgets its way for a time," the young woman said.

Daniel's gaze turned from the lone bird and settled on his youngest son.

"But don't worry," she said. "It always finds its way home."

Chapter 43

Ivy turned away from the grave as a bent old man began to shovel dirt on the casket, already deep in the ground. She began to walk among the tombstones.

Sometimes only the family waited to see the mound of earth, adorned with flowers. But a few friends still clustered around her parents, around Nikki and Russ. Connor was standing under a shade tree, smoking. Drew and Owen had followed him.

Ivy passed a couple of white-haired women, touching the worn names on the stones. One said in a high, thin voice, "Oh, my Lord! Here's Stanton Burdette, my Aunt Lucille's second husband. They buried her over in Mt. Heron by her first husband, though she always said Stanton was the great love her life. She told her children, 'Lay me down by Stanton Burdette.' They said it was dementia talking, but there was nothing wrong with Aunt Lucille's mind!"

All at once, someone said, "Your grandmother sure knew how to make an exit." Ivy stopped. Skip Garrison stepped up beside her. Tall, still lean, but the years showed in his eyes, in his shoulders. Like life was heavy now. "You're looking good, Ivy. Real good," he said.

"Hi, Skip. Thanks for being here."

That same old smile, that she once would've given almost anything for. Now Ivy was wiser. What she could see now was *you're-so-lucky-to-be-in-the-light-of-my-smile.*

"Heard you were back," he said.

"Just for the summer."

"I've been hoping we might run into each other," he said. "Maybe go for a drink."

"Mercer County's dry," Ivy said, and she began to walk away. She turned toward the old part of the cemetery, the headstones blackened by the years.

Skip hung by her side. "Durbin Falls has a nice little restaurant looking out over the falls. We could have dinner some night, catch up, remember all the good old times."

Ivy decided to put a stop to his little game. "Aren't you married, Skip? I saw your wife's picture in the *Gazette,* advertising her real estate business. She's beautiful."

"She sure works hard enough at it," Skip said. "Her body is a magnificent specimen of starvation. She spends all her earnings on potions that put fear and trembling into wrinkles."

Ivy had to laugh. Skip's smile this time was more genuine, and she couldn't help seeing the boy he'd once been.

Skip Garrison was the star forward who'd taken the Eagles to the State Basketball Tournament twice, who scored the three-pointer that gave them the championship, once. Ivy was not a star on the basketball court, but she was a tall, athletic, smart player who practiced shooting baskets with the same discipline she applied to most anything she did. All the players, boys and girls, and the cheerleaders rode the bus to away games. Skip Garrison always commanded a seat at the back of the bus, with a girl, a new one each game.

After a big win for the boys over their rival, Durant High, Ivy was the chosen one. She was a junior. Seventeen. She'd been kissed, but never the way Skip Garrison kissed her. The bus was well-chaperoned, the coaches, their wives, and an old-maid female teacher who kept glancing back, clearing her throat. Not much would happen but kissing and some roaming of hands, but Ivy was sure it all had to mean something. How could it not?

But at school Skip never looked her way. He didn't call her. She suffered that mix of heartache and anger and despair that hits with tornadic force when you're seventeen and you don't know yet about the earthquakes and tsunamis of love. Then — another away game, and another — and Skip kept choosing her for the back of the bus. She thought this had to be the first miles of forever, but it was always over the minute the bus pulled up in the school parking lot.

Ivy's mama had told her, "Watch out for boys who kiss and run," but she never said anything about boys that kiss and just walk away.

The season ended. Basketball, and that season of first heartache. Time came to line up dates for the prom, and Skip asked cheerleader Celine Taggart.

It surprised Ivy how quickly it all came back, there at the cemetery, where memories were put to rest. Ivy was finally in the position to say no. No to drinks. No to dinner. No nothing. "You're lucky an accomplished woman like your wife puts up with you," she said. "I wouldn't."

"Ah, Ivy." Still playful, he said, "*I'm* not accomplished? You must not know I'm a highly sought-after attorney here in Montpier."

"I heard something about that. What's your specialty?"

"Criminal defense."

Ivy had assumed Skip Garrison's legal practice would be wills, deeds, divorces, small town stuff. She wouldn't have thought Montpier had enough crime to keep a criminal defense attorney busy, but Skip explained, "I hit the circuit. Got cases in all the counties around here."

"Lots of drug cases," Ivy said.

"Some are drug related. Not all. Whatever the charges are, I believe everyone deserves a rigorous defense." He held up his forefinger, as if the thought had just struck him. "If Connor had stayed in Montpier or come back before the statute of limitations was up, I would've represented him. Whatever happened at that market, I'd a damn sure kept him out of jail."

"He didn't shoot that boy at the Back Home. It was not Connor's gun," Ivy said.

Skip nodded, thoughtfully. "I always thought the whole thing was squirrely. And now Joe Ray Loomis is missing. And I heard what happened at your house Sunday night."

Ivy wasn't sure how they'd come around to Connor, the shooting, and Joe Ray Loomis, but she had an inkling Skip had meant to arrive at this destination all along.

He said, "You know I'm here if Connor needs my help."

"Your help?" Ivy said. "Why do you think he might need your help?" Ivy said.

"Don't get riled up, Ivy. I don't have any inside information, nothing like that. But I have a bad feeling about Loomis." Skip raised his eyebrows. "And my hunches are usually right-on."

"If you think Connor is involved in Joe Ray's disappearance, you're out of your mind, Skip," she said.

"You're not hearing me, darlin'," he said, keeping his voice low, patient. "If something has happened to Joe Ray, Connor *will be a suspect.* Because they have a history, and it didn't end ten years ago. I'm just telling you; he'll be first on the list."

Ivy saw her family, flanked by friends, making their way to the lonely grave site. Dirt heaped into a mound, covered with flowers. The gravedigger was gathering his tools.

"Give your family my condolences, Ivy," Skip said. He started to walk away.

For fifteen years, Ivy had wanted Skip Garrison to tell her why, at seventeen, when she didn't know her own worth, she had only been good for the back of the bus.

"Skip?" she said. He turned around.

She hesitated, thought about it, and said, "If Connor needs a lawyer..."

He said, "Gimme a call, darlin'."

Audrey Brown was one of the last mourners at the grave. With a final wistful look, she said, "Oh, Lord, if we didn't have some great times, Lady and me." Her cackle of a laugh sounded older than her appearance suggested. She was a large, imposing woman with bangles and diamonds, red lips, and thick silver hair. Audrey was the same age as Lady, eighty-four, and they were doubles partners for years. Lady always mentioned their ages when telling one of her elaborate tales about a win over a much younger doubles team. Ivy was often annoyed by her grandmother's obsession with tennis, but today she wished she could see Lady, with her skinny old legs, in her ridiculous little tennis skirt.

Whatever her performance on the tennis court might have been in those days, Audrey seemed a little wobbly as she walked down the slight slope to her car. The sight of her big Mercedes brought something to Ivy's mind, and she caught up her.

"Mrs. Brown," she called. "Do you need any help?" The woman was as independent as Lady, but she didn't seem offended.

"Oh, not really, dear, but you can come walk with me to my car," she said.

"You drove Lady home from the country club on Thursday, didn't you?" Ivy said.

"Oh yes! Exactly one week ago." Mrs. Brown immediately went into an account of that afternoon, and then, in a mournful voice, said, "It was the last time I saw her."

"Did you go inside the house with her?" Ivy asked.

Mrs. Brown gave her a dubious look. "No. We'd already had lunch at the club. And she was expecting a visit from her daughter-in-law."

They had reached the Mercedes. Mrs. Brown touched the door handle. "Isn't this wonderful? I was always looking for my keys and now I just have to know they're in my purse."

"Mrs. Brown, I think you mean Lady's granddaughter," Ivy said. "*Me.* I was supposed to visit, but when I got there and rang the bell, there was no answer."

"No, it wasn't *you* she was expecting." Mrs. Brown gave a sheepish laugh. "And not Kitty. No, it was her grandson's wife, the tennis player. She was expecting Nikki."

Ivy didn't move until after the Mercedes had pulled away.

Why, she wondered, hadn't Nikki said anything about that?

Chapter 44

Death in a small town has its rituals. Growing up a preacher's son, Connor understood. Death leaves a hole that can only be filled by the living. Mourning is a kind of weight that can only be lifted by many. And Connor knew all the gestures that came together around food were the measure of a common unspoken hunger for some kind of healing.

Neighbors crowded into the kitchen, trying to fill loss, one mouthful at a time. The pies, cakes, and cookies, providing a memory of sweetness to offset the bitter taste of grief.

All day long Connor had been feeling the tightness of the town around his neck. Now he pulled off his tie and stuffed it in his pocket and took the first easy breath of the day.

He told himself, at least it's over. The hard part. Visitation, funeral, burial, finally over. The Burdettes would not be left alone while their sorrow was raw, but somehow, here at the parsonage, Connor didn't feel the same need to put on a face.

Not like anybody had said anything to him, more than a passing word, but he'd seen it in their sidelong glances. Like he didn't belong. Like he had some answering to do. Some avoided him altogether, and he was fine, avoiding them, too.

Connor saw that his parents were eased by the dishes clattering, and gentle voices soothing, then laughter rising.

Comforted, he guessed. Not like him, just getting through, best he could.

In the living room, Boone was holding court. Through a mouthful of coconut cake, he claimed that Lady didn't like him much. He said, "She told me, 'You're like a big termite. Like the rest of the GOP, eating away at our country's foundations. It's a wonder you get anything done.' She said that, by God! I thanked her for noticing that I damn well *do* get things done and asked her if she'd donate to my campaign. She said, 'When pigs fly, Boone, I'll support a far-right candidate.'"

Connor figured most in the room were far-right-leaning, but everybody laughed. Everybody but Mr. Hardaway, the neighbor, standing in the corner, arms crossed. Under his breath, he said, "Sounds about right."

Connor went outside to smoke, and he saw Nikki.

She was at the Suburban, the door open, and then she stepped up and sat in the back seat.

He walked toward the SUV and called, "You OK?"

"Yeah, I'm fine." As he came closer, she said, "Just changing my shoes."

Connor could see why. He knew she always wanted to be taller than five-foot-two, but for a funeral, four-inch heels were ridiculous.

She wiped her forehead with the back of her hand and took a deep breath.

"You look like you're gonna be sick," he said.

"I feel kinda sick. The heat, I guess." She slipped her small foot out of a shoe and put on a sandal, then laughed a little. "At least it's all over."

"I was thinking the same thing," Connor said. But somehow, he didn't believe it would ever be all over.

He watched her take off her other high heel and slip into a sandal. And he noticed a white dress, crumpled, laying on the seat. Looked like a stain on the skirt that somebody had tried to blot away but only made worse. He wasn't going to mention it, but Nikki said, "Cut myself at the funeral home yesterday. I couldn't do much about it then, but maybe the cleaners can."

Connor nodded. "Reminds me of something else."

Nikki fooled with her sandal, and Connor held his breath. And then he heard her almost whisper, "Grape Nehi."

"That Fourth of July. Yellow sundress. I can see it all, still." And then he wished he hadn't said it.

Nikki looked up, met his gaze. "That stain never came out. Some just won't."

"Ain't it the truth," Connor said.

She tossed her high heels into the back and started to step down but stumbled. Connor caught her. "Whoa," he said, as she leaned into him, and for an instant he leaned into her, too.

He tried not to think about her bare arms.

And then they stepped back. Both. Quickly.

Without a word, she turned and crossed the yard.

That was a long time ago, he thought. Why does it still seem so close?

But as he watched her walk away, somehow, he knew she was thinking the same thing.

Chapter 45

"It just felt so right," Ivy heard her mama say. "The music, the sermon, the doves."

Ivy had thought the same thing. But what had felt right that day had started to slip away, like the late afternoon light was slipping into shadows. Something felt wrong. Every time Ivy glanced at Nikki, she heard Audrey Brown's words. "*She was expecting Nikki.*"

The parsonage had finally emptied of all except family. Ivy kept thinking she and Nikki might have a moment to themselves. Nikki kept glancing at the door but didn't move from the table. From time to time, she touched Russ's arm, but if she wanted to leave, he didn't get it.

"We might've had a fire code violation," her daddy said. "Guess it always helps to have the Fire Chief standing in the back. I don't think he was counting heads."

Ivy's phone rang. She picked it up and headed through the hall to her room.

"Hi, Sonny," she said, "I mean Sheriff."

"You got it right the first time," he said. She could almost feel his smile. "Sorry I missed you today. I managed to get to the funeral, then got called away before I could pay my respects."

"I understand," Ivy said.

"Heard about the doves," he said.

"Yes. It was..." She searched for the word. "Powerful."

There was a pause. "We had those doves at Paula's service. I've never seen anything like it." Sonny cleared his throat, and Ivy heard something in his voice. Remembering. "I know what it's been like today. For your family. For you. And this is prob'ly the wrong time, but I can't help but think it's the right thing to ask." He took a deep breath. "Maybe we could have dinner tomorrow night? You never said yes — or no."

"I was about to, when we saw Connor on the porch," Ivy said. "About to say yes."

"I thought you might have forgot."

"Forgot? How could I?"

"Then I'll see you about six."

"It's a date, Sheriff Bellingham."

Ivy felt herself smile. Until her thoughts turned to Nikki.

Russ and his family were crossing the yard. Ivy hurried to catch up with her sister-in-law. "Hey, Nikki, can I drop by in the morning?" she asked.

Nikki waited a beat too long to answer. "I'll be home after I take the boys to tennis camp. Is anything wrong?"

"Just something Audrey Brown said. She drove Lady home, the day she died." As soon as she said it, she wished she'd waited.

But she knew she had touched a nerve.

Nikki drew herself up to all her five-foot-two, and said, "Mrs. Brown is nice enough. Wicked backhand for an old lady, but she gets confused. Has trouble staying between the lines. If you know what I mean."

She turned away.

"You're probably right," Ivy said.

But all she could feel was the wrong of it.

Chapter 46

When you're born poor, more is never enough.

Nikki figured out when she was just a girl that there was only one way up. You had to climb.

Her mama was the first to see it. That summer, when her friends carried trays at the DQ, Nikki worked in Hibbett's Jewelry, showing customers trays of gold watches and diamond rings.

"How long till you dump the Hibbett boy?" her mama said one day, blowing a smoke ring into the stale air of their apartment. "How long till you climb past that one?"

Not long, it turned out. Summer and summer job ended, and Nikki no longer needed Wayne Hibbett's sweaty hands and small dreams.

Nikki's mama, long dead now, had been a single mother since Nikki was two. A factory worker, always juggling rent and water and electric, she never saw the importance of designer jeans, manicures, and salon haircuts, as Nikki climbed to the future she imagined. Nikki didn't resent her. How could a woman like that understand? What mattered wasn't what you are. It was what you wanted to be. What you dreamed of.

By the time she'd climbed as far as high school could take her, Nikki thought she had figured out men. There were men with big futures, and there were men who made your heart race, and there were men who were just plain decent.

Russ Burdette was a little bit of each. Nikki knew it from the day he showed up for occupational therapy. Nikki was in the O.T. program, and there he was with a busted arm and a lost baseball career. And from the first, Russ let Nikki dream for them. Like he knew they could have the moon if *she* put her mind to it, and she loved that about him. He would never have pushed for Holly Hills, where Nikki knew they belonged, or for the country club, but he was sure proud to see his kids swimming in the club's Olympic-sized pool.

Just outside the city limits, Holly Hills was home to young families with swing sets, barbecue grills, and thirty-year mortgages. As Nikki turned into her street, a boy not more than seven turned his bike right in front of her. Nikki felt her brakes catch along with her breath, and the car stopped along with her heart. The boy pedaled away, oblivious. Sweet Jesus! Was she the only mom who hammered bike safety into her boys' heads?

The street was nice enough, tidy split-level houses on small, well-groomed lots. But from the day they'd moved in, Nikki had her eye on the upscale homes at the top. She was sure the higher the street wound up the hill, the better life became. Everybody town knew *outdoing-it hill.* Nikki was sure — in time she'd outdo them all.

Lady could have pushed them up a few rungs on that ladder if she'd been the kind of grandmother Nikki had expected when she married Russ.

Climber was just another way to say you were ambitious, reaching for your dreams. But it was such a cruel word when Lady said it. "You're just a little climber," the old lady spat, "and you do your climbing on the backs of the Burdettes!" How could Nikki ever forgive her for that? And how could she forgive her for the will?

What she could never say to Russ was that she didn't really blame Connor for his sudden good fortune. Not the way Russ did. Connor had missed out on so much, on all the things Russ had. Maybe it evened things out.

The memory washed over her like a flood as she pulled into her driveway. At the same time, a surge of nausea hit her. Nikki sat there, head in hands, and let the wave pass over her. After a few minutes, she made her way to the kitchen.

Inside the house, another kind of flood.

It wasn't like Nikki knew nothing about busted pipes. She knew how much could be ruined by one small break.

Ivy called from the kitchen door, "Oh my God, Nikki, what happened?"

Nikki was on all-fours, leaning into the wet space under the sink. "I was running the dishwasher while I took the boys to tennis camp. Came back to this."

"You need a plumber?"

Nikki scooted back and looked up. "I called Russ. He said he could fix it. I turned off the dishwasher and shut off the water valve. That's all I can do except clean it all up."

Ivy asked if she could help, and Nikki told her she could bring some more towels from the bathroom. She worked in silence for a few minutes more. Then she stood up, the knees of her jeans soaked, and she remembered why Ivy was there.

"What was it Audrey Brown said, anyway?"

"She told me Lady was expecting you at her house that afternoon," Ivy said.

"Audrey Brown said that?"

"Yes. She drove Lady home from the club and Lady said you were coming to her house."

Nikki went to the broom closet, got a mop, and began to mop the wet floor.

"Were you there?" Ivy asked. "Were you at Lady's house the day she died?"

Nikki kept mopping. Finally, without looking up, she said, "Yeah. I was there."

The words were in the air, impossible to take back.

Nikki wished Ivy would say something, but she was quiet. Too quiet, as she took hold of the back of a kitchen chair, like maybe she needed to steady herself. After a minute Nikki stopped mopping and fixed her with a hard look. "Lady's death was an accident."

Finally, Ivy spoke. "Well, *that's* good to know. You could've told us about it."

"Maybe I shouldn't have kept it all to myself, but don't judge me, Ivy," Nikki said. "You don't know the whole story."

"So tell me."

"It's a long story."

"I'm in no hurry."

Nikki looked around the kitchen, the floor still wet. Scattered all around were rolls of paper towels, dishwashing detergent, and cleaning supplies from under the sink. The towels were soaked. "What a mess. What a goddamned mess," she said.

"I called Lady. Told her I wanted to come over," Nikki said. "Lady was at the club, in the Ladies Lounge. I said some things I didn't mean to say, not on the phone anyway. But you know Lady could dish it out, too. She said some things that were not fair."

"What things?" Ivy asked.

"Doesn't matter now." Nikki made another swipe at the floor. "She must've been alone at first, then I heard talking and laughing, and Lady's tone changed. She wanted to tell me about her car and the tow truck, and when I offered to come out there and take her home, she said in that put-on honey-sweet voice you've heard, I know you have" — and she glanced at Ivy — "she said, 'Oh, no, dear, Audrey's giving me a ride. I don't want you to trouble yourself.' I got the message she sure didn't want to see me."

"Why wouldn't she?" Ivy said.

"Because I knew what was in her new will."

Nikki saw the change in Ivy's eyes, and she knew her sister-in-law was wondering *How did you know what was in the will?* And Nikki began to think she'd made a huge mistake, telling Ivy any of this, but she'd gone too far to quit now. Something told her she had to explain.

"I told her, 'I'm coming to your house.' I was pretty insistent," Nikki said, "and she told me to bring the boys, still so fake, all for the benefit of the women that could hear her. Lady never cared that much about my boys, and I was always afraid they'd break some tennis trophy at her house." She gave a low, caustic laugh. "I guess she thought if I had the boys with me, I wouldn't talk about the will, but that was the only reason I wanted to see her."

"What time did you go to Lady's house?" Ivy asked, like she was trying to come up with a timeline. Questions, like she was interrogating.

Nikki had thought she could make Ivy understand. She hadn't realized before how much she needed to say it, and Ivy had always kept secrets.

"I don't know. Two-thirty? Maybe later. The boys had gone to a swim meet over in Riverside, and I had to be at the club by three-thirty to pick them up." Nikki stood the mop against the wall. "You're sure you want to hear this? It's a long story."

"I'm listening," Ivy said.

Nikki stepped into the laundry room and grabbed a basket. "Remember Olivia Smartt?"

Ivy frowned. "Not much."

"No, you wouldn't. I guess you'd call her a wallflower. A nobody. But she was a somebody to me. Livvy and I came up together." Nikki stared at her French manicured nails and whispered, "Ruined."

Looking up at Ivy then, she said, "How did all of this happen? You do your best... then all at once it just goes to hell."

Chapter 47

A long story sometimes meant an excuse — even a confession. Truth didn't have to be drawn out. Ivy felt a kind of dread creeping up her spine as she listened to Nikki ramble on.

"Kids used to tease us about our names. Nikki Rich, Olivia Smartt. My family was not rich, and hers was not smart." Nikki gathered up a pile of soggy towels and dumped them in the laundry basket. "She had a bunch of stepbrothers and sisters and half-brothers and sisters, must have been about ten in all. And at least two second-hand daddies. I'm a mother now. I know how people look at little girls like Livvy and me, like we'd never amount to anything. No ribbons, clothes from the Thrift Store, nails needed trimming."

Ivy could feel Nikki trying to push away that memory as she pushed the basket aside. "But things got a lot better in high school." She gave Ivy a sideways glance. "Things are always better if you look good."

"And you did," Ivy said. She remembered Nikki Rich, cheerleader with blue eyes, long, blonde hair and cute little figure, walking through the halls, all the boys taking in every move.

Nikki reached for the mop again. "It was always hard for Livvy, with that family of hers, and she was so shy, but she had some friends in high school." Ivy had the feeling Nikki hadn't been one of those friends who stuck by her, and now maybe she was sorry for it.

"She studied hard, trying to be something better, like I did," Nikki said. "Married Toby Phillips. He's a mechanic. I hadn't seen her in years when she called. But she's doing fine."

Ivy waited past all the not-my-faults that she could hear coming. Listening hard, trying to keep up with the threads of this disjointed tale.

Nikki made a few swipes with the mop, then leaned against it.

"I went to Lady's house," she said, switching gears again. "I had something to say, and it couldn't wait. The front door was open a crack, so I went in and called to her. She answered from upstairs. Sounded annoyed. I just marched right up there. That was the mood I was in. Lady came from her bedroom, with something in her hand." Nikki grew quiet, like she was measuring her words, then gave Ivy a long look. "That's where things got a little crazy."

The dread had worked its way from Ivy's spine into her throat. But she waited.

"Nobody needs to know this," Nikki said. "It wouldn't make a difference. Not one bit."

The excuse, Ivy thought. And a confession? Now she was sure her sister-in-law had been waiting to say all of this. Wanting to say it. "Look, Nikki, if there's something the sheriff should know, I can't promise — "

"The sheriff? Oh my God! What are you saying? I told you! Lady's death was an accident. It doesn't matter what I did or didn't do!"

"The truth matters!" Ivy said.

Nikki looked underneath the sink, where the pipes were showing. Where the leak had caused the flood. Then shut the cabinet door, hard, with her foot.

Ivy tried for a patient explanation, a gentle admonition. "The sheriff already knows Lady's bracelet didn't break in the fall. They found two of the little diamonds at the top of the stairs. Something happened up there, didn't it?" Ivy couldn't help it — she felt her voice rise. "Can't you just tell me the truth?"

Nikki was mopping again, furiously, at water – or dirt – that no one else could see. "The truth is, I *hated* the old lady. I wished her dead!" she said. After a minute, she threw down the mop. The handle hit the floor with a sharp whack. She looked up. "But I didn't kill her."

It seemed to Ivy that time slowed down, as her heart sped up, beating like a hummingbird's wings. Trying to hope it was the truth. Afraid to hope. "What else?"

Nikki leaned on the edge of the counter, put her palm on her forehead. "Lady held the copy of her will out to me, slapped at it and said, 'I knew it! I had a terrible suspicion when that little nobody witnessed my signature. *She* told you what was in the will!' Nikki's voice was suddenly shaky. 'Not a nobody,' I said. 'Her name is Olivia. Olivia Phillips.' And Lady crowed, 'Olivia

Smartt! Oh yes, I knew that bunch. Jack always had trouble with the no-good daddy. He worked at the mill. What did she do, ask you to pay her for information?'"

Nikki made a sound of disgust. "I told her it wasn't that way at all. Livvy and I had come up the same way, and she knew how I'd worked to be a good wife and mother. A good *Burdette*! Now my children would get nothing! And then Lady said — called me a *climber.* She said I'd been climbing on the backs of the Burdettes all along, but I wasn't gonna climb on *her* back."

Ivy was still trying to fit all of it together. "Olivia works for Don Petrie," she whispered.

Nikki nodded. She looked down at her chipped nails. "Livvy called me, said there was something I needed to know. It was not some kind of extortion! She was being a friend, a *real* friend. Livvy said Connor was getting everything. I believed there had to be some mistake."

Ivy closed her eyes, imagining. A long, excruciating moment passed.

"I tried to get the will. Lady swung it away and lost her balance. I reached out. I did, but somehow, I caught her bracelet, and it broke." Nikki was blinking back tears now, her blue eyes luminous, but she gave Ivy a straight-on look. Not backing down. "I tried to save her."

Ivy felt something in her was about to burst. "You didn't call 9-1-1. What if she was alive?"

"I checked her. There was nothing to be done." Nikki's voice had suddenly gone cold. She made a little gesture that could have been swatting a fly.

"You put the tennis bracelet in her hand? To make it look like it broke in the fall?"

"Yeah. And I took the will and left."

A silence grew between them. There was a ring of truth to everything Nikki said, but Ivy could not at that moment dredge up an ounce of sympathy for her.

"It was an accident," Nikki said. "I probably didn't handle it right, but that's the truth."

Nikki's voice was more level now as she told the rest of it, how she destroyed the will later, burned it in the fireplace at her house and even gathered the few remaining ashes and flushed them down the toilet. "I guess it doesn't make much sense. Don Petrie still had the original. I wasn't thinking straight. I just had to see if Livvy had missed something."

"You should've called for help. My God! You just left her... like that." Ivy heard her own rising level of doubt. Her sister-in-law seemed in much better shape than she felt. Neither said anything for what seemed like an eternity.

At last Ivy began to feel the change in the air change. Nikki seemed calmer. Resigned.

"Russ doesn't know any of this. He's not good at — " She seemed to search for the word.

"Deception?" Ivy said.

"I don't like to think of it that way. I was just hoping it would all blow over. Maybe it has. None of this has to come out." She gave Ivy a look that seemed to ask, *Can't you keep this between us?* "I love my husband," she said. "I love Russ. I do."

It sounded true. The first completely true thing Ivy had heard from her.

"I sure hope I don't wind up in trouble over this. Something that wasn't my fault at all," Nikki said. She sounded almost flippant. "Think about Russ and my boys. Your brother and your nephews." The words hung in the air a moment before she said, "And in case you hadn't figured it out yet, I'm pregnant."

Chapter 48

What have I done? Nikki kept asking herself. What was I thinking?

Long after Ivy was gone, Nikki mopped with a manic kind of energy.

Russ always said Ivy was like a vault. Mistakes and heartbreak, foolishness and sins were whispered to her and locked away deep inside her forever. Will Ivy feel the same loyalty to me? Nikki wondered. Ivy's only promise was not to mention anything about the baby yet.

"I was waiting for the right moment to tell Russ," Nikki had said. "All that's happened — Lady dying, Connor coming back, the will — I didn't want the news about this baby to get all twisted up with everything else."

Ivy had hurried away, like something was smothering her and she had to get some air.

Nikki grabbed a rag and got on her knees. She rubbed at the stain no one else could see. Except perhaps now, Ivy. She stood up at last and inspected the tile, shining like new. What do I do now? she asked herself. Always, she had found a way. Whatever she put her mind to. But she was so tired. Tired of it all. Hope seemed to be waiting at the top of an endless hill.

A memory washed over her. Being pregnant the first time. A baby was growing inside, and a baby didn't let you keep it a secret. Russ had already given her a ring. Once she told him about the baby, he forgot all about the rocky path they'd been on, and they just hurried up the wedding. Russ was so trusting, even to a fault.

Nikki picked up the phone. Once more she'd have to climb past her mistakes. Russ believed in her — like only a preacher's son could. And Nikki did love that about him.

In her sweetest voice, she said, "Let's go out tonight. Just you and me. I'll call a sitter. Let's go somewhere special. It's been such a long time."

Chapter 49

Nothing mattered more than family. Not success, not happiness, not love.

Ivy had been raised to believe family was the hard rock bottom of everything. Like the foundation of the parsonage that her daddy kept worrying about. Like the Scripture he quoted about a house built on solid rock, the only house that would withstand the storms of life. Family was that rock.

Over and over Nikki's words ran through Ivy's mind as she ran through the neighborhood. Trying to outrun the worry that chased her.

How much truth was there to Nikki's story? And how much was excuse?

Ivy knew the hard edge of truth. She knew how it felt. And almost all of Nikki's story felt like putty. Stuck in the holes around a window, just trying to keep the cold out.

If her parents or Connor — or even Russ — knew what Nikki had told her, the damage could be permanent, the kind that could never be mended like the cracks Russ kept patching at the parsonage. Not even a baby could right that kind of wrong.

And then there was Sonny Bellingham. A sheriff should know. And hiding the truth from him was just another kind of lying. A silent assent to deception.

But Ivy still believed in keeping secrets. To her a secret heard was a confession and even perhaps a kind of love.

Ivy ran to the far side of town and back in the ninety-five-degree heat, and finished soaking wet, still worried. She showered and dressed for the evening with Sonny, unable to get past that tangle of loyalties. And something new. Not exactly a wish, but a thought. That it would be such a relief to let someone else carry the weight of all she knew. Someone like Sonny Bellingham.

"I hope you like catfish," Sonny said, as Catfish Heaven came into sight.

Ivy laughed. Laughed at what she'd been thinking – remembering the place Skip Garrison had mentioned. She'd imagined an upscale restaurant with dim lighting and long-stemmed wine glasses and a menu with entrees like *tenderloin medallions au jus.*

"Who doesn't like catfish?" Ivy said.

Waiting for seats, she took in the scene of a long table, a party of diners who had cleaned away the work week and washed the tired from their eyes. Their faces content and sunburned, they seemed happy as a middle-aged waitress delivered catfish, hushpuppies, and slaw, platters that she balanced expertly on her forearms.

Ivy and Sonny found a table by a window overlooking the river. Another cheerful, much younger, waitress lost no time bringing them tall glasses of water. "Ready to order?" she asked.

Ivy realized there were no menus. A blackboard covered the wall behind the cashier. Not many choices, easy to read the large chalk lettering.

"I like the catfish plate. The large," Sonny said. "Whatever you want, Ivy. It's all good."

"Catfish plate sounds good, but I'll take a small one," she said.

"Small? You'll be sorry," Sonny said.

"Sweet tea?" the waitress asked.

"Tea's fine. Unsweetened," Ivy said.

"Sweet tea's like liquid air around here." He shook his head and gave a little laugh. "You've been away too long."

Again, Ivy thought of how she had imagined this date, but now she was glad it had not turned out that way. She hadn't lied about liking catfish, though she hadn't tasted it in years, but Sonny's company mattered much more than the food.

The usual number of men had passed through Ivy's life. She had come to know that some men were like tornados, a gale-force storm that would leave only wreckage behind. And some were a gentle steady wind, the kind you could count on to blow away life's debris.

Looking into Sonny Bellingham's face, she could feel the gentle steady breeze of him.

The waitress brought the drinks and food at the same time, and said, "I'll check back about dessert. Special's peach cobbler and pecan pie."

Sonny said, "My son always wants pecan pie."

Ivy said, "Tell me about Michael."

Sonny beamed with pride and talked about Michael for a while, then mentioned Paula, and Ivy said, "Tell me about her."

Sonny wiped his mouth, took a drink, and said, "Well, she was my heart."

The sorrow in his voice was the clearest indication of all that Sonny Bellingham would not be ready for another woman in his life for a long time. Somehow that comforted Ivy. No pressure. No weighty expectations.

Sonny said, "I was at the Academy in Nashville. Paula was a reporter. She was doing a story on the female cadets. Somehow, I wrangled a date with her. We got married the next year."

Someone knocked a glass off the long table, and it shattered, an ear-splitting noise. For a moment, the room fell quiet. Sonny was looking down, like he was a million miles in the past.

Ivy said, "I didn't mean to... intrude... on your memories."

He blinked a couple of times. "No, I'm glad. I want you to know." He started up again. "For the longest time it looked like we weren't gonna have kids, but then Michael came along. We were back in Mercer County by that time. Paula wanted me to run for Sheriff. I admit, I wasn't keen on it at first, but I won, and it seemed like everything was falling into place. Having an autistic child was hard sometimes, but things were good. Real good. Until Michael was four."

He took another long drink and waited a moment to go on. "We lost Paula eighteen months ago. Sometimes it seems like it was just last week. People say you have to let grief go. I guess I thought it would get better. Sooner." He ran his finger down the condensation on his glass. So much sadness in his face. "It's always with me. Probably always will be. But Michael helps. The job helps. Sometimes I can lose myself."

Ivy said, "I think you just have to let grief take its own time. There's no right timeline." The tenderness in her voice surprised her.

"You're pretty smart, Ivy." Sonny's gaze turned back to her, and he shifted in his seat. "How's the catfish?" he asked.

Talk was easy, between bites. Sonny asked how Ivy liked teaching at the college, and they talked about that. Ivy said what she'd said so many times. "I'm just here for the summer."

"Are you really going back to the Gulf?" he said. "How can you leave all of this behind?" His gesture took in the room as a short, squat, ancient waitress passed by.

Ivy laughed, and then found herself confiding. "I was a different person when I went to Wexler-Fitzhugh. Everything's black and white there, no questioning what you were taught from the time you were born," she said. "College ought to be about opening a window to the wider world. But I became part of the machinery that kept slamming that window shut."

The talk seemed more natural between them than she could have imagined. She found herself saying, "I was engaged. He was the Academic VP. I thought he was in love with me, but it turns out he was in love with a harem of grad students. When I finally stopped lying to myself and confronted him, he managed to get me removed from two key committee positions. Showing me *he* was the one with power. I'm sure he's put an end to my hopes for tenure."

Ivy could feel Sonny listening hard. He said, "Was he afraid you'd tell the administration what he was doing with students? Surely, they have rules about that kind of thing."

"Oh, they do," Ivy said. "And they knew. I didn't have to tell them anything. For all their Puritan preaching, the administration turned a blind eye. I hate hypocrites. They're the worst." She thought about the letter Lady had written to her daddy a long time ago. *Jesus had no patience with hypocrites.*

"Yep," Sonny said, and then, earnestly, "I'm sorry all that happened to you, Ivy."

Suddenly, a helicopter appeared in the sky, above the river.

"That's Life Flight," Sonny said. "They have a base near here. Looks like they're headed toward Montpier." As he spoke, his phone made a vibrating sound. He took it from his shirt pocket and stepped away from the table. "No, I hadn't heard."

His expression darkened. Something the caller had said. Ivy couldn't make out the rest.

The waitress was on her way to their table, but she stopped short when Sonny said, "Have to take a rain check on the pie. Come on, Ivy."

"What's going on?" Ivy crumpled her napkin and stood up. Sonny pulled out some bills and threw them on the table. "What is it?" she asked again.

"There's been an accident," he said. "A boy's been seriously hurt. Car hit his bike."

Sonny put his hand on the small of her back, a gentle touch that suggested — what? — suggested protectiveness, Ivy decided. That was it. A sudden shiver ran through her as he guided her to the door. Ivy knew, just knew. She could feel the solid ground beneath her about to shift.

Sonny waited until they were seated in the car to tell her. "It's your family, Ivy."

Chapter 50

It's the suddenness of the news that shakes the ground, Daniel thought. You feel something fracture beneath you, and you think nothing will ever feel solid again.

He was at the church, in a meeting about Vacation Bible School, when he got Nikki's call. She was on the verge of hysteria, so he didn't catch everything, but he heard enough.

"It's Drew... a car hit him... he's unconscious. The ambulance is pulling in. I've gotta go. Pray for him, Daniel!" Then, almost a whisper: "Pray God will forgive me."

For Nikki to call him, not Kitty — to want prayer when the only time you'd see her in a pew was Christmas and Easter — it had to be bad. And what about God forgiving her?

Daniel prayed. Driving to the hospital, a road he could've traveled in his sleep, but now, this time he was not just praying. He was *begging* for his grandson. Letting up only to answer a call from Kitty. She'd found out from Nikki's neighbor, who had seen it all and called to say Owen was with her. Kitty was going to get him.

Sometimes a preacher got special treatment. In the E.R., a woman in scrubs that he didn't know called out, "Brother Burdette," and motioned him straight through the doors that said, "Authorized Personnel Only." That too bright, too quiet, too sterile environment that always seemed too cold.

The woman stopped in front of a drawn curtain. "Wait here," she said. "They'll be coming out. Life Flight's gonna take them to Vanderbilt." She was gone before Daniel could ask how bad it was. But Life Flight — he knew how close that was to death. It made him weak.

No place to sit, not even a wall that he could lean against. As medical personnel hurried in and out of the cubicles, passing within inches of him, Daniel dared not move from where he'd been told to wait. He closed his eyes and offered that age-old bargain to God. Take me, take every minute I have left, but let that boy get up and walk through the rest of his years.

A swing of the double doors and a soft "Daddy!" jolted him.

Ivy was there with Sonny Bellingham. Special treatment for the sheriff, too.

Daniel took a couple of long strides to meet Ivy and folded her into his arms. He could feel the trembling in her as much as he could feel his own, but somehow, they steadied each other. It surprised him, what a relief it was that his daughter was there.

"They're about to put him on Life Flight, taking him to Vanderbilt." The words tumbled out. "Nikki called, said he's unconscious. I came as soon as I could, but I haven't seen him."

Ivy let go, and Sonny stepped up. "I'm sorry about this, Daniel," he said. "Your grandson was on his bike. Dispatch said the driver's at the station. I'm going there now, unless there's something I can do here for you."

"There's nothing any of us can do but pray and wait," Daniel said.

Sonny nodded. "Call me if I can help." He turned away, touched the button to open the doors, then looked back. "You too, Ivy. Let me know if you need me."

Daniel caught something that passed between them. "You were with Sonny when he got the call?" he asked Ivy, as the swinging doors closed.

"Yes," she said. "He talked to somebody in the sheriff's office on the way here. The driver that hit Drew was a teenager."

"Oh, Lord," Daniel said, and he thought, *There's another family fractured.*

From the opposite end of the room came a flurry of dark uniforms pushing a gurney. Had to be from Life Flight. The curtain to Drew's cubicle swept back and they went in. Something in Daniel's blood turned icy. Ivy crossed her arms and shivered, like she was feeling it, too.

A moment later, Nikki came out. She was wearing jeans, carrying a jacket and purse and a plastic bag that must have been Drew's belongings, her hair pulled back in a scraggly ponytail. Not the image-conscious Nikki that they all knew.

Ivy embraced her. Nikki looked as rigid as a mannequin.

"How is he?" Ivy asked.

Nikki's voice wavered. "Head trauma. We're going to Vanderbilt."

Daniel tried to remember how a pastor should act. How he'd behaved so many times when a family was having a crisis. A heartbroken grandparent was no good to Nikki.

He stepped up to her and squeezed her arm. "What can we do?"

"Owen's with my neighbor," she said.

"Kitty's got him," Daniel told her.

Ivy said, "Don't worry about Owen. We'll take good care of him."

"What about Russ?" Daniel said.

"I can't reach him," Nikki said. "Last time we talked, he was going out on a sales call. Sometimes he has to go through the boonies to get to those places. Cell phone service is spotty."

"We'll keep trying," Daniel said.

Once again, someone pulled back the curtain, and this time, the gurney carried a small body. That's too small for Drew! Daniel thought. Their boy was nine, tall and healthy, but here he was, a helpless little soul under a white sheet, tubes everywhere. Daniel shifted to try to get a closer look. He wanted to touch that little-boy face, pray over his fractured body, but what mattered now was getting him on Life Flight. The gurney turned toward the hall, and Daniel saw the wings insignia on the backs of the dark uniforms. Angels, he thought. Angels taking our boy.Nikki started to follow, took a few quick steps, then turned. "Does Connor know?"

"Connor?" Daniel let the word settle.

"Make sure he knows," Nikki said, and she ran to catch up with her little boy.

Chapter 51

Connor couldn't remember when he'd fixed anything for anybody. Not even for himself. Anything he'd tried to fix had seemed to end up in broken pieces all around him.

Still, he could not help but try.

He was at Russ and Nikki's house with his mama and Owen. They'd found the water shut off in the kitchen and Owen told them how a leak had flooded everything before his mama could turn off the dishwasher and the valve under the sink.

"Daddy's s'posed to take care of it tonight," Owen said.

Connor had worked framing houses, roofing, hanging drywall. Grunt work. Dragged lumber and shingles in place and nailed it down. Plumbing and electrical took more than muscle and a strong back. It took know-how.

But he said, "Let me see what I can do."

Connor went to the garage and found a wrench. He leaned up under the sink and turned the water on. The plumbing looked tight, like someone cared about the work. What you'd expect from Russ.

Owen, squatting beside him, soaking it all in, asked, "Can you fix it?"

"Maybe. Might just be a loose connection," Connor said. "Sometimes big problems have small fixes."

He checked the pipes and tightened the fittings. The dishwasher's supply hose and drain line felt dry. He made sure the connections were secure.

And that was about all he knew about fixing.

"Let's give her a try." He stood up and turned on the faucet. No leaking.

Then he turned on the dishwasher. It started up where it had left off. Before Connor could get it stopped again, a jet of water spurting from behind the dishwasher had soaked the cabinet under the sink.

Owen was quiet as they mopped up the water. Disappointed, Connor could see.

He wondered why he'd believed he could fix something, anyway.

Night fell and darkness settled all around, and another kind of darkness seemed to seep into the house. Connor played half a dozen hands of Go Fish with Owen, trying to keep his nephew's mind occupied — and his own — while his mama was on the phone with the family.

After she'd talked to Russ, she said to Owen, "Your daddy had to go see about Drew, so he thinks you ought to go home with us."

She said they ought to pack some things for him to take, and Owen followed her to his bedroom. He just wanted to somebody to tell him what he was supposed to do. Connor could see it in the small, slumped shoulders. He remembered that feeling. Knowing someone was doing the thinking for you.

Connor was in the garage, putting the wrench back, when his phone rang.

"Nikki?" he said.

"Yeah. It's me. Can you talk for a minute?"

"Sure," he said, though he heard how unsure he sounded.

"Russ just got here, and he's gone in to see Drew," she said. "They've got him in Neuro ICU, on a Decadron drip to shrink brain swelling. He's sedated, but Russ wanted to see him."

Connor figured Nikki must have a reason for calling, so he waited for her to get to it.

"They're watching some internal bleeding," she said. "He might have to have surgery. Might have to have his spleen removed."

Connor groaned. After a moment, he said all he could think to say. "We're with Owen. Mama and me. We're gonna take him home with us."

"Connor," she said. "There's something else."

Daniel had told Russ he and Ivy were planning to come to Vanderbilt the next morning, Nikki said, "Will you come with them? The doctors want the family to donate blood. If Drew needs surgery, it's better to get blood from a family member instead of the blood bank."

Connor heard an urgency in Nikki's voice and something in him wanted to protect her from it. "Mama can go," he said. "I'll stay here with Owen."

"No, *you,*" Nikki said. "Please, Connor."

He heard noise in the kitchen and said, "You want to talk to Owen?"

"Tell him I'll call him before he goes to sleep," Nikki said. "I gotta go. Please, Connor. Let Kitty stay with Owen."

Connor wanted to feel like he had some use to the family. Nikki seemed to think he did.

He said, "All right, if you think that's best."

Owen's backpack, pulling at his small shoulders, looked like it held bricks when he came into the garage.

"Looks like you're ready to go," Connor said.

Owen walked over to his bike and grasped the rubber handles.

After a minute, Connor asked him, "Something on your mind?"

"Is Drew in trouble?" Owen sounded like he didn't really want to ask.

"Trouble? Why?"

Still looking at the handlebars, Owen said, "It was a Range Rover."

Connor stepped closer to his nephew and gave a little laugh. "You know your cars."

"Somebody said it." Owen looked up into Connor's face. "Drew was listening to music. He was wearing his earbuds."

Connor nodded, thinking about how to go on. "Are you saying maybe he didn't hear the Range Rover coming?"

Owen flared a little. "He turned around in the street, right in front of it. He wasn't s'posed to be wearing his earbuds!"

Connor reached for Owen and pulled him to his side. "Everybody just wants Drew to get well. He's not in trouble."

"Mama and Daddy tell us don't listen to music when you're on your bike. They're gonna be mad," Owen said, and Connor could see it was taking something out of him, being brave.

"No, they won't be mad. Don't you worry about that, Buddy."

Owen stared at his bike again. Connor knew he would have nightmares. Hard not to see it all happening, over and over. Connor blinked a couple of times, thinking of the nightmares he'd had after that Fourth of July. Sometimes still did.

Something that changes your life in a big way, there are no small fixes.

His mama came out carrying a duffle. "Did you fix the leak?" she asked.

"It's coming from behind the dishwasher," he said. "Wasn't a simple fix."

"My daddy will fix it," Owen said.

That's right, Connor thought. Nothing to do now but leave it to Russ.

He wished he hadn't even tried.

Chapter 52

Russ could feel the worry coming off them like sweat. Some would get a miracle. Some would leave to plan a funeral.

The atrium with its large skylight and rooftop patio was the waiting area for the Neuro Intensive Care Unit. Russ had seen the skylight go dark and light again. He had drunk gallons of bad coffee and knew more than he would have ever cared to know about some of the families whose world had suddenly cracked down the center. Like the woman whose husband was in a coma eight days now, hay-baler accident, and she was knitting a scarf for his Christmas present. Like the guy with his arm in a cast, whose wedding plans had been crushed along with his fiancée's spine, when their car collided with a tractor trailer.

And now Russ's heart felt a tug-of-war between the threat of a child who might never grow old, and the promise of the baby Nikki had told him she was carrying. She'd leaned into him last night, there in the corner where they'd tried to sleep in those big, overstuffed chairs. "This isn't how I wanted to tell you," she whispered, "but you're gonna be a daddy again."

He drew her tight against him, murmured words he didn't remember, buried his face in her hair — but she must have felt his dread. Because he couldn't manage the pure joy that he knew he ought to feel. Not like with Owen. Not even like with Drew, when it was a shock, but nothing that shook their plans to get married and the happiness he was sure would follow.

Now, how was a man supposed to feel, pulled between terrible and wonderful?

The elevator doors opened. There was Ivy, putting her arms around him. There was Connor, hard to read him except the worry at the edge of his eyes. And there was his daddy standing back, nodding, like he was seeing once more how tragedy can mend a broken family.

Russ headed toward the rooftop patio.

"Did you get any rest?" his daddy asked.

Russ nodded toward the chairs in the corner. "We stayed over there. Not much sleep."

Ivy patted the bag that hung from her shoulder. "Nikki wanted me to bring clean clothes. Brought some for you, too."

"That'll help." Russ figured he looked like hell and probably smelled worse.

He slid the glass door open. A breeze from the south met them. "It's quiet out here. Almost peaceful." He stood with arms folded. The others went to the rail and leaned on it.

"How is he?" his daddy finally asked.

"They don't tell us much," Russ said. "They put him in a kind of coma. Nikki said he woke up on Life Flight, he was yelling and fighting, and that was a good sign. But they don't want him awake yet. Trying to keep the brain swelling down."

Russ heard the rise in his voice, the frustration he'd held back. "For all their medical know-how, they sure do a lot of don't-knowing. Don't know when they'll bring him out of it. Don't know if he'll ever be right. Don't know if he'll need surgery. He broke a rib. They say he might lose his spleen. Surgery might stop the bleeding. Nikki knows more about it than me."

"Is Nikki with him now?" Ivy asked.

"She's back there. Hoping to talk to the doctor."

His family turned from the rail and gathered around him. They weren't just listening anymore. They had become a kind of safety net.

"It's damn hard to get straight answers," Russ said. "God isn't even answering."

His daddy started to say something but didn't. Russ was relieved he wasn't gonna get one of those Sunday morning sermons.

"Nikki's better about pulling out information than me," he said. "She says we can trust these docs. They won't give false hope. I get it. But last night the one they call Dr. O — nice enough woman but everything was *watch* and *might* and *wait and see,* and I finally said, 'Why can't you give us *something* to hang on to? Cause I don't feel a drop of hope coming off you!"

Russ could see that they didn't know what to say to him. Connor shifted from one foot to the other, like he was wishing he was anywhere else. Russ thought, me, too, brother. Me, too. Ivy looked down, and he couldn't be sure, but she might've been trying not to cry. Even his daddy, so full of the gospel, didn't have one solitary word of wisdom. He just smiled a sad smile and said, "So hard. All this waiting. All this not knowing."

"They're watching Drew's numbers," Russ went on, and his voice finally began to grow steady. "His hematocrit. Watching how much it drops. That's how they decide about surgery and how much blood he needs. Nikki says there less chance of a reaction if he gets family blood."

Connor, who'd been so quiet, was quick to say, "We're here. We're family blood."

Russ glanced from face to face. "Nikki can't give blood," he said. "She's pregnant."

A quiet fell over them. He knew they'd say all the right things, and they did. But it was awkward. Russ could tell how hard they were trying to get enough air behind the words.

Ivy asked if they could see Drew. "I'll find out," he said, and they headed back inside.

His daddy touched him on the shoulder and whispered, "Every life's a gift, son, and God surely knows this baby is the gift you and Nikki need most now."

Russ searched his daddy's eyes but couldn't feel anything but doubt. Why would God send him another child when he couldn't even protect this one?

An eerie silence filled the waiting area. Russ looked around and saw that the woman who'd been knitting was gone. Cleared out all her things. Another one, he supposed, gone to plan a funeral.

Chapter 53

The room was so cold. Like death was near. Drew was so still that Ivy had to tell herself he was alive.

She had thought she was prepared for this, but she wasn't.

His hands and head were wrapped, a tube down his throat. The ventilator made a gasping murmur, again and again, like it was unsure how to breathe. The other machines pulsed with numbers. The room had a medicinal smell, and beneath it, a whiff of disinfectant.

Nikki was holding on to the rail of the bed. Ivy had a feeling that without it she would have collapsed to her knees. She had the unmistakable air of worry and dread. The way it presses down on you. The way it forces you to lift it again and again.

"Drew, honey — Ivy's here. Ivy came to see you." Nikki began to stroke his thin arm.

Drew's face, so innocent, was as flawless as an infant's skin except for one ugly scrape just above his eyebrow. Eyes closed, absolutely motionless.

"He's going to be all right. He just needs time," Nikki said, smiling a brave smile that made something in Ivy crumple.

She had seen Nikki kiss a hurt finger that was caked with mud. Climb a tree to rescue Owen when he'd gone up too high. March a neighborhood bully home after he'd smashed Drew's science project. Ivy knew Nikki's love for her boys was fierce.

She saw the exhaustion in her sister-in-law's face. Even her clothes were tired. This heartbroken mother is who Nikki is, who she really is, Ivy told herself. This is what matters. Only this. None of the rest of it matters.

And then tears began to slide down Nikki's face. Ivy slipped an arm around her. Nikki leaned in for a moment, then moved back. "Go on. Talk to him," she said, her voice shaking.

Ivy came closer. She touched his arm, the cool, dry skin, and let her hand rest there a minute. And then she bent down, her face next to his ear. "I know you can hear me. You can't answer right now and that's OK. But soon you'll be telling me all about your helicopter ride. Owen will want to hear about it, too."

She thought she detected a flutter of his eyelids at the mention of Owen, but a moment later, there was that same little twitch for no reason. Ivy rubbed his arm, lightly, with her fingertips, the way Nikki had done. It was unnerving that he was so unresponsive.

"You're too young to hurt like this, but it will all be a memory someday," she said. "You're going to laugh again, and play. And then you'll grow up. You'll be a man with a girl who loves you and children that dream of being just like you. You just have to get through this."

A nurse entered, came over to check the wheezing ventilator, and darted a glance at Ivy.

"There's a whole life ahead of you," Ivy whispered. She kissed Drew's forehead, just under the bandage that wrapped his head, said, "You know I love you," and stepped back.

Nikki wiped her eyes. She said, "Let's go down to the chapel."

The chapel was a small, simple room, paneled in dark wood, with a few unlit candles. An arrangement of white flowers, real flowers, gave off a scent a little too reminiscent of funerals. Ivy followed Nikki to the altar, knelt, and prayed. She prayed for Drew. For Nikki and Russ and Owen. Though silent, she knew her plea sounded cross. *"It's a hard time for the Burdettes, God. Can't you help us?* Then she took a seat on the first pew. Nikki was still at the altar.

And she thought of the last time she'd seen her sister-in-law praying. One day last summer Ivy had come by their house and found them in the back yard, Nikki digging a small grave, Drew holding a shoebox-coffin, Owen with a clump of wilting wildflowers.

"It's a bird," Nikki said.

Drew held up the shoebox, showing a child's printing on the lid: *Solo.* "His name is Solo, because he liked to sing," he said. "But we found him dead this morning. God let him die."

"He perched outside the kitchen every morning and sang the prettiest little tune," Nikki said. She reached up and squeezed Drew's arm. "Like I told you, honey, every solo has to end. Solo sang all the songs God put in him. That was what God put him on earth to do."

Ivy watched Nikki smooth out the dirt, her manicured nails a mess. Owen laid the flowers on the grave. Still kneeling, Nikki said, "We ought to pray over Solo, don't you think?" Ivy remembered what she prayed. "God, thank you for sending Solo to sing for us for a little while."

Nikki stood up at the altar and came to sit on the pew.

"God's punishing me, isn't he?" she said.

The words stunned Ivy. "What are you talking about?"

Nikki was looking down at her ruined nails. "I've been thinking about it, ever since I saw Drew lying in the street. I know about brain injuries. God's punishing me."

Ivy made a soft, groaning sound. "What happened to Drew was a horrible accident." Was Nikki thinking about Lady's brain injury? "An accident, like Lady — that was an accident, too." Ivy held her breath, waiting for Nikki to say yes, an accident.

"I didn't help her. Just left her there like a dead dog."

She turned to Ivy, her eyes dry, but tortured. "I keep messing up. I don't mean to, but I keep messing up people's lives. And now look at my little boy."

Nikki's phone rang, and she grabbed it from her pocket. "Russ?" Standing up, looking like she was about to fly out of the room, she listened, and the color drained from her face.

Ivy's heart lurched. She waited for Nikki to scream or faint, but it didn't happen, and Ivy knew the call couldn't be what she'd feared. Nikki listened, then put the phone away.

"What did Russ say?" Ivy asked.

Nikki was calm, but unsteady. She reached for the back of the pew. "I was afraid of this."

"What is it?"

"Dr. O says they need to do surgery. To remove the spleen. His rib punctured it."

"But that'll make things better, won't it? The surgery's supposed to stop the bleeding." Ivy touched Nikki's arm. "Why don't you sit down for a minute."

"You don't understand," Nikki said. "He may need blood."

"We're all gonna give. I know you can't, but some of our family blood ought to match." Ivy said. "Russ is probably a match, anyway."

"You don't understand," Nikki said again. She put her hands over her face and moaned, "Oh my God. What's gonna happen to us?"

Ivy put her arms around Nikki's shoulders and felt the trembling in her.

Nikki breathed in gasps, holding back sobs, then finally pulled back and met Ivy's gaze. "You don't understand," she said. "Russ's blood won't be a match."

"I'm A positive," Ivy heard Russ say, as he pulled out of the parking garage.

"Probably the only time you were ever A plus," Connor said. "I'm B negative. It's a rare blood type. Not many in the world like me."

"Figures," Russ said. "You'll prob'ly always be negative."

Ivy knew her brothers were trying to lighten the mood as they made their way to the Red Cross, but she wished their banter didn't involve blood.

Her daddy, in the back seat with Connor, said, "I've donated several times for church members' families. I don't believe they ever told me what my type is."

Russ said, "Only reason I know mine is cause they were doing a blood drive when I was having physical therapy at the hospital. Where I met Nikki. She convinced me to donate."

Ivy remembered. Russ had busted his arm and lost his baseball scholarship. Wound up leaving college, coming back to Montpier. He met Nikki Rich and brought her to Thanksgiving dinner. Lady had not approved. Told him so, later. But Russ and Nikki kept up their on-again, off-again romance. Ivy never knew when she came home from college whether it would be on or off, even after they were engaged.

"I sold my blood a few times," Connor said. "I'm ashamed of it, but I needed money."

"I guess you could've done a lot worse for money. How about you, Ivy?" her daddy asked. "You know what type you are?"

"No," she said.

Connor reached over the back of the seat and gave her shoulder a little punch. "You've been awful quiet."

"Just worried," she said. It felt like she'd slammed a door. Everyone turned quiet.

Ivy thought about that Spring Break she was home, and Russ and Nikki had a loud argument at a baseball game. Russ stormed off somewhere, leaving Nikki with Ivy and Connor. Nikki in tears, Connor more consoling than Ivy, his arm around Nikki's shoulders. Ivy was just embarrassed by the whole thing. She remembered — Connor was always in the picture as Nikki and Russ fought and made up. Connor disappeared on the Fourth of July, and Russ and Nikki married finally at a small, private wedding in August. Drew was born six months later.

Ivy had wanted to ask Nikki, If not Russ's blood, whose? Now she was thinking, Was I blind? God help us all, she thought. She knew whose blood would match.

Chapter 54

A long-faced doctor in green blood-streaked scrubs said, "I'm sorry. So sorry."

Nikki jerked and gasped, then opened her eyes. Ivy was shaking her awake.

"You were dreaming," Ivy whispered. "Must've been a bad dream."

Nikki sat up quickly and tried to push strands of hair back behind her ear. "Guess I drifted off," she said, her voice raspy. She couldn't believe she'd gone to sleep. How could she have slept, with her little boy in surgery?

There was a sameness to every waiting room Nikki had been in, the past twenty-four hours. The same merciless fluorescent lights. The same heavy air of unease. The same way time blurred. The waiting lounge for families of surgical patients had cleared out, except for a few clusters of anxious faces. Routine surgeries might be over for the day, but surgeries like Drew's were not routine. They had taken him in at four o'clock and now it was six-thirty.

"Where's Russ?" Nikki asked.

"He and Daddy went down to get something to eat. We thought you needed to rest," Ivy said. "You and I can go when they come back."

Nikki shook her head. "I couldn't eat a thing. What about Connor?"

"What about him? He's probably outside smoking."

Nikki caught something in Ivy's eyes. A shift. And then Ivy looked down at her hands, at her nails. Nikki looked at them, too. Clean, unpolished, neatly trimmed. Not like hers.

She thought for a minute, then said, "I guess you've got it all figured out."

"We don't have to talk about it now," Ivy said.

"You *know,* but you don't understand. You shouldn't judge me, Ivy."

"I don't. I don't mean to," Ivy said.

Nikki turned away. Whatever it was in the eyes of the preacher's daughter, she didn't want to see it. Even pity – *poor Nikki – she tried so hard to be a good*

Burdette but couldn't help ruining people's lives. Nikki didn't want see that in Ivy's eyes.

She looked at the circular stairs outside the glassed-off lounge, nurses chatting and smiling, like it was any typical day, like they didn't know her boy's life was hanging by a thread.

"Russ and I love each other. We do. We just got off to a rocky start," Nikki said. "I made a big mistake. Thinking I needed more, a gentler spirit. Russ is a good man. But back then he was so used to hearing how wonderful he was, you know, he was the golden boy." It came out all in a gush, and it was a kind of relief to say it. "And then he couldn't play baseball anymore. It was hard on him. And me. It wore me out trying to keep being his cheerleader. I guess I needed somebody to cheer for me."

She was remembering how it felt it for someone to be so sweet to her. Telling her she was the best thing that ever happened to Russ, that Russ didn't deserve her. Someone putting her on a pedestal, for a change. A comfort — no, it was a rush. She clasped her hands and brought them to her forehead. Closed her eyes. "I'll never forgive myself for how I hurt him."

Ivy said, "You mean Connor."

Nikki kept on talking. She couldn't stop now. "I told him, that day at the picnic. Not that I was pregnant. No. I couldn't tell him that. I just said I *had* to marry Russ. We were engaged, and I had to go through with it. I think Connor went a little crazy. You know what happened at the Back Home, and then he went away – all these years. I blame myself."

"Connor doesn't know Drew is his son?" Ivy said. "And Russ doesn't know?"

Nikki shook her head, but she could not look at Ivy, still. "I broke Connor's heart, and now if Russ finds out the truth, it'll break his heart, too. I've caused so much damage. I deserve to be punished. But Drew — No! God should punish me, but not my little boy!"

A long-faced doctor in green scrubs was suddenly standing in front of her, saying, "Mrs. Burdette?"

Nikki felt a little cry in the back of her throat. It was *him.* From her nightmare. But she got hold of herself. He was the doctor who had talked to them before they took Drew to surgery. No wonder he'd been in her dream. Nikki reached out to Ivy, and Ivy took her hand. They stood up together.

"Your little boy's not out of the woods yet, but he's on the right path," the surgeon said.

Chapter 55

Russ watched the blood flow into his boy's arm. Bags of blood and saline and other clear liquids hung from a metal pole, but it was the blood that held Russ spellbound as it drained through the tubing. *His* blood, probably. Blood, life-saving force. Blood between father and son.

Time didn't mean much. All Russ knew was that it was late, really late. His daddy, Ivy, and Connor had headed home once they knew Drew was out of surgery and was stable. And Nikki — Nikki was about to jump out of her skin when someone finally came for them and took them to Recovery.

He and Nikki stood on each side of their boy, touching the bare skin of his arms and the cotton hospital gown that hung on his thin shoulders. Drew looking like he was resting, not in any pain, the ventilator breathing for him. Not so different here from the Neuro ICU. Just the thought that he was cut on and stitched up, under the crisp white sheet. Tubes and monitors, but now he had to have blood.

Nikki leaned down to Drew's face and whispered, "You came through that like a champ, honey. Everybody said so. You are so brave."

Russ wanted to say something to his boy, but his throat felt like it was closed off.

And then a nurse came in with a cart, and Nikki started asking her questions. How long would he be in Recovery? Would he go back to NICU? How much blood would he need? Thank God for what she knew and what she knew to ask and for the way she just kept on asking.

Russ couldn't stop staring at the blood, the nearly depleted bag. He would give his blood, his life, for his son.

The nurse had brought a replacement bag. She was patient with Nikki but finally stepped up to the metal pole to make the switch.

And Russ had a glimpse of the label on the new bag of blood.

B. Rh negative.

Russ was tired. Beyond tired. And he knew he wasn't thinking right. But his blood type was A. He was sure of that. Nikki's was O. He was sure of that, too. That day at Mercer County General — another lifetime — when they donated at the blood drive, they both got cards and compared.

How was it possible for a child's blood type to be B when his parents were A and O?

How was that possible?

It was not.

Drew was B negative.

B negative, a rare blood type, not many in the world...

Chapter 56

From the moment the first E.R. doctor at Mercer County General said, "Internal bleeding," Nikki had been thinking about blood.

Hers. Russ's. Connor's. Drew's.

Blood, such a silent thing, but Nikki could almost hear her blood roaring in her veins.

If only Drew hadn't needed surgery. If only he hadn't needed blood.

These past days, she'd had so much time to think. And she'd thought about how you were sometimes forced to do the right thing, something you never wanted to do.

Tuesday morning, when Drew woke up, Nikki believed God had given her a miracle. She'd taken to praying, during this awful time. Going down to the chapel, where she felt a spirit she'd never felt in a church pew.

The extent of Drew's brain damage was still unknown, but he was no longer teetering between life and death. Doctors spoke of getting him out of NICU, into a regular room at the Children's Hospital, within the next twenty-four hours. There would be tests and more tests — but he was alive. God had saved her boy. And now she promised God she'd try to do the right thing.

Given a respite from the all-consuming fear that had defined these four days, Nikki began to think of the child she'd left in Montpier. "Maybe I ought to go home for a day," she told Russ. "I know Owen's missing us. I need to see him, too."

"I'll stay here," Russ said. "My boy might need me."

Nikki wasn't sure what she heard in his words, saw in his eyes, but it troubled her. What if he'd seen the type on the bag of blood? Just that once, in Recovery, when Drew was getting a transfusion. But Russ didn't usually pay attention to details like that.

If she could wait — *please God* — another silent prayer. And this time it was not for herself. It was for Russ. From the time Connor came back, it had been one shock after another. Too much, even for a strong, good man like Russ. *If I can just wait to put this on him...*

That afternoon, Nikki drove to Montpier. As the Suburban wound past farms and small communities on the twisting state highway, she kept praying. Praying she would have the words — for Connor, and for Russ when the right time came. Cell service was not reliable, there in the hollows, but somewhere outside Montpier, she got a signal and dialed Connor's number.

"Meet me at the park," she said. "You know where."

Just once.

Behind a screen of trees and underbrush in the far reaches of the city park, Nikki had stretched out in the cool grass with Connor. And everything they'd held back let go. Just one time. Because of Russ, because of guilt — hers, yes, but Connor's, too.

And it was here, also, that Fourth of July, that Nikki told him she was going to marry Russ. But not before he'd brought her a Grape Nehi, there under the hot sun, and she'd managed to spill it when he told her he loved her, pulled her into his arms a little too hard, and said, "Nikki, you never say you love me, but I know you do."

That was another lifetime, yet it felt like she'd just blinked, as she waited for Connor in that secluded spot. Nothing — and everything — had changed.

"What's this all about?" Connor's voice startled her, drew her back to now. His gray t-shirt was soaked, his face slick with sweat.

"How'd you get here?" she asked.

"Walked. Ran, really."

Connor looked around, like he was taking it all in, the tangle of green that isolated them and the rocky bank that led to a creek bed, nearly dried up, this hot summer. Nikki knew he was remembering, too. He shifted from one foot to the other. "Why'd you want to meet here?"

Nikki bent down and broke off what she thought was a four-leaf clover. But no. She never had that kind of luck. She tossed it. "You know, every time I hear fireworks, I remember."

"Fireworks sound like gunshots to me," Connor said, not a trace of mercy in his voice.

"I think about that day. Right here. I told you I was going through with it, the wedding," she said, "but I didn't tell you why. I was pregnant."

For a moment she was still and silent, and so was he. Nikki thought his glare softened a bit, but he still sounded cross. "I kept going to the library, checking the *Gazette,* looking for anything about Joe Ray or Raleigh. And guess what. Here comes an announcement. A baby born to Russ and Nikki Burdette." He made a sound that could've been a laugh, had it not been so full of self-loathing. "But that Fourth of July, I was still playing the fool, thinking you might break it off with him. Thinking you might want me."

"I tried to do the right thing. I did," Nikki said. "But somehow the right thing always turns out wrong for me." The words didn't ring true, not even to her. All she'd done was take the easy way out. Marry Russ and let everyone assume the baby was his. Even Russ.

"There was a lot of wrong between you and me, Nikki. It felt right, but it was the wrong kind of right." Connor took a step toward her, and she thought he might touch her, but he didn't. "You and me, we were fireworks for a while. Lit up the sky, then it all went black. You and me, that's all in the past." He sounded like he'd just that minute decided. "You did the right thing, marrying Russ." It was the first time she'd heard any kindness in his voice.

Nikki thought, I promised God. I can't go back on it...

She steeled herself. "Drew is yours, Connor."

She could see shock take over. Feel it, charging the air. "I never meant to hurt you," she said, reaching toward him, and but he stepped back, looking confused, then angry.

He pushed at the air with his palm, like he was trying to keep the truth away. "Don't! Just *don't!*" he yelled. Breathing hard for a minute, then turning away from her.

"I'd make it right if I could. But I don't know how." This was not like before, when he'd begged her not to marry Russ. When she might have made it right.

"I *loved* you!" The words came out of him like a howl. Finally, he faced her again. "Why didn't you tell me? We could've raised Drew — *my* son — together! I wanted you to marry me! Soon as I could buy a ring, I was gonna ask you to take off Russ's ring and put on mine!"

Nikki put her hands to her face. She tried to pray again, one of those silent prayers that she'd been so sure God heard, but now she was afraid her prayers would never reach His ears. Because she just couldn't keep from ruining everything around her.

"You let me spend all that time alone. Not knowing there's a boy out there with my blood!" Connor wailed. "And I'll never, *never,* get all of those years out of me!"

Nikki began to cry softly. She could barely hear, in the distance, a siren that screamed for a minute and faded. And then there was nothing but silence. She wiped her eyes and saw through the blur, Connor's face. The way he looked at her. A look she could never forget.

"Please, Connor," she whispered — but what did she want from him? Please forgive me? Please don't let Drew find out? Please don't try to take Drew away from Russ?

He didn't wait for her to ask for anything. He whirled around and walked fast, the way he'd come.

"Connor!" she called. "Please!" But he was already gone.

Just like before.

Chapter 57

"Joe Ra-a-a-a-ay, I'm comin' for you!" Connor howled, tossing another empty, "I'm comin' for you, boy!"

There wasn't enough alcohol in the world to kill this kind of pain. Hurt in a way he never thought he could be. Not a drop of whiskey in this dry county, and too far to the county line, but he'd spent the last dollar in his pocket on a twelve-pack of Coors. Not enough to get him where he wanted to be, but enough to make him swing away at the world.

And all that heartbreak was rolled up into something with Joe Ray Loomis's name tattooed on it.

At the Back Home, where he'd bought the beer, the clerk who looked older than his mama would just not shut up. "Everything's on sale," she'd said. "Beer, too. Going out of business. One of them big oil companies is buying the property. They'll be tearing down the Back Home."

"Bout time they took it down," Connor said, as he grabbed his beer. He shotgunned one in the parking lot, then headed out for the trailer park where he was sure he'd find Joe Ray.

The Four-Ten bus rolled by, traveling toward the highway.

I oughta be on that bus, Connor thought. I oughta be anywhere else. Why did I think I could ever come home? There's no place for me here. Never has been.

Now just past the city limits, his twelve-pack lighter, he still had a thirst no beer could ever satisfy. "Comin' for you, Joe Ra-a-a-a-ay!" he hollered at the sky.

He stopped and stared down the side road that led to the Montpier Memorial Gardens.

He and his buddies used go there to drink. A graveyard, as alone as it gets, nobody around but the dead. He was feeling a little unsteady. Maybe it was the beer. Maybe it was the way his heart had started to throb, back there with Nikki. Felt like it was dying for a rest.

And seeing the graveyard, he knew there were a few things he wanted to say to Lady, too.

Five days since the burial, Lady's grave was still a mound of dirt covered with dying flowers. Connor stumbled toward it. His legs buckled and he fell to his knees in the grass. He opened another beer. Took this one slow. He was beginning to feel like he was thinking straight for the first time in a long time.

Thinking how different life could've been. Lady must've known in her bones, those same bones now deep in the ground, how she could've changed things for him. He'd somehow found the courage to go to his almighty grandmother and ask for money. "You didn't even want to know why I needed it!" he yelled to the grave. "It was for a ring. It was for Nikki."

Lady's words still clanged in his ears: "Get back home and start acting like a Burdette instead of some piece of white trash! And don't expect anything from me!"

He laughed to himself. "Now you've left me your fortune, old woman. Now you want to give me the money you can't spend anymore!" he cried out. "Like you thought you could make up from this grave what you wouldn't give me when you were alive. When I needed it!"

Connor made his way through a couple more beers. He stretched out on the grass, thought about how it could've been if Nikki had just told him she was having his baby and wondered how he could have ever loved someone who didn't give a damn about him.

It wasn't right. His son, *his* son, growing up thinking Russ was his daddy. Connor didn't know how he could let that lie just be, now that he knew the truth. He tried to weigh it against what the truth would do to Drew. But he kept coming back to how wrong it was that all this time, there was a boy in the world with his blood who never knew it.

His phone rang, but he turned it off. Didn't care who it was.

His head began to spin. He closed his eyes, meant to rest, just for a minute — but sometime later he opened them and saw daylight had faded to dusk. Fireflies hovered above the grave. He sat up and reached for the last beer. He'd forgotten how lonely a graveyard could be.

Finally, Connor staggered to his feet and looked out across the dark tombstones. "Maybe this is where I belong, here with all you dead and buried!" he called out. "You don't have to feel anything!" Some part of him had died ten years ago but tonight he'd felt it start to come back alive, and he wished it had just stayed dead. "I don't want to feel anything anymore!" he yelled.

A rising yellow moon gave some light as he made his way back to the main road.

A car flew by. "Sonofabitch!" he yelled, staggering into the gravel at the edge of the pavement. "Watch out!"

He glanced back toward town, then at the open road. Seemed like one more crossroad. Then he remembered the trailer park. And Joe Ray. He clenched his fists and thought, Now I'm ready to give that bastard what's coming to him.

The dim lights made the trailer park seem far away, but Connor knew he was close. Wished he had another beer. His mouth felt like it was stuffed with cotton. As he dragged himself along, wobbling, his legs could barely carry him, but there was no quitting now.

A car edged up behind him. Connor turned as the car slowed. With his hand, he shielded his eyes from the high beams. The driver killed the lights and opened the car door.

"Get in, Connor," Sonny Bellingham called.

Connor snorted. "Well, if it ain't the sheriff. Am I under arrest for something?"

"I can make that happen."

"I ain't done anything. Not yet. And you can't arrest me for what I was fixing to do."

"Somebody reported a drunk out here, trying to get himself run over." Sonny walked up to him. "I could run you in for public drunkenness, just smelling you, but I don't want to."

"What is it you want to do?"

"I want to take you back where you belong. Home," Sonny said. "Seems like you can't get there on your own."

Connor said, "Ain't that the truth."

The sheriff walked around to the passenger side, his voice suddenly kinder. "Come on. Let's get some coffee in you." He opened the passenger door.

Suddenly all the fight went out of Connor. He sure couldn't fight kindness.

"Guess you must like coffee," Connor said, when Sonny ordered four coffees at the drive-through, three black and one with sugar.

It was the first time he'd spoken since the sheriff hauled him away. To Red Pete's, it turned out. Connor could remember when Red Pete's was the place to go, before McDonald's came to town. Looked like it was barely hanging on now. Selling early bird dinners to the old crows, he supposed.

"Anything else?" the girl at the window asked.

"Water," Connor mumbled.

"Biggest you got," Sonny told her.

The order came, and Sonny pulled into the empty back parking lot.

Connor drained the water in a few gulps. Sonny reached for his cup and said, "Better get started on those. We don't have all night."

"I do," Connor said. He picked up the steaming hot coffee. Tried it and winced as it burned his tongue. "Why didn't you just leave me out there by the trailer park?"

"That's where you were headed? Dammit, didn't I tell you to stay away from there?"

"You're not doing nothin' to find Joe Ray."

"Joe Ray's not there," Sonny said. "And that trailer park's not a safe place. Stay away from there, man! Too much meth dealing. You don't want to get crossways with that bunch."

"And you can't make an arrest? So you come after me?"

"We'll get 'em. There's more to their operation. That's what we're after. Just let me do my job."

Silence settled between them. Sonny looked annoyed, but his frown smoothed out as he drank his coffee. Connor finished his first and started in on the next.

"I was at the parsonage earlier," Sonny said, finally. "Ivy kept calling you."

Connor looked straight ahead. Remembered his phone ringing.

"You sure know how to keep your folks twisted up with worry," Sonny said.

"Don't mean to. It's not their fault. None of it." And don't ask me why I got loaded, Connor thought. Just don't ask.

He set his coffee, half of it gone, in the cup holder and slumped against the door.

Sonny said, "Still one more."

"I'm all full up." Connor said. "You want me to puke all over your car?"

Sonny flipped on the lights, shifted into reverse, and backed out.

"Where're you taking me?" Connor asked.

"Where you want to go?" Sonny pulled up to the street and waited.

After a minute, Connor said, "Home. I just want to go home."

Chapter 58

The silence that hung in the kitchen was louder than any words.

Kitty hadn't expected Connor to be up at a decent hour, not after last night, the way he'd staggered in, smelling like he'd been swimming in a river of beer. No excuses. Just mumbled, "Sorry I made you worry."

Daniel hadn't needed to speak. He'd had that look — Kitty knew it well — like there was a sermon in him but he didn't have the words for it yet.

"I'll put on a pot of coffee," was all Kitty knew to say.

Connor shook his head. "I've had my fill of coffee," he said and stumbled into the hall.

Now here he was, barely eight o'clock, silent, sullen, but wolfing down bacon and eggs.

Ivy was still asleep. Daniel had already gone to the church for an early meeting. It was just Kitty and Connor, and Kitty had something on her heart, something she needed to say, and she was going to say it. She refilled her coffee and pulled out the chair across from her son. Whether he wanted to talk about it or not, he was going to listen.

"Connor," she said, "I know you can take care of yourself. You've been out in the world. It's not like you're a teenager, and we're worried you're drinking and driving."

Connor broke in. "Last night was not about drinking, Mama. It wasn't about running away. It was about trying to figure out where I belong."

Kitty could see he wanted to say something else, but he couldn't seem to get it out.

After a minute, she said, "You're a grown man. Twenty-nine years old. You don't need our permission to come and go. You don't have to tell us when you'll be back." She suddenly felt her voice quiver. "It's just that — " she fixed him with an earnest gaze — "one day you left and didn't come back for ten years. And those ten years are hard for us to forget."

Connor looked down, began rubbing his hands, that nervous habit of his.

"I can feel the wound in you, Son," Kitty said. "A mother knows when her child is hurt. Seems to me it's only getting worse. Worse than when you first came home. And I don't know what to do. Your daddy doesn't. We just want to stop the pain, Connor. That's all we want."

She reached out across the table, and he raised his head, his eyes bloodshot but something genuine in his expression that made Kitty feel like she'd connected with her boy, at last.

Connor took her hand. "That's all I want, too, Mama," he said. "All I ever wanted."

"You know, you could do worse than Sonny Bellingham," Connor said when Ivy sat down with her bowl of cereal.

Kitty thought so, too. She smiled, the first time that morning.

Ivy pretended to scowl at her brother, then took a bite.

"Sonny came by last night with a copy of the final autopsy report," Kitty said. She was at the sink. She reached for a manilla envelope tucked behind the cannisters. "You want to see it?"

"I don't feel like wading through it now," Connor said. "Just tell me."

Kitty pulled out two pages and scanned it. "Not much different from the preliminary autopsy. Acute intracranial hemorrhage, blunt trauma. Accidental death."

"So it's official. An accident." Kitty left it at that.

"Guess I'm off the hook." Connor took another bite and pushed back his plate. "Not that I was anywhere near Montpier that night. The sheriff checked it out. But if there was a murder investigation, you know half the town would believe I did it. Like the Back Home."

No reason to mention what Sonny had said. *I'm not completely satisfied, myself. Just have this feeling there's more, like somebody else was there.*

Ivy, who must have been thinking the same thing, said, "I just wish it was over."

"It *is* over," Connor said. "Accidental death. How's it not over?"

The phone rang, and Kitty answered. She didn't expect Nikki's sharp words. "I tried to call your cell phone. Ivy's, too."

"What's wrong?" Kitty said.

"Can I bring Owen over? I have to head to Vanderbilt," she said. "Drew had a seizure."

Kitty waited in the yard as Nikki's SUV pulled into the driveway. Owen jumped out, carrying a backpack, his face showing he did not want his mama to leave. Nikki seemed so distracted. Kitty hoped she'd loved on her boy before they left the house.

Kitty drew Owen against her for a moment, hugging. "Connor and Ivy are inside, waiting for you," she said, trying not to let her worry show.

She knew Nikki was anxious to get on the road, but she couldn't resist leaning into the open car door, asking, "Anything else about Drew?"

"All I know is he had a seizure and they're keeping him in ICU. I talked to Russ about an hour ago. The neurosurgeon told Russ these setbacks just happen sometimes with a TBI." Nikki glanced at the kitchen door. Connor had opened it to let Owen in. He did not look Nikki's way. "I've gotta get there, try to find out what this means. How bad it is," she said.

A rumble of thunder sounded in the distance. Kitty looked up. A bank of dark clouds in the west looked like black smoke.

"Be careful, Nikki," Kitty said. "Looks like rain. Maybe a storm."

"I feel like I've been in a storm. Still am," Nikki said.

"I know, honey." Kitty closed the car door and waved, as raindrops began to fall.

Chapter 59

Daniel figured he was about to be fired.

The Colonel's call had come at a bad time last night. The family worrying that Connor was missing — again. Sonny Bellingham, who had delivered a copy of Lady's autopsy report, said, "I wouldn't be alarmed just yet," but how could he know what that familiar dread felt like? Sonny also brought news about Drew's accident. He couldn't charge the teenage driver. The neighbor's eyewitness account had confirmed that Drew made a sudden turn, right in front of the Range Rover, that the driver wasn't speeding and couldn't have avoided the bike.

All of that going on, and right in the middle, Frank Steele calling, saying in short, terse terms that he needed to meet Daniel at the church first thing in the morning. Like an order he'd issued when he was in the Army. It hadn't been a good time to get into anything with Frank.

Daniel always started his day with prayer, but today he was in his office earlier than usual. He knelt on the worn carpet, not that he had to kneel to pray or pray out loud, but it was how he felt closest to God. The prayers rolled off his tongue. For Drew. *Heal him. Let him be the boy he was.* For Connor. *Strength to win the battle over whatever demons he's fighting.* On and on. Russ and Nikki and Owen. Kitty and Ivy. He prayed for grace, for all of them. "Oh Lord, our family is hurting! Help us!"

It was so natural to give God his wish list. That's how Daniel sometimes thought of his prayers. The Scriptures did say, "Ask and you shall receive," and he took it to heart. Asking, again and again. He was grateful, as well. Drew was still alive. Connor had come home. Daniel was blessed — blessed with his family, blessed to serve his church.

That brought him to the hard part of praying.

He could pray that God would let him stay at First Baptist, finish out his ministry there. He surely could. But to pray, "Not my will, but yours, Lord," that was the hardest prayer. So difficult, even for a preacher. If the deacons had voted him out, as he expected the Colonel was about to tell him, he would have no choice but to look for another pulpit. And if a church in another town called him, how could he and Kitty leave Russ's family in their time of crisis?

Preachers were supposed to trust in the Lord — and Daniel did trust. But this morning, kneeling on that threadbare carpet, where he'd sent up so many pleas, he grasped a truth about himself that had never been so clear. He didn't trust God enough. It was easy to trust with somebody else's heartaches. How many times had he said, "Just put it all in God's hands"? But now that the heartaches were his, all he felt was his lack of faith. Tears filled his eyes. All he could manage was, "Forgive me. Help me. Have mercy on me."

The heavy knock brought him out of his prayers. He wiped his eyes and made his way to the door, trying to straighten his back. Opened up for the Colonel and said, "Morning, Frank."

Behind the commanding presence that was Frank Steele stood a teenage boy, looking like a lamb being led to the slaughter.

"This is Tyler Estes, my sister's boy," the Colonel said. "He was driving the Range Rover that hit your grandson."

Daniel couldn't be sure why the Colonel brought in his nephew. Tyler Estes was not going to face any charges. Sonny Bellingham had made that plain. Could Frank be thinking there was going to be some legal recourse from the Burdettes?

But the boy's intentions were pure. Everything Daniel knew about confession, years of experience with honesty and deceit, told him so. Tyler was a six-foot beanpole, just sixteen. Wearing khakis and a button-down shirt, prep school attire. Looked like a fresh haircut. Daniel imagined the Colonel had orchestrated it all. Wanted to make his nephew look squeaky clean.

"The boy wants to tell you what happened. He wants you to know the truth," Frank said, as Daniel shook hands with the young man.

"I see," Daniel said. He motioned toward the upholstered chairs, the setting he preferred for talking like this. When they were seated, he asked Tyler. "Tell me why you came to see to me, Son."

The boy swallowed hard. His voice cracked a little as he said, "I feel bad about Drew. Is he gonna be all right?"

"He's not admitting any guilt, you understand," Frank put in.

Daniel raised his palm to hush Frank but did not look at him. "He's making progress," Daniel said. "Do you know Drew?"

"Yes sir. I mean, we're not friends, you know. He's a lot younger. But we're both on the swim team at the club. He's fast. I hope he can come back, you know, when he gets well."

Daniel could feel the Colonel's stare, like a laser. It would be easier if he could just talk to Tyler in private, but he knew the Colonel would never allow it.

"Where do you go to church?" Daniel asked, thinking the boy was really wanting a pastor.

"Nowhere," Tyler said. "I used to go to the Methodist youth group, but not now."

Daniel shifted in his chair, leaned forward, and said, "Tyler, your uncle probably thought it was a good idea to meet with me, but I'd like to know what *you* want. How can I help you?"

Tyler glanced at the Colonel, back at Daniel, then stared at his hands. Rubbing his palms together, just like Connor. After a moment, he looked up. "I tried to stop. Drew turned in front of me, like he didn't know I was there, and I tried, but I just couldn't!" His voice shook. Daniel waited for him to go on, waited through an awkward silence. "I guess you could pray," Tyler said, finally. "I mean, you're a preacher. I guess you could pray that Drew won't blame me."

"Yes, I can do that," Daniel said.

"I mean, it wasn't my fault, but — " He darted a look at his uncle again. Clear to Daniel that the Colonel had coached him well on what to say, what not to say. "I keep seeing it, over and over," he whispered.

Daniel couldn't help but think of Connor. Unable to forgive himself for the Back Home.

"I think we should pray that you won't blame yourself, either," Daniel said. "It was a terrible thing. Terrible for Drew. Terrible for you, too."

The boy nodded and closed his eyes. And Daniel prayed with him, for all kinds of forgiveness.

It began to rain, a few heavy drops. The Colonel stood up quickly after the Amen. "We might beat the storm if we skedaddle," he said. He darted a quick glance at Daniel, like he wanted to say something else, but all that came out was a grunt and "Thanks."

At the door, Daniel said, "Tyler, you'd be welcome in the youth group here."

The boy stuck out his hand, like he'd figured out what a man might be supposed to do.

Only after Daniel was back at his desk, opening his Bible, did it come to his mind that the Colonel hadn't fired him. He felt his spirits lift. For a moment.

And then he listened to the message Kitty had left. About Drew and the seizure. And Daniel felt that grip of fear that just would not go away.

He didn't kneel again, nor did he pray out loud, but he finally felt the words coming from the deepest part of him: "I trust you, Lord. I put it all in your hands. All of it."

Chapter 60

Sometimes the world seems so soaked that it can't take another drop of rain. Then somehow it does. Why won't God just let up? Ivy wondered. He keeps throwing these pails of water down on us.

Sitting cross-legged on her bed, she stared at her laptop, trying to make sense of the world for tomorrow's class but all she could think about was her brother's family. Nikki, how she'd had to take those hairpin curves on the state road this morning, with the rain beating down. Drew, pale and motionless and stone-silent in the ICU. She'd studied some medical sites about TBIs and seizures. So frightening, all she'd read, and thinking of Drew.

And she kept thinking about Russ. "I'm A positive," he'd said. Something sank in the pit of her stomach as she thought, he shouldn't be so positive. And she wondered, *Did Russ know*?

Ivy pushed her laptop aside. Nikki ought to be at Vanderbilt by now. She would've had time to see Drew and talk to Russ and to doctors. It should be all right to call her. Make sure she'd arrived safely. Get the latest on Drew's condition. Ivy picked up her phone.

But it was her big brother's number that she called.

"Yeah, Nikki's here. She's with Drew," Russ said. "Seemed exhausted. Said the rain was coming down so hard, she couldn't see anything but the blur of somebody's taillights for forty miles."

"I couldn't quit thinking about her," Ivy said.

"Nikki knows how to take care of herself," Russ said.

Ivy thought she heard something else beneath the words, but maybe she'd just imagined it — because she knew too much.

"What about Drew?" Ivy asked.

"Lot of don't knows and wait and sees," Russ said. "They still can't tell us if he'll ever be right. The CT scan yesterday looked a little better, but then came that damn seizure."

Ivy had the feeling it was a relief to her brother, talking to her. "They cut back on the meds the night before, and yesterday he opened his eyes, like it was any other morning." Russ took a breath and let it out long and slow. "Nikki was hugging on him, about to smother him, crying and all, and he looked up at me and said, 'Daddy?'"

Ivy heard the tremble in her brother's words, heard him try to clear his throat twice, to get his voice back. "He doesn't remember any of it. We tried to tell him he had an accident on his bike, but I don't know how much is getting through. He seems drowsy. Confused."

Ivy remembered what Nikki had said, and she repeated now, "He just needs time."

"Time." Russ grunted. "A social worker came by yesterday. She's part of Drew's treatment team that's supposed to meet with us next week. Left some information about Stallworth Rehabilitation Center. It hadn't entered my mind that he'd need rehab after he leaves Children's Hospital." A pause, then, "And he can't even get out of ICU yet!"

Before Ivy could shape anything hopeful to say, Russ's voice fell to a whisper. Almost as if he was talking only to himself, he said, "This will not be over soon."

The driving rain gradually turned into a steady downpour. Ivy kept hearing Russ's words: *This will not be over soon.*

She pulled up an email that Gwenna Wallis had sent yesterday. A kind note, prayers for the Burdettes, and then, *Just wanted you to know we've advertised the English position. We'll be getting loads of applications.*

Ivy had been too distracted to think about applying. To think about what it would mean to stay in Montpier, make this her real home again. She had come back to lick her wounds. Now her wounds didn't seem to matter so much. With all the other storms Ivy and her family were weathering, Preston Gorman was fast becoming a blur, like taillights that she no longer needed to follow.

She clicked on the link Gwenna had sent. She hadn't tried to see Dr. Keller yet, but here was a basic form, easy to fill out. A request for a resume. Ivy could update hers in no time. References. Not everyone at Wexler-Fitzhugh would give her a reference, so many administrators loyal to Preston, the Academic VP, but she had loyal colleagues, too.

It couldn't hurt to try.

Because she could not predict — none of them could — how much her family would need her. And she would need them.

Chapter 61

Sooner or later every storm runs out of rain, Russ thought. That's one thing you can trust. The creeks were still rising along the state road after two days of torrential rain, thunderstorms and flooding, but today the sun was trying to come out.

He'd been thinking about so many things he couldn't trust. He used to trust the helmets his boys wore, riding their bikes, but now he knew helmets weren't foolproof. One of the docs had explained that when a child's head hits the pavement, the hard blow causes the brain to rebound inside the skull. The bounce against the other side was what caused Drew's injury. Helmets didn't protect against that kind of thing.

He used to think he could trust Nikki.

He used to think he could trust God.

Russ had been in a kind of trance for a whole week. Consumed with worry, with blood. Glaring hospital lights and medicinal smells, waiting for a word of hope or the slightest change in Drew, a signal that he might be all right. Now, somewhere between Nashville and Montpier, Russ had started remembering there was a world beyond the hospital.

A house in Holly Hills with the water shut off in the kitchen.

A job at the Sports Emporium.

And a son who was waiting for him at the parsonage.

He hadn't expected the rush he felt when Owen ran to him, calling, "Daddy!" How a heart could ache with love. How easily he'd scoop his eight-year-old into his arms, and how tight he'd hold on till he felt his boy gasp to breathe.

His mama stood on the front porch, a sight that cheered him more than he would've imagined. In the week he'd been away, it seemed he was seeing it all with fresh eyes.

"Is Drew coming home?" Owen asked.

"It'll be a while longer," he said. "Go get your things. We're going to our house!"

Russ could see Owen's body practically quiver with excitement as he ran past his grandma.

"Hi, Mama," Russ said, giving her a hug.

"How're you holding up, Son?" she said, hanging on to him a little longer, the way he'd wanted to hold on to Owen. And then, "How's Drew?"

"They finally moved him into a room this morning. I guess Ivy told you he'll have to spend some time in a rehab facility near Vanderbilt. Stallworth."

"She mentioned it."

"We don't know when or how long."

His mama smiled, a brave smile, more than a cheerful one. "We're here. Whatever you need. You know that."

He did. It was another thing Russ could trust.

"Is Daddy at the church?" he asked.

She shook her head. "He and Connor are in the basement. All this rain — it got in and the sump pump might not be working." She looked at him, almost apologetically. And he knew the rain had come in through the cracks in the foundation.

"Aw, Mama," he said. "I'm sorry. I should've finished what I started, back in the spring."

"It's not your fault. All this rain," she repeated. "Don't worry. Daniel and Connor will figure it out."

"Connor couldn't even fix the leak in my kitchen," he said. He hadn't meant to sound so cross. He raised his palm, like he wanted to wipe out what he'd said.

Owen came out, smiling big, with his backpack and duffle. "Let's go!" he said.

"I need to see about my house," Russ told his mama. "Tell Daddy I'll be back in the morning to deal with the basement."

And the foundation. That was the heart of the problem.

On Saturday morning Russ loaded the wheelbarrow with the supplies he'd brought to the parsonage. His mama came out to meet him in the back yard.

"Daniel called you about the sump pump, didn't he?" she said.

"He said he fixed it."

"*They* fixed it," she said. "Daniel checked it this morning. Said the basement's drying out."

"Good. We can get on to the other problem," Russ said. "Where's Daddy? This is a two-man job."

"He was called away. Beauregard Tulley died. His family called at six o'clock. Beau was a hundred and four, but they said he was in perfect health. They were all torn up, like they couldn't believe it. They were planning a grand celebration for a hundred and five next month."

Russ unloaded a bag of mortar mix in the yard.

"You know how it is with a preacher," his mama said. "Get Connor to help you."

"I can manage by myself," he said.

"Why would you want to?" It was Connor, coming around the corner of the house. Russ faced his brother, with a glare, and for a moment everything seemed to come crashing down on him. What he knew now about his brother and his wife. The boy he would give his life for. How much did Connor know?

Connor was looking at him the same way.

After a silence, Russ said, "I guess you can help if you want to."

"I wouldn't know how to be the foreman," Connor said. "But I'm a damn good helper."

Russ looked around and thought about the job before them.

"Well, then, let's get at it. We've got work to do."

In the basement, on his knees beside his brother, Russ ran his hand over a long, deep crack in the foundation that was still damp from the rain. "Worse than I thought," he said.

They had already spent an hour of tedious patching outside, on the above-ground concrete. "I thought that was all it needed," Connor said. "Didn't look too bad out there."

"Guess that's the way of the world," Russ said.

"What do you mean?"

"Cracks everywhere, but the worst are the ones you can't see from the outside."

"Didn't you know about this?" Connor's voice changed to a kinder tune. "I don't mean anything by it. All I'm saying is it looks like it took a long time to get in this condition."

Russ thought about the work he and his daddy had done in the spring, filling the crevices outside. His daddy said they needed to work on a bad crack in the basement wall, but he was anxious to finish. Promised he'd come back. "I put it off. Should've known it would only get worse."

They went up into the yard, emptied more mortar mix into the wheelbarrow, added more water. Together they carried the wheelbarrow into the basement. Russ pointed Connor to the corner, under a hanging light. "Trowels over there," he said. "A chisel, too."

And then, pushing the mixture around with the hoe, Russ said, "You didn't say anything about Drew."

Connor's back was turned to him, but Russ imagined he might've flinched a little.

"Don't know what you mean. Every piece of news the family gets — we're all in it together." Connor returned with the tools. "Drew hasn't been out of my mind for a minute."

Russ grunted. "You didn't say anything." If Connor knew, this was the time to get it out.

Connor's gaze was steady. Earnest. "You don't know how much I love that boy."

Russ waited. Maybe there was more. But no. Connor wasn't going to say it.

Russ laid down the hoe, took the trowel, and looked at the long crack again. "Feel it. See how deep it goes. You've got to feel it before you can fix it. And chisel out the debris."

Connor put his hand on the joint, pushed his fingers into the gaping fissure, the problem that threatened the structure of the house. "I get it," he said, and he stuck a trowel in the mixture.

Russ chiseled out the joint. "It takes real work. Can't just smooth it over to make it look good. Hand me that trowel," he said. "Gotta get your hands in it, too. Like this." He used the trowel and then with his hands, pushed the mix into the heart of the crack.

"Let me," Connor said. Russ watched his brother follow his lead.

They worked like that for a while. Then Russ said, "I wasn't sure about us when I asked Nikki to marry me. I did what I thought was right. Marriage is hard work, watching out for things that go wrong, trying not to let everything fall apart."

"I can see you and Nikki are right now," Connor said, and after a minute, "I've made some mistakes. Came home to try to fix what I did ten years ago. But I don't know if I can."

Russ slapped more of the mixture onto the wall and stuck his hands into it, felt the crack filling up.

"We can fix this," he said. "We're gonna fix it somehow."

Chapter 62

The world tears itself apart in a million ways every day and a man goes about fixing what he can, Connor thought, as he rested in the swing on the porch. He had fixed a few cracks today.

Working with his hands brought back how he always felt after a hard day's work. A hot shower after sweating. The squeak of the swing and a breeze stirring as the sun went down brought a kind of solace you could only find on a front porch in a small town.

And then the sheriff pulled off the street, into the edge of the yard.

Sonny Bellingham might be here to see Ivy, Connor thought, but as he watched the sheriff walk toward the porch, he could see something in his stride that said bad news.

"Connor," Sonny said with a nod, coming up the steps.

Connor stood up. "Sheriff. You look like a man on a mission."

"You could say that."

"Can't think of anything I've done lately," Connor said.

"No, not that I know of." The sheriff paused, then said, "Joe Ray Loomis is dead."

Connor felt his heart pound against his rib cage. "Joe Ray, dead?" he said under his breath, but the words still didn't sound real. He hadn't wanted Joe Ray to die. He'd wanted to punch his lights out, but he hadn't wanted him to die.

"He was shot. We're still trying to piece it all together." Sonny took a long breath, and Connor had a feeling it would be a long story.

Sonny said, "I've been trying to track him down. Don't know where he hid out since the night he shot through your window. But he showed up at Ted Brisco's this morning. That's Lonnie Briscoe's daddy. Lonnie's wife ran off and left him and the kids. His stepmother, Amanda, helps with the kids when Lonnie's on a long-distance haul."

Connor nodded that he was following, though he didn't know why all of that mattered.

"Amanda was taking care of the kids, there at Ted's house. Four little ones."

"They saw what happened?"

Sonny kept on in the same patient voice. "Joe Ray came to the house. Hadn't been there for a long time, but it was the house he'd lived in, growing up. Lonnie's family raised him after his daddy killed his mama."

Connor could see there was no hurrying Sonny.

"Amanda said Joe Ray showed up wanting money. She told him he'd have to wait for Lonnie to come home. Wait on the porch. She said Joe Ray looked like he was wearing a month's worth of dirt. So he went out there and dozed off."

Sonny took a breath and he looked like it was not easy to tell to rest. "The little boy found a gun in the tomato patch behind the house. Must have washed up in all this rain. He took it to where Joe Ray was. I guess Joe Ray was startled. Best we can figure, he grabbed at the gun." Long breath. "You wouldn't think it would fire, buried all that time. You can't trust an old gun."

"Oh God," Connor whispered. "The boy?"

"By the grace of God, the little boy wasn't pointing it at himself or his sister when it fired."

The screen door opened, and Ivy came out. Smiling, but only for an instant. "What's the trouble?" she asked.

And Connor had to listen to the sheriff go over it all again.

Ivy gave a little cry. "How old is that child?"

"Five. Same as Michael," Sonny said. "Amanda ran to the porch when she heard the gunshot. The little girl was out there, screaming, but the boy — Amanda told us he hadn't made a peep since it happened."

It seemed like a long time before Sonny took up the story again. When he did, Connor had the feeling he was getting to the point, finally. A report, coming to an end.

"Looks like Joe Ray must have buried the gun on their property ten years ago. Ten years, and God only knows how many storms, but today in all this rain, it washed up somehow. We'll wait for ballistics, but it's a fair bet the gun's the same one that shot Raleigh Dalton at the Back Home Market."

The fireflies came at dusk and danced around with their lights, and then they disappeared as night wore on. Connor sat in the swing for a long time after the sheriff left.

Much later than his parents' typical bedtime, his daddy opened the screen door. "Just came out to say goodnight, Son."

"Goodnight," Connor said. He waited, knowing there was more, as there usually was when your daddy was a preacher.

His daddy stepped out on the porch and closed the door. "I was thinking about that night Joe Ray shot up your window. You were out here, asleep. Saved your life."

Connor pushed the swing a little. Joe Ray was not going to shoot at him ever again. Joe Ray, who had lied, lied, lied. Somehow the truth found its way to the surface, with the rain washing up the evidence of ten years past.

Some things just won't stay buried, Connor thought. Guns. Mistakes. Secrets of all kind.

He ought to feel a weight lifted.

"Why does it all still feel so heavy?" he asked his daddy.

"A man died today. And a child will be living with that tragedy for a lifetime," his daddy said. "It's enough sorrow to make any heart heavy."

Connor thought for a few more minutes. His daddy didn't go anywhere, just stood at the rail, staring at the stars.

"You think this town will ever forgive me?" Connor said. "I didn't pull the trigger, but I was fool enough to be in that market. Is that all anybody in this town will ever think when they see me? That young punk. That shooting on the Fourth of July."

"It's not the town that won't forgive you, Connor." His daddy turned to him. "It's you."

Connor didn't say anything. Maybe that was what he'd been carrying all this time. He'd listened to his daddy's sermons for years, about atonement and forgiveness and redemption, but he still didn't know how to get there.

After a while his daddy said, "Did you hear about the Back Home?"

Connor had a hazy memory of a woman selling him a twelve-pack, telling him a big oil company had bought the property. They'd be tearing down the Back Home.

"It's about time they took it down," he said.

Back Home was nothing but a dream, anyway.

Chapter 63

The air in the kitchen was the heavy quiet that settles after a storm.

Kitty was thinking about the storm that had flooded the basement, the one that washed up Joe Ray Loomis's gun. That one long gone, but not the storm in the Burdette family.

Starting with Lady's death and quieting only for a brief time before another round of thunderclaps and lightning hit with even more strength. And now the electricity that had charged the air was replaced by a quieter current. Quieter, but with an undeniable force all its own.

"Six weeks?" Kitty said into the phone as she set a plate of pancakes in front of Owen.

Russ was back in Nashville. He and Nikki had met with Drew's treatment team.

"Six weeks at least," Russ said. "Rehab for motor and cognitive skills. He might get to come home then, but he'll need outpatient therapy at Mercer General." Kitty heard the weariness in her son's voice. "He'll go to Stallworth Friday. Exactly two weeks since he ran and played and rode his bike. Things he might not ever do again."

"He will," Kitty said. She had no basis for thinking it. But she had to hope because what else could she do but hope?

Russ and Nikki had rented a room in a residence hotel near Stallworth. Mostly it would be Nikki staying there, he said, but she'd come home from time to time. "I need to work when I can. But we're trying to do the right thing for both boys," Russ said. "Is Owen there?"

Kitty let Owen talk to his daddy. She heard him ask what he always asked: "Is Drew coming home?" Then "Can I go to see him?"

Kitty knew the answers. Russ had told her Drew never spoke of his brother. Didn't respond when they mentioned Owen. "I think he knows who Owen is,"

Russ had said. "But there's something missing. It's like he doesn't remember what's supposed to be between them."

This time, Owen didn't sulk when his daddy answered. He cut the call short. "I gotta get my racquet. Ivy's taking me to tennis camp," he said, and handed the phone back to Kitty.

Now in the aftermath of the storm, the days were settling into a routine that could go on and on, Kitty thought. Only God knew how long.

The time had come to go back into Lady's house, to deal with her personal effects.

Kitty started in the walk-in closet, making fast work of boxing up clothes and shoes and purses that were expensive and fashionable — decades ago. Now it would all go to the Clothes Closet at the church. The neediest woman in Mercer County might come out in a fine linen suit, still in good condition, and she'd be glad to have it.

Lady's closet fit into six banker boxes.

Kitty went downstairs to join Daniel and Connor in Lady's library. A few shelves of books, but the two metal file cabinets made it seem more like an office than a library.

Kitty looked at the folders strewn all around.

"More financial records," Daniel said, glancing up from a document. "A lot of this goes back to the mill, when Daddy sold it. But some of it, we'll need to get to Don Petrie."

"I never knew having money could be so hard," Connor said. "How did she manage it all?"

Kitty noticed a stack of photo albums and pulled an empty banker's box over to the shelves. "We'll take these home," she said.

What pictures would Lady have kept? she wondered. What were the significant moments that she'd wanted to capture? Kitty couldn't resist flipping through the albums. The first was full of tennis photos. She didn't linger over it.

She'd want to spend time with the others. Lady and Jack and Daniel as Daniel was growing up. Family holidays when Russ, Ivy, and Connor were young. It was not lost on Kitty that Lady had fewer pictures of her grandchildren than Kitty had of hers, in just nine years.

In the last album, Lady was a child and then a pretty young woman, before Jack. Black and white photos, some so faded that they were hard to make out.

One oval five-by-seven studio portrait, in a fancy mat, made Kitty catch her breath.

"Look at this!" she said. "Who is it?"

Connor came over. "I'd say me if I didn't know better."

Daniel raised his eyebrows when he saw it. "Lady's brother. Has to be her brother. Her twin."

"Lady never mentioned how much Connor resembled her brother," Kitty said.

"Mr. Petrie said something about her twin that died young, that he'd been on her mind lately," Connor said.

"Landon." Daniel nodded. "Don Petrie said Lady talked about him being lost to her."

"She told Mr. Petrie I was the spittin' image of her lost brother," Connor said.

Kitty gave an exasperated sigh. "Why have I not heard anything about this? All these years I've been in the family, I never heard a word about her brother."

Daniel said, "I didn't know much about him. He died before I was born — *tragically,* Don Petrie called it. All I remember Lady ever saying about him was that she didn't even get to bring him home to bury him. I don't know the circumstances."

Kitty felt a shiver. That could've happened to Connor. She saw a shadow come into Connor's eyes, like he was thinking the same thing.

Connor walked over to Lady's desk, leaned against it, and crossed his arms. After a minute, he said, "You know, I asked Lady for money once. She called me white trash."

Kitty felt a little groan in the back of her throat. "What a *cruel* thing for a grandmother to say! Lady had a sharp tongue, but even for her..." She let her voice trail off.

She saw Daniel's face grimace in pain. And she heard the pain in his voice when he asked Connor, "Why were you wanting money, Son? When was that? Was it so you could leave home?"

"It was a few days before that Fourth of July, before the Back Home... and everything. But it was the last time I saw her."

Kitty knew Connor would tell it in his own time, or not. It wouldn't do any good to ask. She closed the album on the face of the lost boy, the boy named Landon. "We always knew Lady favored you over Russ and Ivy when you were a child," she said. "Now it makes more sense, if she was seeing her brother in you." She stacked the albums in the box and put on the lid.

Connor waited a moment, then left the room, pulling out his pack of cigarettes.

Daniel went back to the document he'd been poring over and stuck it in a file folder.

"Can we wind this up?" Kitty said. "I've had enough for today."

Daniel seemed to still be trying to figure it all out. "It was like her brother's story all over again. Connor left home, too young, like Landon did. How she must've feared it was life repeating itself. She couldn't save her brother. Couldn't even bring him home to bury him. Maybe she believed she should've tried harder to save her grandson."

"You think that's why she made him her heir?" Kitty said.

"She wasn't long for this earth. It was the last thing she did. Tried to bring him home."

Kitty heard something like a plea in Daniel's voice, a plea for her to forgive his mother, when he said, "Lady was trying to atone."

Chapter 64

A real date, Ivy thought. "Kinda uptown," Sonny had said about the place in Durbin Falls when he'd called her and wanted to know if they could try again.

The restaurant reminded Ivy of places on the Gulf. White tablecloths, soft lights, servers in white shirts and black pants.

"You approve?" Sonny asked.

"I do," Ivy said. "Not that I didn't approve of Catfish Heaven."

"I thought it might be bad karma to go there again," he said.

He picked up the wine list and handed it to Ivy. "I'm more of a beer guzzler than a wine sipper," he said. "Something tells me you might be a wine connoisseur."

Ivy cut her eyes at him. "You don't fool anybody with that 'I'm just a country sheriff' act, Sonny Bellingham." She glanced at the list, which was not extensive, and chose a label that was moderately priced. "I haven't touched wine since I came to Montpier," she said.

"Then I'm thinking it's about time," Sonny said.

A young woman took the order and left menus. And then Ivy saw Skip Garrison coming toward them from the bar in the far corner. Maybe this was the place Skip was talking about, that day at the cemetery, when he said they should go to Durbin Falls for a drink. Ivy wouldn't have been surprised to know he was a regular.

Skip pulled up a chair beside Ivy and sat down without asking. A presumptuous gesture, she thought, but Sonny just said, "Hey, Skip."

"Nice place, don't you think?" He darted a look at Ivy, supposed to be a meaningful glance, she guessed. Seemed it was not lost on him that she'd turned him down but now was here with Sonny. "I'm not gonna break up your little party. Just wanted a sidebar with the sheriff for a minute." He grinned at Ivy. "That OK with you, judge?"

Ivy picked up the menu. "Go ahead."

Skip went right to it. "I've been on a little vacation in Maui. Haven't seen you since old Joe Ray took that bullet. Shot with his own gun, a gun he buried ten years ago. Shot by that little boy. Now that's the stuff of a Hollywood movie."

"It's sad, is what it is. Think of what that child has to carry the rest of his days." Sonny's voice was flat, with an undercurrent that ought to make Skip feel foolish.

But the remark seemed to float right over Skip's head. He looked at Ivy. "And now Connor Burdette's in the clear. Joe Ray always said it was Connor's gun and Connor did the shooting, but now we know the truth. Case closed."

"Raleigh Dalton said it was Connor, too," Sonny said.

"Yep, I believe he did," Skip said.

They had Ivy's attention now. She laid down the menu and leaned forward.

"You oughta know he did." Sonny's tone not so cordial now. "You were his attorney."

"Skip?" The word escaped from Ivy's lips.

"Hold on now." Skip raised his palm and pushed against the air. "All I did was sit by the boy's bedside there in the hospital while he talked to the Chief of Police at the time, who was trying to get it straight what happened. Raleigh's granddaddy called me and asked me if he could hire me. I told him Raleigh was the victim. He just needed to tell his story. But Mr. Dalton thought it was a good precaution to have an attorney present, seeing how Raleigh was a black boy. Justice is supposed to be blind, but my experience is, it sure can see black and white."

The server came back with the wine, and everyone was quiet while she uncorked it, let Sonny taste, and poured. "Do you need another glass?" she asked Sonny.

"I'm not staying, darlin'," Skip said.

"You didn't tell me you were Raleigh Dalton's attorney," Ivy said.

"Nothing to tell." Skip gave an elaborate shrug. "I spent a few hours with the boy. Making sure nothing went south when the Chief was asking him questions in the hospital, and then when Sheriff Talbot took over the investigation, we did it all over again."

He looked back at Sonny, at Ivy again, back and forth. After a long moment he said, "Guess I oughta leave you kids to your evening."

"Skip," Ivy said, "did Raleigh tell you the truth, that Joe Ray was the one who shot him, that the two of them had planned the robbery, and Connor didn't know anything about it?"

A broad grin spread across Skip's face. "Ah now, Ivy," he said, raising a cautionary forefinger, "you know it wouldn't be ethical for me to divulge what a client told me."

Ivy felt her cheeks turning hot with anger. "What was that about, at the cemetery, telling me you would have represented Connor? You said you could've kept Connor out of jail."

He started to say something, but Ivy didn't let him finish.

"You would've given up Raleigh Dalton. That's how you could've gotten Connor off." She felt her voice rising. "You don't give a damn about ethics, Skip. You don't care about clients. Or anybody. You're just an opportunist." She glanced at Sonny, who had the faintest smile curling one corner of his mouth.

"I think we've done just about enough rehashing of old times," Skip said, trying for his good ole boy voice, but not quite keeping the irritation out of his tone. He scooted back and stood up. "Y'all have a nice dinner now."

Ivy watched him go and said, just above a whisper, "He'd better stay away from my family." She touched her cheek. Her hand was cold against her flushed face.

"Piece of work," Sonny said, "but I think you got to him a little bit."

"Nobody does," Ivy said. "Nobody gets to Skip Garrison."

Sonny was easy to talk to, too easy. Ivy had to watch herself when he brought up Lady's death again later that night, as they were sitting in the swing on the front porch of the parsonage.

"Everybody that investigates cases has those where all the pieces don't quite fit," Sonny said. "A murder where you have evidence against the suspect, but you know in your gut he's innocent. Or a rape case where the scumbag that you know did it has a trumped-up alibi you can't break. You just know all the pieces will never fit together right. This one feels like that."

Why are you so sure the pieces don't fit?" Ivy asked. "Why can't you just let it go?"

"I think someone struggled with Lady at the top of the stairs. That's when the bracelet broke," he said. "Lady's wrist was fractured. I don't see how she could've held on to the bracelet with a fractured wrist. My theory is, somebody put the bracelet in Lady's hand, and closed her fingers around it. Whoever did that didn't know about the two small diamonds at the top of the stairs." He paused, and a little wrinkle etched itself between his eyebrows, like he was thinking harder. "Now I'd say the chances are good that it was an accident, but if somebody tampered with the evidence, that puts another slant on it. Makes it seem a little more — sinister." He looked at Ivy.

"Not me," Ivy said.

"No. The timeline tells us you were at the college when she died."

"Not Connor."

"No, the manager of the apartments where he was living, two hours away from Montpier, said he was complaining about the AC unit not working, right about the time Lady died."

Ivy waited, and finally Sonny said, "Daniel was at the church. Kitty was at the Farmer's Market. I haven't had a chance to talk to Russ and Nikki."

"They have all they can manage right now, Sonny. Surely you understand that."

"I do," he said.

He kept trying to hold her gaze, or was she just imagining it?

"Are you going to keep investigating?" she asked. "Can't you just close the case?"

Sonny rubbed his jaw. He sounded like he'd rather not say it. "Ivy, there's a whole lot of money involved, a new will, and an accident where the facts don't all line up."

"You're kind of like a terrier, Sonny," she said.

He gave a little laugh. "Yeah, I guess I am."

"Nobody's going to blame you if you let it go."

"You're probably right," he said. She waited, but he didn't say he would let it go.

"My vacation's coming up next week," he said. "I'm taking Michael to El Paso to see his other grandparents for a few days. Paula's parents. When are you going back to the Gulf?"

"Not sure," she said. A pause. "I've applied for the English position at the college."

A big smile spread across his face. "I never believed you when you said you were just here for the summer."

Ivy was not expecting what happened next. He touched her cheek. Then he took her face in his hands and kissed her.

And she kissed back. For a moment. Then pulled away. The swing squeaked on its chain.

"I guess I know what you're thinking," he said.

No, Ivy thought. He couldn't know the secret she carried: Nikki was the missing piece in the case he wouldn't give up. And Ivy couldn't tell him. She couldn't ever be absolutely honest.

"What do you think I'm thinking?" she asked.

"That you've been hurt. And so have I. Not the same way as you, but we might not be ready to start something new. Either one of us."

"Are you?" Ivy asked. "Ready to start something new?"

He made a face, an exaggerated frown. "Sometimes I think, yeah, I am. Right now is one of those times." A smile, full of tenderness. "But I'm about to go where Paula grew up, visit with her parents, do a lot of remembering Paula with them. Michael and I have done that a couple of times since she's been gone, and it always sets me back. Sometimes I start hoping, and then it feels shaky like I'm trying to climb a ladder that has a few rungs missing." His voice trailed off.

Ivy said, "I've been on that ladder."

For a few minutes the only sounds were the squeaky swing, crickets croaking, and down the street, music playing, like there was a party.

After a while, they walked to the edge of the porch. The music from down the street had turned to something slow, full of longing. Ivy wished she could ask

Sonny to give her time, give himself time, and if she stayed in Montpier, maybe they'd both be ready to start something new.

But she was a secret-keeper. That was not likely to change. And she would not let herself get close to a man when she knew from the get-go that she was keeping a huge secret from him.

He took both her hands and looked at her for a long moment. The music pulled at her, but her secret pulled her another way. It made her heart ache a little to let this good man go.

"Have a good trip, Sonny," she said. "You and Michael, have a good trip."

"I hope the college hires you, Ivy," he said. "I hope you stay in Montpier."

And then he took her in his arms, and they began to dance on the porch of the house with the cracked foundation.

Chapter 65

"It's so hard to find your way home."

Daniel closed his Bible after he'd read the prodigal son parable from St. Luke. He grasped the podium and began the sermon he'd wanted to preach ever since Connor had come back to Montpier. But he had not felt the Lord's whisper saying it was time, not until yesterday. As he'd watched Connor and Russ work on those cracks in the foundation, the story of the lost son had come to him in a new light. Preachers always mined the parable for the lesson that the Heavenly Father welcomes any wayward child who returns and repents, just as the father in the scriptures opened his arms to the son who'd gone astray. But the Lord had laid something else on Daniel's heart.

"Everybody gets lost some time." He spoke gently to his flock, his voice instructive, not accusatory. "We fail each other. We fail ourselves. And we fail God. We measure the miles between what we were and what we are, and we try to find our way home."

Daniel could see he'd struck a chord with the congregation. The hush, the solemn faces, even now and then a nod.

Looking out over the sanctuary, he saw five hundred prodigals, contemplating his words.

He let his gaze fall on Kitty. Always there, near the front. He counted on it. Took it for granted, he supposed. Russ and Owen beside her — and, today, even Ivy.

And then his heart lifted, like he was hearing the Mormon Tabernacle Choir sing the *Hallelujah Chorus*, when Connor slipped in the side door and into the pew beside Kitty.

And Daniel knew for certain that this was the sermon God had meant him to preach.

"How many times have we read this story about the prodigal son? It's so tempting to put on our pious faces and say, 'Look at that lost boy! What was he thinking? All that riotous living, and look how he wound up, eating with the hogs!' It's so tempting to point a finger." Daniel's voice quietened even more. "Friends, you don't have to break the law. You don't have to flee to a far country. You can be lost, sitting right here in your pew on Sunday morning. Some of you might be feeling a little lost right now. Some of you might've felt part of yourself lost, for years, and you don't know if you can find your way back."

A middle-aged couple he'd counseled, the Kimbroughs, occupied the same pew every Sunday, going through the motions of worship like going through the motions of marriage. Daniel noticed Clay slip his arm around Dana's shoulders.

"Now there's no map for finding your way home. Never has been. Just these old writings." Daniel held up his Bible. "The Word of God tells us the Heavenly Father is waiting to forgive. But you have to find your own way back."

The Carlton brothers, both in their eighties, had sat on opposite sides of the sanctuary for years. Some old feud that Daniel wondered if they even remembered. Nobody else did. He noticed Floyd glance toward Luther. A minute later, Luther glanced toward Floyd.

"This Sunday morning, some of us in this church are trying to find our way back from our failures," Daniel preached. "Trying to forgive each other, trying to forgive ourselves. Some are waiting for loved ones to find their way home, and that's a lost feeling, too."

He glanced at Connor but passed over him quickly. Scanning the sanctuary, he saw the Carlton brothers, from across the room, look at each other and let their gazes linger.

"We are all prodigals," Daniel said. "We get lost in countless ways and spend our time on earth trying to return to what feels like home. We are forever trying to find our way back."

Daniel preached his heart out. He had the feeling his whole ministry had been preparing him for this sermon.

The altar call was at times a formality. A hymn sung, two verses. Some new residents in town might join the church. Occasionally someone would come to the altar and kneel. If somebody walked the aisle and grabbed Daniel's hand and said, "I want to be saved! I want to be baptized!" it was a good day.

Today, men, women, even some young people walked down the aisles and knelt at the altar. Praying silently, a few tears shed, as voices lifted in the old hymn, *Softly and Tenderly.*

Daniel, feeling the spirit among them, motioned to the organist after the second verse and she continued to play the chorus. No voices, but the words everyone knew seemed to fill the room.

Come home, come home. Ye who are weary, come home.

Daniel watched Billy Dell Sykes, who had thrown his pregnant, unmarried daughter out of the house, walk across the sanctuary toward her. The big, rough welder put his arms around her, and Daniel saw his lips move. Maybe, Daniel hoped, he was telling her, *Come home.*

The line was long at the end of the service, everyone wanting to speak to Daniel at the door. He shook hands, hugged the old women, and kept saying, "Just what the Lord laid on me today."

Daniel did not expect Connor to linger, and he didn't. But Daniel's heart was full of gratitude. Something had brought his son, the prodigal, home at last. God had led him there, Daniel knew, as he shook hands with Floyd and Luther Carlton. They came out together.

Chapter 66

It came to Ivy during her daddy's sermon.

That must have been why she'd felt the nudge to go to church. Her daddy would say God's whisper. She supposed God had been whispering all morning. And now that Ivy was certain she knew the right thing to do, a sense of peace washed over her like cool water.

Her family would be so pleased.

But as they were gathering at the Sunday table, the old phone interrupted.

Ivy could always tell when her mama was speaking to Boone. A particular cadence, the tone she used with her brother. "We're fixing to have Sunday dinner, but what's on your mind?" she said, and then, "Uh huh... Uh huh."

Ivy darted a smile at Connor. He rolled his eyes. Her daddy pushed his chair back and went to the never-ending coffeepot, while they waited.

Her mama ended the call and came to the table. "I suppose that was worth disturbing our meal," she said. "Boone was bragging that Frank Steele showed up at his church this morning. Pumping hands and grinning like he was running for office, Boone said. Stopped short of kissing babies, he said. He figures the Colonel is looking for another church home."

Ivy thought Boone ought to know about pumping hands and kissing babies.

"Somewhere else he thinks he might get to run things would be my guess," her daddy said. "He didn't have to leave First Baptist. After he brought his nephew to my office, I took that as an olive branch. I was hoping we could work together from now on."

"You have too much forgiveness in you, Daniel," Ivy's mama said.

"Didn't you pay attention to Daddy's sermon?" Connor said.

Ivy hadn't seen her daddy's face light up like that in a long time. "Just preached what the Lord laid on my heart." His eyes glistened a little as he gave Connor a lingering, earnest look.

"I had to twist my sister's arm to go," Connor said. "You know what a sinner she is."

Though it was the other way around, Ivy had not had to twist Connor's arm as hard as she might have expected. "I wasn't the one that came dragging in late," she said.

"Warmed my heart to see you there," her daddy said. "Both of you."

He blinked, then said, "Your mama's fine meal's getting cold," and he bowed his head and prayed, "Thank you, Lord, for small mercies."

"I'm not going back to Wexler-Fitzhugh," Ivy announced, as the pot roast went around.

A moment passed, like something under the words had to sink in.

"You're coming home?" her mama said.

"My sister, the prodigal," Connor said, and he smiled, almost like his old self.

Ivy thought, I've always been coming home. "That's what struck me this morning. Your sermon, Daddy. This is where I belong."

And she told them she'd applied to teach full-time at the college. Her mama was sure she'd be hired, but her daddy frowned. "Frank Steele's in tight with the powers that be at the college. He told me about the summer class you're teaching. Remember? He made it sound like the position was his to offer. If you'd just talk to his friend — Keller, was it? But Frank might be singing a different tune now. All because of what he thinks of me. I hope not, Ivy."

"Doesn't matter. I'll find something to do," she said. "Russ and Nikki and the boys will need a lot of help. But I'm not going back to Wexler-Fitzhugh."

Sunday dinner stretched out longer than usual. And then Ivy wrote her letter of resignation to Wexler-Fitzhugh. The rest of the afternoon slid by like so many languid summer Sundays. That night Ivy's parents went to the funeral home, a visitation for one more soul looking for heaven's door, her daddy remarked on his way out. He said the church had lost four of their old darlings during the summer, but God had sent four babies to young couples in the congregation. Funny how it evens out, he'd said.

The heat was too much. The old air-conditioner at the parsonage couldn't keep up. Ivy and Connor wound up on the porch, Ivy in the swing, Connor on the top step, leaning against the rail. Ivy remembered another night, early July, he'd just come home — seemed so much longer than a month! — and she'd wondered if she could ever trust him again. Looking at her brother now, she could see he'd changed. And she had changed, too.

"I need to go back for the rest of my things," she said. "You want to go with me? I was thinking Friday. Close out my apartment and come back Monday."

"Sure," he said. He lit a cigarette and shifted a little. "I'll drive."

"You don't have a license," she said.

"I plan to change that. Going to the DMV tomorrow. And I've decided to buy a truck."

"A truck would be great," Ivy said. "I was wondering how to get my furniture to the consignment. And I'll have boxes to bring home." Home, she thought. Finally home.

"I'm glad you're staying, Ivy," Connor said.

"It feels right," she said.

The fireflies were coming out. Ivy watched their lights flicker and thought about her tender-hearted little brother who had cried when she caught them, so many years ago. She thought about the squeak of the swing that nobody seemed inclined to oil. And the way the soft night air felt on her skin. And about the little bit of light between her and her brother.

Chapter 67

"I need some money," Connor said.

Don Petrie leaned forward and peered at him over his wire-rimmed glasses.

"I got my driver's license this morning," Connor said. "I want to buy a truck."

The old lawyer gave him a good looking-over. "Going somewhere?"

Connor met his keen gray eyes. "Had about enough of walking."

Petrie finally sat back in his desk chair. He was so thin that the chair, framed by shelves of dusty law books, seemed to swallow him.

"It shouldn't be a problem. It's my money," Connor said. "All coming to me anyway."

"In due time." Don Petrie's brow furrowed. "In due time, Son."

Connor leaned forward, toward the big, cluttered desk. "I know you told me probate could take six months, maybe up to a year," he said, trying now to sound like he was asking, not demanding. "You've been good to me, Mr. Petrie, explaining all the stuff I woulda never understood. I don't mean to cause you any trouble. I just thought you could give me an advance till probate goes through, cause you know I'll be good for it."

The old man's frail shoulders relaxed a little. Connor remembered something his daddy always said about a kind word. Maybe that was all the old man needed. Just a kind word.

Petrie made his long reedy fingers into a steeple. "Four months for probate, best case. Lady's estate is not complicated. We worked through it all when Jack died. You're the sole beneficiary. Nobody has opposed the will and they're not likely to." He gazed at the long window with its heavy drapes pulled back, letting in a slant of sunshine. "My hands would be tied if there was an open investigation, but the autopsy report ruled her death an accident."

Just be quiet, Connor told himself. He's just checking off the boxes in his own mind.

A minute passed before Petrie turned back to Connor. "When you're my age, you blink a few times, and four months" — he snapped his fingers — "gone like *that.* It's not a long time to wait for a fortune, or what passes for a fortune here in Montpier. Not a long time at all." He shifted in his seat. "Unless you're needing to get out of town in a hurry."

His gray eyes narrowed again. Connor knew he was really asking a question.

"Four months is a long time for me to walk everywhere I go. Or depend on my family to drive me," Connor said. "I think Lady would want me to have wheels. She left everything to me. Why would she want me to be walking the streets?"

Petrie sat up as straight as his crooked skeleton would let him. He put his bony hands on his desk. "You can sign a note. When probate goes through, you can repay the debt."

"Fair enough."

"What amount did you have in mind?"

"Fifty," Connor said. Too quickly, he realized. "Fifty thousand ought to do it."

Petrie grunted, and his brow furrowed. He waited a beat to answer. "Sure as hell ought to. You must be wanting all the bells and whistles." His words sharp with disapproval.

"Fifty's a drop in the bucket, Mr. Petrie, when you consider Lady's estate," Connor said.

"Fifty thousand dollars is never a drop in any kind of bucket, Son." One side of the lawyer's mouth turned up a little, like it wanted to grin but couldn't quite manage. "Check back tomorrow. Unless there's an urgency I don't know about." Those eyes, peering from above his glasses, still questioning.

"Tomorrow's fine. I appreciate it." Connor shook Mr. Petrie's hand, not too hard. He sure wouldn't want the old bones to crack. He'd wait until he had the money to mention the rest. About that old debt. What he owed. A debt he intended to settle soon.

Chapter 68

Bittersweet was the feeling, as Ivy walked through the halls of the Humanities Building.

The students and most faculty had not returned yet. Ivy unlocked her office, and Connor gave a low whistle. Maybe thinking about what she was giving up. The thought flew through her mind, for just a moment. She cleared some books and took from the walls an award and a few pictures students had given her. The next occupant would appreciate that she left the bookcases nearly full. It would have taken more than the weekend to go through her file cabinet as she should have, but she was confident nothing she shredded mattered too much. She managed to leave with only one box of records she might need if matters came up about student grades.

Staying at her apartment was the hardest part. All the reminders, like the bed she'd shared with Preston. But that was all in a dark past. She packed clothes, some dishes and pots and pans. Her TV. A good reading lamp. Someday she might live somewhere besides the parsonage.

"I couldn't have done this without your truck," she told Connor, when they were taking the last load of furniture to the consignment.

"And my muscle," he said, flexing his bicep.

"That, too."

On the way home, Connor reminded her of the summer trips their family took in a Datsun station wagon. "The three of us stuffed in the back seat," he said. "Me in the middle. Y'all always made me take the middle."

"You never complained," Ivy said. "You didn't complain about much of anything then."

"Not till later," Connor said. "I got to where everything made me mad."

Ivy didn't want to dig up Connor's past. She didn't want to spoil a good trip. And so they cruised on in silence. Ivy saw how Connor focused on the road, his gaze intense, like he was seeing something far beyond the flat terrain of lower Alabama.

Then, just south of Tuscaloosa, her brother said, "I'm gonna be leaving soon, Ivy."

Ivy felt the words hang in the air, like she couldn't bear to let them sink in. "No, Connor. Please. You don't have to leave."

"I do. Best for everybody." He glanced at her with that old smile of his. "Hey, at least Mama and Daddy are getting one of their kids back."

"Connor," she whispered. "Not again."

"Don't worry," he said. He made it sound like it was no more than a weekend trip. "It's not like before. I'll come home for Christmas. We can sing *Joy to the World,* all one big happy family like we used to be." He gave a cynical laugh. Then, "Seriously, this time it's for good."

"Where will you go?" Ivy asked, after a moment.

"I'll head back to the last place, with the Mexicans. They were good to me. I want to see what they need, now that I can do something for them. And then, I don't know. I left here ten years ago with no plan. Couldn't do much worse than that."

It was a while before Connor spoke again. Still looking to something far beyond the blacktop, he said, "It matters to me. It's important. I'm trying to do the right thing. Give me that, Ivy. Trust me, even if you can't understand."

Ivy was a secret keeper. She carried the burden of Nikki's secrets. And now she would carry her brother's secret, too. About the son he was giving up, the son who would always believe Connor was his uncle. The sacrifice he was making. For Drew. And Russ. And Nikki.

She wouldn't say it, he didn't need her to say it, but she understood.

The silence was comforting as they headed on, toward home.

Chapter 69

Some things in the past need a wrecking ball.

Connor had said his goodbyes that morning. Promised his family he'd be calling. On his way out of town, he made one last stop at the Back Home Market. Going down next week.

On three of the gas pumps, block-printed signs said, "No Regular." Connor pulled up to one of them for the higher grade. No bells and whistles on the old Chevy Silverado. He'd bought it for just seventeen thousand. Exactly the kind of truck he'd need if Juan Luis would take him back. In the week he'd had it, he'd added nine hundred miles to its hundred and five thousand, driving to the Gulf with Ivy. So far, it was reliable, which was more than you could say about Juan Luis's clunker.

Connor waited beside the pump, feeling that old regret creep up once more, the weight in his heart when he thought about how grief and miles and time roar down together and leave you far from all you ever knew or wanted.

Across from him, at the only pump that sold Regular, he saw Raleigh Dalton's grandfather pull up in his old Ford Ranger, rust and rattle.

Mr. Dalton climbed out of his truck, looking more crippled than Connor remembered from just a few weeks ago when he'd mowed the old man's yard. Bent over, legs spraddled like a baby learning to walk. He took out his wallet and a credit card as he limped up to the gas pump.

Connor took a few steps toward him and said, "Mr. Dalton, it's me. Connor Burdette."

The old man squinted like he was trying to place him. Or maybe his eyesight was failing.

Then he said, "I know who you are." His voice had a hard edge. When he had the gas pumping, he glanced at Connor's truck. "I thought you came into some money. What I heard."

"Guess you heard right. My grandmother died."

"You didn't buy no fancy car."

"I'm spending my money the way I want to," Connor said.

He watched as the old man seemed to consider, then turned to the pump. The numbers flashed, slow-moving. At around three dollars, Mr. Dalton looked back at Connor. "A lawyer, white shirt, striped tie, more years on him than I got on me, he showed up at my place with a big cashier's check. Wouldn't say who it was from." Then, a sideways glance, "But I had a notion."

"I still think about Raleigh," Connor said. Words that sounded like they came from a long way off, from another time. A plea from the boy whose life lost its map, here at the Back Home.

"Cain't buy your way outta grief, son," Mr. Dalton said, his voice sounding like old hurt poured in wet long ago, hardened now.

"You know you could buy a new truck with that check," Connor said.

"Nah. It came in handy though. There's young people at my church that can't afford college, so I set up a little fund in Raleigh's name." He rested his hand on the battered hood. "I don't need new. I trust dents. They feel true to me."

Connor finished up. Mr. Dalton was still pumping. "Living's all about collisions," he said. "I can see you know that."

A black Dodge Charger with a lightning bolt on the side pulled into the lot. Mufflers long gone, music blaring, the car zipped around the bays twice before finally parking behind the Ford Ranger. A rail-thin kid with long, greasy hair stepped out from the passenger side. "Hey you! Look at me, old man. I'm talking at you!"

The scowl on Mr. Dalton's face told Connor that he had no trouble hearing the jeers, but he kept staring at the numbers' slow crawl on the pump. Twenty-six-sixty-nine, seventy, seventy-one. Connor didn't wait to see what Mr. Dalton would do. He called out, "I'm finished here. You can have this pump."

"We want Regular!" The kid moved closer to Mr. Dalton. "Why you taking so long with that old beater? Why don't you just push it out of the way and let a real car get some gas? Do yourself a favor. Send it to the junkyard. You and that rust bucket are just old scrap."

Connor took the measure of the young man and was not surprised to see skittering eyes and rotten teeth. Not as young as he'd sounded, though. Prison tattoos on skinny arms. Connor put him at twenty-five. Halfway to judgment day, like every other junkie he'd ever seen. The driver, wearing a red do-rag, stepped out of the Charger. He was older, probably early thirties, steroid muscled, his arms ringed with prison tattoos.

Connor raised a calming hand as he approached the junkie and spoke like he was dealing with a wounded animal. "Nobody wants any trouble. Give it a minute. Just back off."

"Who you telling to back off?" He glanced at Connor, barely. He kept edging toward Mr. Dalton and when he was close enough, he kicked the leg the old man favored.

Mr. Dalton yelped, almost fell, but before Connor could get to him, he righted himself. "Take twenty years off me and I'd whip your ass, you no good little punk!" he called out. "Yours, too!" He pointed a crooked finger at Do-rag. A towering figure, hard, cold eyes, something dead there. He made the slightest movement, his body suddenly rigid, and Connor wished Mr. Dalton didn't have such a mouth on him.

But it was the little punk who puffed up, stepped forward, and with one shove pushed the old man to the pavement. Mr. Dalton's head hit the concrete edge around the pump.

"Hey! *Hey*!" Connor jerked the punk away, his arm as slight as a stick, and flung him against the Ranger. With one hand, he grabbed him by the throat and forced his head against the window. Feeling rage boiling, Connor wasn't sure what he would do next. He wanted to push that scrawny neck right through the glass.

Breathe, he thought. *You don't want to do this.* The trapped animal's eyes were wide with terror.

With a shove, he let him go. He had no words. The punk, rubbing at his throat, stumbled toward the Charger.

Connor rushed to the old man and saw his head was bleeding. "I'm gettin' help," he said, punching in 9-1-1.

Mr. Dalton rubbed at the ugly slash, gushing blood, matting his hair. "I've had worse. Get that punk," he mumbled, then pointed a bloody finger, "That no good goon, too!"

It was Do-rag at the open rear door of the Charger. He turned, raised his hand, and pointed a gun at the old man.

In that moment, all Connor could see was Joe Ray, handgun drawn. He thought, I won't make the same mistake again, and he moved to shield Raleigh's grandfather.

A flash, and Connor heard the sound that almost always changes everything for someone.

Chapter 70

The next Fourth of July

Time roars by like a freight train. But if you're Drew Burdette, ten years old, and hurt in a way you'll never get over, Time is as slow as pushing your bike uphill with flat tires.

Each summer day you spend working with a therapist or with Ivy, who tutors you. Sometimes playing video games with your brother, younger but as tall now, when he's not earning ribbons on the swim team or taking tennis lessons from the pro at the club who said you were the one who could be a tennis phenom. You can't remember what *phenom* meant, just that it made you feel good. But all that ended last summer. Dr. O says, "No competitive sports. Maybe for fun, eventually."

Running used to seem as common as breathing. But you don't breathe that way now. The air has changed, and you might never run that way again. You can't skateboard or climb trees or ride your bike. So you count the weeks till you can go to school in the fall. Your brother says it's stupid to want school, but he doesn't know what it's like when the best part of the day is seeing him burst through the door. And then you hate yourself for being so weak. It doesn't even matter that you've missed a grade and you'll be in the same class with him. Just so you get to do something normal. All you want is normal. Sitting in a classroom with kids like you. Like you used to be.

But Time — if you are Connor Burdette, thirty years old — Time is a freight train rattling on each day's tracks. Once more a year has roared by, and it's the Fourth of July again. You used to love the Fourth, but now all you see is Raleigh Dalton lying behind a cash register and all you hear is the echo of a single gunshot. You tried to think of a good excuse not to come back. There's still that bullet in your leg. It'll never be normal. You have a limp, and you always will. Somehow that feels right.

But your family keeps calling, saying how much they miss you. And some nights you whisper to yourself, *I miss me, too.* They keep going on about how this is your first time home since Christmas, the first time you'll be seeing Russ and Nikki's baby girl, and your mama is making your favorite pie, and there's something about a family that dammit just won't give up on you, that keeps pleading, *Come home... come home... come home.*

The homecoming is familiar, Connor's family waiting, rising to greet him, arms thrown around him. Russ and Nikki, more standoffish. And Drew. The first sight of him makes Connor's heart clinch, but he remembers Christmastime when Drew looked so weak. So broken. He seems a little stronger now.

Everybody talking at once, and coffee, then piling into cars to go to the parade.

The parade feels familiar, same tired floats, same perky majorettes. Connor wouldn't have imagined how glad he is for the sameness, how comforting the same can be when all you've felt are strangers' eyes running over you. He wouldn't have expected to care so much that the old vet Artie Logan is gone, marching now with his long-dead buddies from the Korean War.

Predictable, too, is the picnic. The laughter, high-pitched kiddie voices, too much food, folding lawn chairs, just-bearable heat and then the gradual cooling down. A few surprises, though. The sheriff has brought his son, Michael, and the little boy runs to Ivy, calling her name, hugging on her. Now what is that all about? Connor is glad he let Ivy have Lady's house. She might need it for a family of her own someday.

Nikki takes the baby and Drew home for a while. Connor feels a stitch of worry about Drew, wondering if the day has been too much for him. But he hears his mama say, "The baby needed a nap. And Drew can't join in with the other kids. Might fall and start a new bleed."

Ivy must've read his worry. She said, "He wanted to go home."

They've all seen that look in Drew's eyes. The yearning, when his friends and his brother are whooping and hollering and chasing each other.

"They'll meet us at home for the fireworks," Ivy says.

Connor wanders off to smoke, and Russ follows. Connor has a moment of familiar unease, he and his brother don't just chat, but when Russ begins to talk, it isn't about anything that would end in a fight. It's about Drew.

"Holes in his memory, they say. He's had to learn new ways to do the same thing. Used to like to read, which a lot of boys don't, but Drew did. Now he sees words backward." Russ sounds like he's saying things he's needed to hear himself say, and Connor feels a sudden, strange surge of warmth toward his brother. "It's been a year now, but he's nowhere near right. Might never be," Russ says, looking down at his shoes, and then, "Gimme one of those."

Connor grins and holds out his pack of Marlboros. "When'd you start?"

"Right now. Starting and stopping, right now," Russ says.

"Good idea, the stopping."

Russ lights up. A gentle wind stirs the air. He raises his face, like he's feeling the breeze cool the sweat on his forehead.

"You didn't have to do what you did, Connor," he says, after a moment. "But it saved us." His voice is suddenly filled with weight. "You wouldn't believe the medical bills. And buying Boone out means my family has a future. My boys have a solid foundation."

My boys. Connor feels an instant of envy and regret tugging at each other.

You always hear the echo of the past. You can't change it. It never goes away. But you try to make up for your mistakes. Connor did what he could with what he'd been given. It was only right to split up the inheritance. Lady should've known that. What he kept for himself was far more than he'd imagined he'd ever have. And what he got by giving up so much was far more than he deserved.

His mama and Ivy can't end a phone call now without getting teary about what he's done for his family. Even his daddy brings it up every time they talk. Embarrassing, how they all go on about it. But this is the first word from his brother, and somehow it means the most.

Connor says, "What did I need with all that money?"

Russ takes another drag. Connor, too. They smoke for a minute more. The silence is easier than Connor would've thought.

"How's that leg?" Russ says.

"Stiff. Hurts some. Could've been worse."

Russ rubs the back of his neck. "Never will forget seeing you there at the hospital. They thought you might lose that leg. So much blood. I told them, 'B negative. I'm his brother. He's B negative.'"

Something catches in Connor's chest. Don't go there. Not the blood. Just let it be. Let us be. The words are loud in his head. There're more things between brothers than just blood.

Russ's eyes say there are words loud in his head, too. Somehow Connor knows Nikki has been truthful with her husband. Something liberating about that. But some things are better left unsaid.

They toss their cigarettes, crush them in the dirt, and begin walking. Russ asks, "You leaving tomorrow?"

He glances at Connor, and there's something in his eyes. Something beneath the words. Hope that Connor won't stay. Fear that at any time he could lay claim to his son and turn the world upside down for all of them. But gratitude, too, that he hasn't. And trust that he won't.

Connor nods. "Bright and early."

There's no mistaking the relief in Russ's voice when he says, "Don't be a stranger."

As they walk toward the crowd, Connor has the deep-down feeling that he's home. Finally. Like he had to leave to come home.

Evening slides into soft darkness, and the Burdettes gather on the front porch and in the yard of the parsonage. Drew and Owen are catching fireflies. For the first time that day Connor hears Drew laugh.

And then the first *pop*. Not so different from a gunshot.

The boys look up. The adults shift, find the best spots to watch, on the edge of the porch and the steps.

More *pop pop pop*. *Fizz* and *whistle*. "Ah-h-h!" and "Oh-o-o-o!" and "O-o-o-o-o! as sparkles burst against the sky. Above and below, Connor's world is suddenly brilliant. Brilliant with light. The fireworks fill the darkness. The faces of his family around him shine.

At last, the grand finale, constant exploding colors and *boom boom boom!*

Drew and Owen holler and the adults clap and smile. It might be the best Independence Day the Burdettes can remember.

Connor joins the boys in the yard. He stands between them and puts his hands on the narrow shoulders that are years yet from carrying grown-up weights, though he imagines Drew already carries his share.

Finally, the sky fades to black.

"I wanna be one of the firemen that shoots off the fireworks," Owen says, before he skips away to pick up his jar where the fireflies are blinking their phosphorescent lights.

But Drew lingers. Maybe he doesn't mind the warm hand on his shoulder. For a moment, Connor can almost feel the same blood pulsing between them. He can almost feel the slowness in Drew, the part that won't ever be right, even as his own pulse seems to speed up and his leg begins to ache.

He squeezes the small shoulder. And then he lets go.

Time keeps running one way, a freight train into tomorrow. But yesterday follows on the same old track. A little boy crying for his sister to let the fireflies go. Fireworks above, a gunshot below. And always, the voices that have carved themselves into you.

Drew spots his jar of fireflies and picks it up. "Daddy, look!" he calls and hurries to the man he knows as his father, holds up the jar so Russ can see the fireflies blink blink blink like they're sending out some kind of S.O.S.

And then Drew takes off the lid and lets them go.

As Connor watches, his heart swells. His mama's words echo in his ears, incandescent in his heart. *It's a blessing to free a firefly.*

There is so much darkness in this world. Even the tiniest light is precious. But there's no holding onto it. Any little bit of light you've caught, you've got to let it go.

And letting go is the hardest part.

Suddenly the fragile, flickering lights rise all around them, shimmering in the night sky, and for just a moment, the fractured light fills the darkness.

Author's Note

Prodigal has been a long time coming into print, and I want to acknowledge the people who supported and encouraged me through it all.

I am fortunate to be part of a longstanding writers group who zoomed with me during the pandemic, read each draft of every chapter, and offered solid critiques: Rita Bourke, Mary Buckner, Ed Comer, Mary Bess Dunn, Doug Jones, Will Maguire, Randy O'Brien, Shannon Thurman, and Jack Wallace.

I appreciate everything the Histria team has done to make this book possible.

The professionals who were gracious in providing technical assistance deserve a special thanks. Dr. Jim McFerrin, Department of Psychiatry, Vanderbilt Medical Center, was a valuable source who helped me to understand the implications of traumatic brain injuries. I am also grateful to Ric Wilson, Sheriff of Wayne County, Tennessee, 2006-2018, who knows all there is to know about law enforcement in a small town and took time to share information that was essential to my story.

As always, my deepest gratitude and affection are for my daughters and their families.

The years I spent growing up in a town like Montpier had a profound effect on my writing, but the characters in *Prodigal* are fictional, not based on any real person, living or dead.

About the Author

Phyllis Gobbell writes a little bit of everything—mysteries, true crimes, short stories, creative nonfiction – and now a Southern literary novel, *Prodigal.*

Her award-winning stories have appeared in *2 Bridges Review, Bellevue Review, Zone 3, Red Mud Review, Coastal Shelf, Tetrahedra,* and *Well Read Magazine*. She received Tennessee's Individual Artist Award for Literature. *Treachery in Tuscany,* the third book in her Jordan Mayfair Mystery Series, won a Silver Falchion Award for Best Cozy Mystery.

Other books in the mystery series are *Pursuit in Provence, Secrets and Shamrocks,* and *Notorious in Nashville.*

Before she began her mystery series, Gobbell co-authored two true crimes, *An Unfinished Canvas* and *Season of Darkness,* based on two high-profile murders that have become part of Nashville's history.

An English professor for twenty years, she served on the faculty at Nashville State Community College, where she taught composition, literature, and creative writing and edited the college's literary journal. Recently she taught creative writing in Lipscomb University's Lifelong Learning Program.

Browse her website, www.phyllisgobbell.com, for more about her writing.